John Clare, John　　　 ... y

Life and Remains of John Clare

The Northamptonshire Peasant Poet

John Clare, John Law Cherry

Life and Remains of John Clare
The Northamptonshire Peasant Poet

ISBN/EAN: 9783337778521

Printed in Europe, USA, Canada, Australia, Japan

Cover: Foto ©Raphael Reischuk / pixelio.de

More available books at **www.hansebooks.com**

LIFE AND REMAINS

OF

JOHN CLARE,

THE

"NORTHAMPTONSHIRE PEASANT POET."

By J. L. CHERRY.

"And he sat him down in a lonely place,
And chanted a melody loud and sweet."
TENNYSON.

WITH ILLUSTRATIONS BY BIRKET FOSTER.

London :
FREDERICK WARNE & Co.

Northampton :
J. TAYLOR & SON.

1873.

DEDICATION.

To his Excellency

THE LORD-LIEUTENANT OF IRELAND.

My Lord :

Among the papers which John Clare, the "Peasant Poet" of our county, left behind him, was one in which he desired that the Editor of his " Remains" should dedicate them " to Earl Spencer, with the author's last wishes." That memorandum was written in the year 1825, when the poet was anticipating, to use his own words, a speedy entrance into " the dark porch of eternity, whence none returns to tell the tale of his reception."

These melancholy forebodings were not realized, for although in a few years Clare became dead to the world, he lived on in seclusion to a patriarchal age. Meanwhile,

Dedication.

the Earl Spencer to whom he desired that his "Remains" should be dedicated passed away, and the title descended first to your lordship's uncle; then to your lordship's father, and lastly to your lordship. But through all these years the Earls Spencer were the steadfast and generous friends of the unhappy Poet, nor did your lordship's bounty cease with his life, but was continued to his widow.

In dedicating this volume to your lordship, as I now do, I am complying with the spirit and almost with the very letter of poor Clare's injunction.

I am, with unfeigned respect,

Your lordship's most obedient servant,

THE EDITOR.

INTRODUCTION.

The Editor begs the reader to believe that he undertook the compilation of this volume with diffidence and trepidation, lest by any defect of judgment he might do aught to diminish the reputation which John Clare has always enjoyed with the lovers of pastoral poetry. He trusts that the shortcomings of an unskilful workman will be forgotten in admiration of the gems for which he has been required to find a setting.

Shortly after Clare's death his literary " Remains" came into the possession of Mr. Taylor, of Northampton. The MSS. included several hundreds of hitherto unpublished poems, more than a thousand letters addressed to Clare by his friends and contemporaries, (among them, Charles Lamb, James Montgomery, Bloomfield, Sir Chas. A. Elton, Hood, Cary, Allan Cunningham, Mrs.

Emmerson, Lord Radstock, &c.,) a Diary, pocket books in which Clare had jotted down passing thoughts and fancies in prose and verse, a small collection of curious Old Ballads which he says he wrote down on hearing them sung by his father and mother, and numerous other valuable and interesting documents.

This volume has been compiled mainly from these manuscripts. The contents are divided into five sections, namely :—I. Life and Letters. II. Asylum Poems. III. Miscellaneous Poems. IV. Prose Fragments. V. Old Ballads.

For much of the information relating to the Poet's earlier years the Editor is indebted to Mr. Martin's " Life of Clare," and the narratives of his youthful struggles and sufferings which appeared in the " Quarterly Review" and other periodicals at the time of the publication of his first volume. From that time the correspondence already mentioned became the basis of the biographical sketch, and was of the greatest value. In the few pages which relate to Clare's residence at Northampton, the Editor was enabled to write principally from personal knowledge. It is almost incumbent upon him to add, that in several important particulars he dissents from Mr. Martin, but he will not engage in the ungracious task of criticizing a work to which he is under an obligation. *

While an inmate of the Northampton County Lunatic Asylum, Clare wrote more than five hundred poems. These were carefully preserved by Mr. W. F. Knight, of Birmingham, a gentleman who for many years held a responsible office in that institution, and was a kind-hearted friend of the unhappy bard. From this pile of manuscripts the Editor has selected those which appear under the title of Asylum Poems. The selection was a pleasing, mournful task. Again and again it happened that a poem would open with a bright, musical stanza giving promise of a finished work not unworthy of Clare's genius at its best. This would be followed by others in which, to quote a line from the " Village Minstrel," were

" Half-vacant thoughts and rhymes of careless form."

Then came deeper obscurity, and at last incoherent nonsense. Of those which are printed, scarcely one was found in a state in which it could be submitted to the public without more or less of revision and correction.

* The Editor has pleasure in acknowledging the kindness of Miss James, of Theddingworth, and Miss Powell, of Thame. The former lady obligingly sent him the manuscript of a lecture on " Dryden and Clare" by her brother, the late Rev. T. James, of Theddingworth, and the latter several letters written by Clare to Mr. Octavius Gilchrist.

Introduction.

The Miscellaneous Poems are chiefly fugitive pieces collected from magazines and annuals. One or two, referred to in the correspondence with James Montgomery, have been reprinted from the "Rural Muse," and there are a few which, like the Asylum Poems, have not been published before. "Maying; or, Love and Flowers," to which the Editor presumes specially to direct attention, is one of these.

The Prose Fragments are of minor literary importance, but they help to a knowledge and an understanding of the man. The Old Ballads have an interest of their own, apart from their association with Clare. The majority are no doubt what they purport to be, but in two or three instances Clare's hand is discernible.

J. L. C.

Havelock-place, Hanley,
December, 1872.

CONTENTS.

Contents.

Contents.

Contents.

GLOSSARY.

Bedlam cowslip, the paigle, or larger kind of cowslip.
Bents, tall, coarse, rushy stems of grass.
Blea, high, exposed.
Bleb, a bubble, a small drop.
Clock-a-clay, the ladybird.
Daffies, daffodils.
Dithering, trembling, shivering.
Hing, preterite of hang.
Ladysmock, the great bindweed.
Pink, the chaffinch.
Pooty, the girdled snail shell.
Ramping, coarse and large.
Rawky, misty, foggy.
Rig, the ridge of a roof.
Sueing, a murmuring, melancholy sound.
Swaly, wasteful.
Sweltered, over-heated by the sun.
Twitchy, made of twitch grass.
Water-blob, the marsh marigold.

Life and Letters.

LIFE, LETTERS, Etc.

JOHN CLARE, son of Parker and Ann Clare, commonly called "the Northamptonshire Peasant Poet," was born at Helpstone, near Peterborough, on the 13th of July, 1793. The lowliness of his lot lends some countenance to the saying of " Melancholy " Burton, that, "poverty is the Muses' patrimony." He was the elder of twins, and was so small an infant that his mother used to say of him that " John might have been put into a pint pot." Privation and toil disabled his father at a comparatively early age, and he became a pauper, receiving from the parish an allowance of five shillings a week. His mother was of feeble constitution and was afflicted with dropsy. Clare inherited the low vitality of his parents, and until he reached middle age was subject to depressing ailments which more than once threatened his life, but after that time the failure of his mental powers caused him to be placed in circumstances favourable to bodily health, and in his old age he presented the outward aspect of a sturdy yeoman.

Having endowed Clare with high poetic sensibility, Nature capriciously placed him amid scenes but little calculated to call forth rapturous praises of her charms. "Helpstone," wrote an old friend of the poet, lately deceased, "lies between six and seven miles N. N. W. of Peterborough, on the Syston and Peterborough branch of the Midland Railway, the station being about half a mile from the town. A not unpicturesque country lies about it, though its beauty is somewhat of the Dutch character—far-stretching distances, level meadows, intersected with grey willows and sedgy dikes, frequent spires, substantial watermills, and farm houses of white stone, and cottages of white stone also. Southward, a belt of wood, with a gentle rise beyond, redeems it from absolute flatness. Entering the town by the road from the east you come to a cross, standing in the midst of four ways. * * * Before you, and to the left, stretches the town, consisting of wide streets or roadways, with irregular buildings on either side, interspersed with gardens now lovely with profuse blooms of laburnum and lilac. * * * The cottage in which John Clare was born is in the main street running south. The views of it which illustrate his poems are not very accurate. They represent it as standing alone, when it is in fact, and evidently always has been, a cluster of two if not of three tenements. There are three occupations now. It is on the west side of the street, and is thatched. In the illustration to the second volume of "The Village Minstrel" (1821), an open stream runs before the door which is crossed by a plank. Modern sanitary regulations have done away with this, if it ever existed, and was not a fancy of the artist.   *   *   *   Clare, whose local attachments were intense, bewails in indignant verse the demolition of the Green :—

> Ye injur'd fields, ye once were gay,
>> When Nature's hand displayed
> Long waving rows of willows grey
>> And clumps of hawthorn shade ;
> But now, alas ! your hawthorn bowers
>> All desolate we see !
> The spoiler's axe their shade devours,
>> And cuts down every tree.
> Not trees alone have owned their force,
>> Whole woods beneath them bowed,
> They turned the winding rivulet's course,
>> And all thy pastures plough'd." *

Clare also wrote in the " Village Minstrel" in the following candid and artless strain,—" a sort of defiant parody on the Highland poets"—of the natural features of his native place :—

> Swamps of wild rush-beds and sloughs' squashy traces,
>> Grounds of rough fallows with thistle and weed,
> Flats and low valleys of kingcups and daisies,
>> Sweetest of subjects are ye for my reed :
> Ye commons left free in the rude rags of nature,
>> Ye brown heaths beclothed in furze as ye be,
> My wild eye in rapture adores every feature,
>> Ye are dear as this heart in my bosom to me.

* " Rambles Roundabout," by G. J. De Wilde.

O native endearments! I would not forsake ye,
  I would not forsake ye for sweetest of scenes:
For sweetest of gardens that Nature could make me
  I would not forsake ye, dear valleys and greens:
Though Nature ne'er dropped ye a cloud-resting mountain,
  Nor waterfalls tumble their music so free,
Had Nature denied ye a bush, tree, or fountain,
  Ye still had been loved as an Eden by me.

And long, my dear valleys, long, long may ye flourish,
  Though rush-beds and thistles make most of your pride!
May showers never fail the green's daisies to nourish,
  Nor suns dry the fountain that rills by its side!
Your skies may be gloomy, and misty your mornings,
  Your flat swampy valleys unwholesome may be,
Still, refuse of Nature, without her adornings
  Ye are dear as this heart in my bosom to me!

That the poet's attachment to his native place was deep-rooted and unaffected was proved by the difficulty which he found in tearing himself from it in after years, and it is more than probable that the violence which, for the sake of others, he then did to his sensitive nature aggravated his constitutional melancholy and contributed to the ultimate overthrow of his reason.

Clare's opportunities for learning the elements of knowledge were in keeping with his humble station. Parker Clare, out of his miserable and fluctuating earnings as a day labourer, paid for his child's schooling until he was seven years of age, when he was set to watch sheep and geese on the village heath. Here he

made the acquaintance of " Granny Bains," of whom
Mr. Martin, quoting, doubtless, from Clare's manuscript
autobiography, says:—" Having spent almost her whole
life out of doors, in heat and cold, storm and rain, she
had come to be intimately acquainted with all the signs
foreboding change of weather, and was looked upon by
her acquaintances as a perfect oracle. She had also a
most retentive memory, and being of a joyous nature,
with a bodily frame that never knew illness, had learnt
every verse or melody that was sung within her hearing,
until her mind became a very storehouse of songs. To
John, old Granny Bains soon took a great liking, he
being a devout listener, ready to sit at her feet for hours
and hours while she was warbling her little ditties,
alternately merry and plaintive.   *   *   *
But though often disturbed in the enjoyment of these
delightful recitations, they nevertheless sank deep into
John Clare's mind, until he found himself repeating all
day long the songs he had heard, and even in his dreams
kept humming—

> There sat three ravens upon a tree,
> Heigh down, derry O!
> There sat two ravens upon a tree,
> As deep in love as he and she.

It was thus that the admiration of poetry first awoke in
Parker Clare's son, roused by the songs of Granny Bains,
the cowherd of Helpstone."

From watching cows and geese, the boy was in due
course promoted to the rank of team-leader, and was

also set to assist his father in the threshing barn. "John," his father used to say, "was weak but willing," and the good man made his son a flail proportioned to his strength. Exposure in the ill-drained fields round Helpstone brought on an attack of tertiary ague, from which the boy had scarcely rallied when he was again sent into the fields. Favourable weather having set in he recovered his health, and was able that summer to make occasionally a few pence by working overtime. These savings were religiously devoted to schooling, and in the following winter, he being then in his tenth year, he attended an evening school at the neighbouring village of Glinton. John soon became a favourite of the master, Mr. James Merrishaw, and was allowed the run of his little library. His passion for learning rapidly developed itself, and he eagerly devoured every book that came in his way, his reading ranging from " Robinson Crusoe" to " Bonnycastle's Arithmetic" and " Ward's Algebra." He refers to this in later life when he thus speaks of the " Village Minstrel :"—

And oft, with books, spare hours he would beguile,
And blunder oft with joy round Crusoe's lonely isle.

John pursued his studies for two or three winters under the guidance of the good-natured Merrishaw, and at the end of that time an unsuccessful effort was made to obtain for him a situation as clerk in the office of a solicitor at Wisbeach. After this failure he returned contentedly to the fields, and about this time found a new friend in the son of a small farmer named Turnill. The two youths read together, Turnill assisting Clare with books and writing materials. He now began to "snatch a fearful joy" by scribbling on scraps of paper his unpolished rhymes. "When he was fourteen or fifteen," to use his mother's own words, "he would show me a piece of paper, printed sometimes on one side and scrawled all over on the other, and he would say, 'Mother, this is worth silver and gold,' and I used to say to him, 'Ay, boy, it looks as if it wur,' but I thought he was only wasting his time." John deposited a bundle of these fragments in a chink in the cottage wall, whence "they were duly and daily subtracted by his mother to boil the morning's kettle," but we do not find that he was greatly disturbed by the loss, for being sympathetically asked on one occasion whether he had not kept copies of his earliest poems he replied that he had not, and that they were very likely good for nothing.

While he was yet in his early youth an important and, in some respects, a favourable change took place in the nature of his daily occupation. "Among the few well-to-do inhabitants of Helpstone was a person named Francis Gregory, who owned a small public-house, under the sign of the Blue Bell, and rented besides a few acres of land. Francis Gregory, a most kind and amiable man, was unmarried, and kept house with his old mother, a female servant, and a lad, the latter half groom and half gardener. This situation, a yearly hiring, being vacant, it was offered to John, and eagerly accepted, on the understanding that he should have sufficient time of

his own to continue his studies. It was a promise
abundantly kept, for John Clare had never more leisure,
and perhaps was never happier in his life than during the
year that he stayed at the Blue Bell. Mr. Francis
Gregory, suffering under constant illness, treated the pale
little boy, who was always hanging over his books, more
like a son than a servant, and this feeling was fully shared
by Mr. Gregory's mother. John's chief labours were to
attend to a horse and a couple of cows, and occasionally
to do some light work in the garden or the potatoe field;
and as these occupations seldom filled more than part of
the day or the week, he had all the rest of the time to
himself. A characteristic part of Clare's nature began to
reveal itself now. While he had little leisure to himself,
and much hard work, he was not averse to the society of
friends and companions, either, as in the case of Turnill,
for study, or, as with others, for recreation; but as soon
as he found himself to a certain extent his own master he
forsook the company of his former acquaintances, and
began to lead a sort of hermit's life. He took long strolls
into the woods, along the meres, and to other lonely
places, and got into the habit of remaining whole hours
at some favourite spot, lying flat on the ground with his
face towards the sky. The flickering shadows of the sun,
the rustling of the leaves on the trees, the sailing of the
fitful clouds over the horizon, and the golden blaze of the
sun at morn and eventide were to him spectacles of which
his eye never tired, with which his heart never got
satiated." (*Martin.*)

8

The age at which Clare's poetic fancies first wrought themselves into verse cannot be definitely fixed. We know from his steadfast friend and first editor, the late Mr. John Taylor, publisher to the London University, that his fondness for poetry found expression before even he had learnt to read. He was tired one day with looking at the pictures in a volume of poems, which he used to say he thought was Pomfret's, when his father read him one piece in the book to amuse him. This thrilled him with a delight of which he often afterwards spoke, but though he distinctly recollected the vivid pleasure which the recital gave him he could never recall either the incidents or the language.

It may almost be taken for granted that so soon as Clare could write he began to rhyme. The Editor of this volume has before him the book in which the boy set down his arithmetical and geometrical exercises while a pupil of Mr. Merrishaw, and in this book are scribbled in pencil a few undecipherable lines commencing, " Good morning to ye, ballad-singing thrush." He was thirteen years old when an incident occurred which gave a powerful impulse to his dawning genius. A companion had shown him Thomson's " Seasons," and he was seized with an irrepressible desire to possess a copy. He ascertained that the book might be bought at Stamford for eighteenpence, and he entreated his father to give him the money. The poor man pleaded all too truthfully his poverty, but his mother, by great exertions, contrived to scrape together sevenpence, and the deficiency was made

9

up by loans from friends in the village. Next Sunday, John rose long before the dawn and walked to Stamford, a distance of seven miles, to buy a copy of the " Seasons," ignorant or forgetful of the fact that business was suspended on that day. After waiting for three or four hours before the shop to which he had been directed, he learnt from a passer-by that it would not be re-opened until the following morning, and he returned to Helpstone with a heavy heart. Next day he repeated his journey and bore off the much-coveted volume in triumph. He read as he walked back to Helpstone, but meeting with many interruptions clambered over the wall surrounding Burghley Park, and throwing himself on the grass read the volume through twice over before rising. It was a fine spring morning, and under the influence of the poems, the singing of birds, and the bright sunshine, he composed " The Morning Walk." This was soon followed by " The Evening Walk," and some other minor pieces.

At the age of sixteen, if we may trust the account given by his early friend Mr. Octavius Gilchrist, in the " London Magazine" for January, 1820, Clare composed the following sonnet " To a Primrose"—

> Welcome, pale primrose, starting up between
> Dead matted leaves of oak and ash, that strew
> The every lawn, the wood, and spinney through,
> 'Mid creeping moss and ivy's darker green !
> How much thy presence beautifies the ground !
> How sweet thy modest, unaffected pride
> Glows on the sunny bank and wood's warm side !

And where thy fairy flowers in groups are found
The schoolboy roams enchantedly along,
Plucking the fairest with a rude delight,
While the meek shepherd stops his simple song,
To gaze a moment on the pleasing sight,
O'erjoyed to see the flowers that truly bring
The welcome news of sweet returning Spring.

As we have traced the poet's history down to his six-
teenth year, the next incident of importance may be
anticipated : of course he fell in love, and the object of
his first and purest affection was Mary Joyce, daughter
of a farmer at Glinton. Little is known of this episode
excepting that the maiden was very beautiful, that after a
few months of blissful intercourse their frequent meetings
came to the knowledge of Mary's father, who sternly
forbad their continuance, and that although " Patty,"
Clare's future wife, was the theme of some pretty verses,
Mary Joyce was always Clare's ideal of love and beauty,
and when thirty years afterwards, he lost his reason,
among the first indications of the approaching calamity
was his declaration that Mary, who had then long been
in her grave, had passed his window. While under the
influence of this delusion he wrote the poem entitled
" First Love's Recollections," of which the following are
the first two stanzas :—

First love will with the heart remain
    When all its hopes are bye,
As frail rose-blossoms still retain
    Their fragrance when they die ;

And joy's first dreams will haunt the mind
    With shades from whence they sprung,
As summer leaves the stems behind
    On which spring's blossoms hung.

Mary! I dare not call thee dear,
    I've lost that right so long;
Yet once again I vex thine ear
    With memory's idle song.
Had time and change not blotted out
    The love of former days,
Thou wert the last that I should doubt
    Of pleasing with my praise.

Clare's engagement at the Blue Bell having terminated, a stone mason of Market Deeping offered to teach him his craft on payment of a premium which, though a very moderate sum, was far beyond the means of Parker Clare. A shoemaker in the village next offered to take him as an apprentice, on condition that Clare found his own tools, but the youth's aversion to the trade was too great to be overcome. After that his father applied to the head gardener at Burghley Park, who engaged Clare on the terms of a three years' apprenticeship, with eight shillings per week for the first year and an advance of one shilling per week in each succeeding year. The engagement was considered by Clare's father and mother to be a very fortunate and promising one, but it proved to be in a high degree prejudicial to his welfare. He was thrown into the society of a set of coarse-minded, intemperate fellows who insisted on his accompanying them in their frequent and forbidden visits to public houses in the neighbourhood. Mr. Martin informs us that it was the custom at Burghley to lock up at night all the workmen and apprentices employed under the head gardener, to prevent them from robbing the orchards, and that they regularly made their escape through a window. On several occasions Clare was overcome by drink and slept in the open air, with consequences to his delicate frame which may easily be imagined.

It would appear that the head gardener set the example of habitual drunkenness to his subordinates, and that he was, moreover, of brutal disposition, which will account for the circumstance of the flight of Clare from Burleigh Park, after he had been there nearly a year. Accompanied by a fellow-apprentice he walked to Grantham, a distance of twenty-two miles, and thence to Newark, where the youths obtained employment under a nurseryman. But Clare very shortly became homesick, and he returned to his parents in a state of complete destitution.

The most lamentable consequence of the roystering life which Clare led with the gardeners at Burleigh was, that he acquired a fondness for strong drink with which he had to struggle, not always successfully, for years. That he did struggle manfully is evident from his correspondence, and at length, acting upon the advice of Dr. Darling, a London physician, who for a long time generously prescribed for him without fee or reward beyond the poet's grateful thanks, he abstained altogether.

It will be seen hereafter that in all probability Dr. Darling's advice was given upon the supposition that Clare was able to procure a sufficient supply of nourishing food, when unhappily he was almost literally starving himself, in order that his family might not go hungry.

On returning from Nottinghamshire Clare took again to the work of a farm labourer, and the poetic fervour which had abated in the uncongenial society of Burghley once more manifested itself. After taking infinite pains to that end, he had the satisfaction of convincing his father and mother that his poetry was of somewhat greater merit than the half-penny ballads sold at the village feast; but his neighbours could not bring themselves to approve John's course of life, and they adopted various disagreeable modes of showing that they thought he was a mightily presumptuous fellow. His shy manners and his habit of talking to himself as he walked led some to set him down as a lunatic; others ridiculed his enthusiasm, or darkly whispered suspicions of unhallowed intercourse with evil spirits. This treatment, operating upon a sensitive mind and a body debilitated both by labour and scanty and unwholesome food, had the natural effect of robbing him of hope and buoyancy of spirits. In a fit of desperation he enlisted in the militia, and with other Helpstone youths was marched off to Oundle, a small town lying between Peterborough and Northampton. *
He remained at Oundle for a few weeks, at the end of which time the regiment was disbanded and Clare

---

* The papers connected with Clare's enlistment are preserved in the Northampton Museum.

returned to Helpstone, carrying with him " Paradise Lost" and the " Tempest," which he had bought at a broker's shop in Oundle. This brings us down to 1812, when Clare was nineteen years old.

Little is known of Clare's manner of life for the next four or five years, excepting that he continued to work as a farm labourer whenever work could be found, that he tried camp life with some gipsies, and speedily had his romantic ideas of its attractiveness rudely dispelled, that he had a love passage or two with girls of the village, and that he accumulated a large number of poems of varying degrees of excellence.

In 1817 he obtained employment as a lime burner at Bridge Casterton, in the neighbouring county of Rutland, where he earned about ten shillings per week. The labour was very severe, but Clare was contented, and during his stay at Bridge Casterton several of the best among his earlier poems were produced. It was probably this period of his life which he had in his mind when he said—

> I found the poems in the fields,
> And only wrote them down.

In the course of this year 1817 Clare fell in love with Martha Turner, the daughter of a cottage farmer living at a place called Walkherd Lodge, and this is the maiden who after the lapse of three or four years became his wife. " She was a fair girl of eighteen, slender, with regular features, and pretty blue eyes." Clare entered into this new engagement with passionate ardour, but the courtship ultimately took a more prosaic turn, and having once done so, there was little in the worthy but illiterate and matter-of-fact "Patty" to elevate the connection into the region of poetry. In his correspondence Clare more than once hints at want of sympathy on the part of those of his own household, and at one time domestic differences, for which there is reason to think he was mainly responsible, and which occurred when he was mentally in a very morbid condition, caused him to contemplate suicide. It is due, however, to the memory of "Patty" to say that Clare's latest volume of poems ("The Rural Muse," 1835) contains an address "To P * *" which is honourable to the constancy of both parties. It is as follows :—

> Fair was thy bloom when first I met
> Thy summer's maiden-blossom :
> And thou art fair and lovely yet,
> And dearer to my bosom.
> O thou wert once a wilding flower,
> All garden flowers excelling,
> And still I bless the happy hour
> That led me to thy dwelling.
>
> Though nursed by field, and brook, and wood,
> And wild in every feature,
> Spring ne'er unsealed a fairer bud,
> Nor found a blossom sweeter.
> Of all the flowers the spring hath met,
> And it has met with many,
> Thou art to me the fairest yet,
> And loveliest of any.

. Though ripening summers round thee bring
 Buds to thy swelling bosom,
That wait the cheering smiles of spring
 To ripen into blossom,
These buds shall added blessings be,
 To make our loves sincerer,
For as their flowers resemble thee
 They'll make thy memory dearer.

And though thy bloom shall pass away,
 By winter overtaken,
Thoughts of the past will charms display,
 And many joys awaken.
When time shall every sweet remove,
 And blight thee on my bosom,
Let beauty fade !—to me, my love,
 Thou'lt ne'er be out of blossom !

Although Clare's engagement to Martha Turner added
to his perplexities, it was really the immediate moving
cause of his determination to be up and doing. He
resolved at length to publish a collection of his poems,
and consulted Mr. Henson, a printer, of Market Deeping,
on the subject. Mr. Henson offered to print three
hundred copies of a prospectus for a sovereign, but he
firmly declined the invitation of the poet to draw up that
document. Clare resolutely set to work to save the money
for the printer, and soon succeeded ; but then there was
the difficulty with regard to the composition of the address
to the public. He could write poetry ; that he knew ;

he had done so already, and he felt plenty more within; but prose he had never yet attempted, and the task was a really grievous one. This is his own account of his trouble, given in the introduction to the " Village Minstrel :"—" I have often dropped down five or six times, to plan an address. In one of these musings my poor thoughts lost themselves in rhyme. Taking a view, as I sat beneath the shelter of a woodland hedge, of my parents' distresses at home, of my labouring so hard and so vainly to get out of debt, and of my still added perplexities of ill-timed love, striving to remedy all to no purpose, I burst out into an exclamation of distress, 'What is life?' and instantly recollecting that such a subject would be a good one for a poem, I hastily scratted down the two first verses of it, as it stands, and continued my journey to work." When he got to the limekiln he could not work for thinking of the address which he had to write, " so I sat me down on a lime scuttle," he says, " and out with my pencil, and when I had finished I started off for Stamford with it." There he posted the address to Mr. Henson. It ran as follows :—" Proposals for publishing by subscription a Collection of Original Trifles on Miscellaneous Subjects, Religious and Moral, in verse, by John Clare, of Helpstone. The public are requested to observe that the Trifles humbly offered for their candid perusal can lay no claim to eloquence of composition : whoever thinks so will be deceived, the greater part of them being juvenile productions, and those of later date offsprings of those leisure intervals which the short remittance from hard and manual labour sparingly afforded to compose them. It is to be hoped that the humble situation which distinguishes their author will be some excuse in their favour, and serve to make an atonement for the many inaccuracies and imperfections that will be found in them. The least touch from the iron hand of Criticism is able to crush them to nothing, and sink them at once to utter oblivion. May they be allowed to live their little day and give satisfaction to those who may choose to honour them with a perusal, they will gain the end for which they were designed and the author's wishes will be gratified. Meeting with this encouragement it will induce him to publish a similiar collection of which this is offered as a specimen." The specimen was the " Sonnet to the Setting Sun," in which a comparison is drawn between sunset and the death of a Christian.

The address was too artless—too honest, and the people of the Fens, taking Clare at his word, subscribed for exactly seven copies ! The state of excitement, caused by mingled hopes and fears, in which Clare was at this time may be seen from the following extract from a letter to Mr. Henson :—" Good God ! How great are my expectations ! What hopes do I cherish ! As great as the unfortunate Chatterton's were, on his first entrance into London, which is now pictured in my mind. And, undoubedly, like him I may be building castles in the air, but time will prove it. Please to do all in your power to procure subscribers, as your address will be looked upon better than that of a clown. When 100 are got you may print it, if you please ; so do your best."

But now fresh troubles came upon Clare in rapid succession. He quarrelled with Patty and was forbidden the house by her parents. He was discharged by his master on the probably well-grounded plea that he was writing poetry and distributing his address when he ought to be at work, and he was soon without a penny in the world. He returned to Helpstone and tried to get employment as a day labourer, but failed, the farmers, who had heard of the publishing project, considering that "he did not know his place." In this extremity he was compelled to apply for and accept relief from the parish. This was in the autumn of 1818, and Clare was twenty-five years old.

Henson declined to begin the printing of the book unless Clare advanced the sum of £15, and this being impossible the negotiation fell through. Clare shortly afterwards, with the two-fold object of finding employment and obtaining relief from mental distraction by change of scene, was on the point of setting out for Yorkshire, when a copy of his prospectus fell under the notice of Mr. Edward Drury, a bookseller, of Stamford. Mr. Drury called upon Clare at his own home, and with difficulty induced him to show him a few of his manuscript poems. Having read, among others, "My love, thou art a nosegay sweet," he was unable to conceal his gratification, and told Clare, to the poor poet's intense delight, that if he would procure the return of the poems in the possession of Mr. Henson he would publish a volume and give Clare the profits after deducting expenses.

On this footing 'the poet became intimate with Mr. Drury, who frequently entertained him at his house. His letters to Clare are cordial, and disclose an honest desire to be of service to him, on which account it is the more to be regretted that, owing to a dispute which afterwards took place between Mr. Drury and Mr. Taylor, Clare's London publisher, Clare rather ungraciously separated himself from his early friend. He was clearly indebted to Mr. Drury in the first instance for the opportunity of emerging from obscurity into public notice, and also for introductions to Mr. Taylor and Mr. Octavius Gilchrist, both men of influence in literary circles, and both of whom took an active and genuine interest in the young poet. Mr. Taylor, as has been already stated, became his editor and publisher, and remained his faithful friend until after Clare had been lost to public view within the walls of a lunatic asylum.

Towards the end of 1819 Clare met Mr. Taylor at the house of Mr. Gilchrist, in Stamford, and the latter gentleman gave the following account of the interview in a patronizing and not very judicious article which appeared in the " London Magazine" for January, 1820 :—" Mr. Taylor had seen Clare, for the first time, in the morning, and he doubted much if our invitation would be accepted by the rustic poet, who had now just returned from his daily labour, shy, and reserved, and disarrayed as he was. In a few minutes, however, Clare announced his arrival by a hesitating knock at the door.—' between a single and a double rap'—and immediately upon his introduction he dropped into a chair. Nothing could exceed the meekness, and simplicity, and diffidence with which he answered the various enquiries concerning his life and habits, which we mingled with subjects calculated or designed to put him much at his ease.   *   *   *

Of music he expressed himself passionately fond, and had learnt to play a little on the violin, in the humble hope of obtaining a trifle at the annual feasts in the neighbourhood, and at Christmas.   *   *   * The tear stole silently down the cheek of the rustic poet as one of our little party sang ' Auld Robin Gray.'"
Mr. Martin gives a somewhat different account of this interview. He states that the poet took decidedly too much wine, and that while under its influence he wrote some doggerel verses which Mr. Gilchrist had the cruelty to print in the article intended formally to introduce Clare to the notice of the English public. Mr. Gilchrist was an accomplished and warm-hearted man, and it was by his desire that Hilton, the Royal Academican painted Clare's portrait for exhibition in London, but he presumed too much upon his social superiority, and his judgment was at fault in supposing that the poet was all meekness and diffidence. On one occasion he took him sharply to task for associating with a Nonconformist minister, and Clare warmly resented this interference and for a time absented himself from Mr. Gilchrist's house. A reconciliation, however, soon took place, and the poet and the learned grocer of Stamford were fast friends until the death of the latter in 1823.

Clare's first volume was brought out by Taylor and
Hessey in January, 1820. It was entitled " Poems Descriptive of Rural Life and Scenery," and contained an
introduction from the pen of Mr. Taylor. In this preface
the peculiarities of Clare's genius were described with
force and propriety, his perseverance in the face of great
discouragements was commended, and the sympathy and
support of the public were invited in the following
passage :—" No poet of our country has shown greater
ability under circumstances so hostile to its development.
And all this is found here without any of those distressing
and revolting alloys which too often debase the native
worth of genius, and make him who was gifted with
powers to command admiration live to be the object of
contempt or pity. The lower the condition of its pos-
sessor the more unfavourable, generally, has been the
effect of genius on his life. That this has not been the
case with Clare may, perhaps, be imputed to the absolute
depression of his fortune.   *   *   *   When
we hear the consciousness of possessing talent, and the
natural irritability of the poetic temperament, pleaded
in extenuation of the follies and vices of men in high
life, let it be accounted no mean praise to such a man
as Clare that with all the excitements of their sensibility
in his station he has preserved a fair character amid
dangers which presumption did not create and difficulties
which discretion could not avoid. In the real troubles of
life, when they are not brought on by the misconduct of
the individual, a strong mind acquires the power of right-
ing itself after each attack, and this philosophy, not to

call it by a better name, Clare possesses. If the expectations of a 'better life,' which he cannot help indulging, should all be disappointed by the coldness with which this volume may be received, he can

'—put up with distress, and be content.'

In one of his letters he says, 'If my hopes don't succeed the hazard is not of much consequence: if I fall, I am advanced at no great distance from my low condition: if I sink for want of friends my old friend Necessity is ready to help me as before. It was never my fortune as yet to meet advancement from friendship: my fate has ever been hard labour among the most vulgar and lowest conditions of men, and very small is the pittance hard labour allows me, though I always toiled even beyond my strength to obtain it.' To see a man of talent struggling under great adversity with such a spirit must surely excite in every generous heart the wish to befriend him. But if it be otherwise, and he should be doomed to remediless misery,

'Why, let the stricken deer go weep,
    The hart ungalled play,
For some must watch, while some sleep,—
    Thus runs the world away.'"

Towards the end of January, 1820, the Rev. Mr. Holland, of Northborough, the minister already referred to, called upon Clare with the joyful news that his poems had been published, and that the volume was a great success. Next day a messenger arrived from Stamford with an invitation to the poet to meet Mr. Drury and Mr.

Gilchrist. They confirmed the favourable report made by Mr. Holland, and at length Clare had an opportunity of seeing the book which had caused him so many anxious days and sleepless nights. He made no attempt to conceal the honest pride he felt on receiving the congratulations of his friends, and acknowledged his obligation to Mr. Taylor for the editorial pains he had taken to prepare his manuscripts for the press, but he was deeply mortified at the tone of the "Introduction," in which Mr. Taylor dwelt, perhaps unconsciously, on Clare's poverty as constituting his chief claim to public notice.

The success of the "Poems" could scarcely be overstated. The eager curiosity of the public led to the first edition being exhausted in a few days, and a second was promptly announced. "The Gentleman's Magazine," the "New Monthly Magazine," the "Eclectic Review," the "Anti-Jacobin Review," the "London Magazine," and many other periodicals, welcomed the new poet with generous laudation. Following these came the "Quarterly Review," then under the editorship of the trenchant Gifford. To the astonishment of the reading public, the "Quarterly," which about this time "killed poor Keats," admitted a genial article on the rustic bard, and gave him the following excellent advice:—"We counsel—we entreat him to continue something of his present occupations, to attach himself to a few in the sincerity of whose friendship he can confide, and to suffer no temptations of the idle and the dissolute to seduce him from the quiet scenes of his youth (scenes so congenial to his taste) to the hollow and heartless society of cities, to the haunts of men who would court and flatter him while his name was new, and who, when they had contributed to distract his attention and impair his health, would cast him off unceremoniously to seek some other novelty. Of his again encountering the difficulties and privations he lately experienced there is no danger. Report speaks of honourable and noble friends already secured : with the aid of these, the cultivation of his own excellent talents, and a meek but firm reliance on that good Power by whom these were bestowed, he may, without presumption, anticipate a rich reward in the future for the evils endured in the morning of his life." The estimate formed by the writer of the liberality of Clare's patrons was exaggerated, and instead of there ·being no danger of his ever again having to encounter difficulties and privations he was scarcely ever free from them until the crowning privation had placed him beyond their influence.

The " Poems Descriptive of Rural Life and Scenery" were about seventy in number, including twenty-one sonnets. The volume opened with an apostrophe to Helpstone, in the manner of Goldsmith, and among the longer pieces were " The Fate of Amy," " Address to Plenty, in Winter," " Summer Morning," " Summer Evening," and " Crazy Nell." The minor pieces included the sonnet " To the Primrose," already quoted, " My love, thou art a Nosegay sweet," and " What is Life ? a reflective poem produced under circumstances with which the reader has been made acquainted. The two compositions last named are inserted here as examples of Clare's style at this early period of his career :—

My Love, thou art a Nosegay Sweet.

My love, thou art a nosegay sweet,
    My sweetest flower I'll prove thee,
And pleased I pin thee to my breast,
    And dearly do I love thee.

And when, my nosegay, thou shalt fade,
    As sweet a flower thou'lt prove thee;
And as thou witherest on my breast,
    For beauty past I'll love thee.

And when, my nosegay, thou shalt die,
    And heaven's flower shalt prove thee,
My hopes shall follow to the sky,
    And everlasting love thee.

What is Life?

And what is Life? An hour-glass on the run,
A mist retreating from the morning sun,
A busy, bustling, still repeated dream;
Its length ?—A minute's pause, a moment's thought;
And happiness ?—a bubble on the stream,
That in the act of seizing shrinks to nought.

What are vain hopes ?—The puffing gale of morn,
That of its charms divests the dewy lawn,
And robs each flow'ret of its gem,—and dies;
A cobweb hiding disappointment's thorn,
Which stings more keenly through the thin disguise.

* * * *

And what is Death ?   Is still the cause unfound ?
That dark, mysterious name of horrid sound ?—
A long and lingering sleep, the weary crave.
And Peace ? where can its happiness abound ?
No where at all, save heaven, and the grave.

Then what is Life ?—When stripp'd of its disguise,
A thing to be desir'd it cannot be,
Since everything that meets our foolish eyes
Gives proof sufficient of its vanity.
'Tis but a trial all must undergo,
To teach unthankful mortals how to prize
That happiness vain man's denied to know
Until he's called to claim it in the skies.

The following lines in the " Address to Plenty" have
always been admired for their Doric strength and
simplicity, and the vivid realism of the scene which they
depict :—

Toiling in the naked fields,
Where no bush a shelter yields,
Needy Labour dithering stands,
Beats and blows his numbing hands,
And upon the crumping snows
Stamps, in vain, to warm his toes.
Leaves are fled, that once had power
To resist a summer shower ;
And the wind so piercing blows,
Winnowing small the drifting snows.

Clare used at first, without hesitation, the provincialisms of his native county, but afterwards, as his mind matured, he saw the propriety of adopting the suggestions which Charles Lamb and other friends made to him on this subject, and his style gradually became more polished, until in the " Rural Muse" scarcely any provincialisms were employed, and the glossary of the earlier volumes was therefore unnecessary.

The article in the " Quarterly " was, with the exception, perhaps, of the concluding paragraph, just quoted, from the pen of Clare's friend and neighbour, Mr. Gilchrist, who wrote to Clare on the subject in the following jocular strain :—" What's to be done now, Measter ? Here's a letter from William Gifford saying I promised him an article on one John Clare, for the ' Quarterly Review.' Did I do any such thing ? Moreover, he says he has promised Lord Radstock, and if I know him, as he thinks I do, I know that the Lord will persecute him to the end. This does not move me much. But he adds, ' Do not fail me, dear Gil., for I count upon you. Tell your simple tale, and it may do the young bard good.' Think you so ? Then it must be set about. But how to weave the old web anew—how to hoist the same rope again and again—how to continue the interest to a twice-told tale ? Have you committed any arsons or murders that you have not yet revealed to me ? If you have, out with 'em straight, that I may turn 'em to account before you are hanged ; and as you will not come here to confess, I must hunt you up at Helpstone ; so look to it, John Clare, for ere it be long, and before you expect me, I shall be about your eggs and bacon. I have had my critical cap on these two days, and the cat-o'-nine-tails in my hands, and soundly I'll flog you for your sundry sins, John Clare, John Clare! Given under my hand the tenth of the fourth month, anno Domini 1820."

Following close upon the complimentary criticisms in the principal monthlies, the condescension of the " Quarterly" completed the little triumph, and Clare's verses became the fashion of the hour. One of his poems was set to music by Mr. Henry Corri, and sung by Madame Vestris at Covent Garden. Complimentary letters, frequently in rhyme, flowed in upon him, presents of books were brought by nearly every coach,* and influential friends set about devising plans (of which more presently,) to rescue him from poverty and enable him to devote at all events a portion of his time to the Muses. On the other hand, visitors from idle curiosity were far more numerous than was agreeable, and he was pestered with applications for autographs and poems for ladies' albums, with patronage and advice from total strangers, with tracts from well-meaning clergymen, and with invitations to lionizing parties. One of these communications was in

* Among those who at this time or subsequently made Clare presents of books were Lord Radstock, Bishop Marsh, Mrs. Emmerson, Sir Walter Scott, Robert Bloomfield, Mr. Gilchrist, Lord Milton, Messrs. Taylor & Hessey, Messrs. Smith, Elder, & Co., Charles Lamb, Henry Behnes, Lady Sophia Pierrepoint, the Rev. H. F. Cary, E. V. Rippingille, Allan Cunningham, Geo. Darley, Sir Charles A. Elton, William Gifford, Mr. and Mrs. S. C. Hall, James Montgomery, E. Drury, Alaric A. Watts, William Hone, &c. Clare's little library, consisting of 500 volumes, was purchased from his widow, after his death, and placed in the Northampton Museum.

its way a unique production, and for the entertainment of the reader a portion of it is here introduced :—

"The darksome daughter of Chaos has now enveloped our hemisphere (which a short time since was enubilous of clouds) in the grossest blackness. The drowsy god reigns predominantly, and the obstreperous world is wrapped in profound silence. No sounds gliding through the ambient air salute my attentive auricles, save the frightful notes which at different intervals issue from that common marauder of nocturnal peace—the lonesome, ruin-dwelling owl. Wearied rustics, exhausted by the toils of the day, are enjoying a sweet and tranquil repose. No direful visions appal their happy souls, nor terrific ghosts of quondam hours stand arrayed before them. Every sense is lost in the oblivious stream. Even those who on the light, fantastic toe lately tripped through the tangled dance of mirth have sunk into the arms of

Tired Nature's sweet restorer, balmy sleep.
Meditation, avaunt !

Respected (tho' unknown) Sir,—Out of the abundant store of your immutable condescension graciously deign to pardon the bold assurance and presumptuous liberty of an animated mass of undistinguished dust, whose fragile composition is most miraculously composed of congenial atoms so promiscuously concentred as to personify in an abstracted degree the beauteous form of man, to convey by proxy to your brilliant opthalmic organs the sincere thanks of a mild, gentle, and grateful heart for the delightful amusement I have experienced and the instruction I have reaped by reading your excellent poems, in (several of) which you have exquisitely given dame nature her natural form, and delineated her in colours so admirable that on the perusal of them I was led to exclaim with extacy Clare everywhere excells in the descriptive. But your literary prowess is too circuitously authenticated to admit of any punctilious commendation from my debilitated pen, and under its umbrageous recess, serenely segregated, from the malapert and hypochondriachal vapours of myopic critics (as I am no acromatic philosopher) I trust every solecism contained in this autographical epistle will find a salvable retirement. Tho' no Solitaire, I am irreversibly resolved to be on this occasion heteroclitical. I will not insult your good sense by lamenting the exigencies of the present times, as doubtless it always dictates to you to be (whilst travelling through the mazy labyrinth of joy and sorrow) humble in the lucent days of prosperity and omnific in the tenebricous moments of adversity." And so on, for several pages, concluding with an invitation to meet a few congenial spirits at dinner. It is not on record that the poet accepted the invitation.

Clare's claim to the title of poet having been established, his noble neighbours at Milton and Burghley invited him to visit them. At Milton Park he was graciously received by Earl Fitzwilliam and Lord and Lady Milton, after he had dined with the servants. A long conversation on his health, means, expectations, and principles was held, and he was dismissed with a very handsome present—an earnest of greater favours to come.

The visit to the Marquis of Exeter was equally gratifying. His lordship made himself acquainted with the state of the poet's affairs, and having read a number of unpublished effusions which Clare had taken with him, told him that it was his intention to allow him an annuity of fifteen pounds for life. The delight of the poor bard may be imagined without difficulty, for now he doubted not he could reconcile Patty's parents to the long hoped-for marriage, and deliver his mistress from anxieties which had for some time made life almost intolerable. He dined in the servants' hall. About the same time Clare also visited by invitation General Birch Reynardson, of Holywell Park—a visit full of romance, as narrated by Mr. Martin, a beautiful young lady, governess to the General's children, having to all appearances fallen desperately in love with the poet at first sight. The only unromantic incident of the day was the customary dinner at the servants' table. Clare's biographer, with excusable warmth, says that his local patrons, however much they might differ on other subjects, held that the true place of a poet was among footmen and kitchen maids. But it should not be forgotten that the noblemen named were life-long friends of Clare and his family, and it would be unjust to reflect upon their memory because the relations of "the hearty and generous Oxford," the Duke and Duchess of Queensbury, and Lord Bolingbroke with the polite and scholarly Prior, Gay, and Pope were not immediately established between the Marquis of Exeter or Earl Fitzwilliam and the gifted but unlettered rustic who had toiled in their fields.

Clare's proud spirit was almost always restive under the burden of patronage, especially if bestowed on account of his poverty, but we may feel sure that he did not expect to dine with these noblemen, that no indignity was intended in sending him to the common hall, and that it did not occur to him that he ought to feel insulted.

Clare was married to Martha Turner at Great Casterton Church on the 16th of March, 1820, and for a time Mrs. Clare remained at her father's house. She afterwards joined her husband at the house of his parents in Helpstone, his "own old home of homes," as he fondly called the lowly cottage in one of his most pathetic poems, and there they all remained, with the offspring of the marriage, until the removal to Northborough in 1832. Flushed with his recent good fortune, Clare distributed bride cake among his friends, and received from all hearty good wishes for his future happiness.

Early in the same month, and before his marriage, Clare accepted the invitation of his publishers, Messrs. Taylor and Hessey, to pay them a visit in Town. He was accompanied by Mr. Gilchrist, and remained for a week, making his home at his publishers' house in Fleet-street. With great difficulty Mr. Taylor persuaded him to meet a party of friends and admirers at dinner. It was impossible for him to overcome with one effort his natural shyness, but the cordial manner in which he was welcomed by Mr. Taylor's guests put him comparatively at his case, for he was made to feel that the labourer was forgotten in the poet and that he was regarded as an equal. The host placed him at dinner next to Admiral Lord Radstock, an intimate friend of Mrs. Emmerson, a lady whose name will frequently occur in the course of this memoir. His lordship had taken great interest in Clare from the first appearance of his poems, and had already made him several presents of books. By mingled tact and kindness he got from the poet an account of his life, his struggles, his hopes, his fears, and his prospects. Clare's share in the conversation made so deep an impression upon Lord Radstock that he conceived for him an attachment approaching to affection, and never ceased to exert all the influence of his position and high character in favour of his protégé. The Editor has before him many letters addressed to Clare by his excellent friend, but is restrained, by a wish expressed in one of the number, from publishing any portion of them. The request does not, however, apply to the inscriptions in books which Lord Radstock presented to Clare, and as the intimacy had a very important influence on the poet's career, those who are sufficiently interested in the subject to read these pages will not look upon the following passages as a superfluity :—In a work by Thomas Erskine on the Christian Evidences his lordship wrote :—" The kindest and most valuable present that Admiral Lord Radstock cou'd possibly make to his dear & affectionate friend, John Clare. God grant that he may make the proper use of it ! " In a copy of Owen Feltham's " Resolves :"— " The Bible excepted, I consider Owen Feltham's

'Resolves' and Boyle's 'Occasional Reflections' to be two as good books as were ever usher'd into the world, with a view to direct the heart and keep it in its right place ; consequently, to render us happy in this life and lay a reasonable foundation for the salvation of our souls through Jesus Christ our only Mediator and Redeemer. It was, therefore, under this conviction that I not long since presented you with both these truly valuable books, earnestly hoping, trusting, and, let me add, not doubting that you will make that use of them which is intended by your ever truly and affectionate friend, Radstock." In a copy of Mason's " Self-Knowledge " :—" I give this little pocket companion to my friend John Clare, not with a view to improve his heart, for that, I believe, would be no easy task, but in order to enable him to acquire a more perfect knowledge of his own character, and likewise to give him a close peep into human nature." In a copy of Hannah More's " Spirit of Prayer " :—" My very dear Clare,—If this excellent little book, and the others which accompany it, do not speak sufficiently for themselves, it would be in vain to think of offering you any further earthly inducement to study them and seek the truth. The grace of God can alone do this, and Heaven grant that this may not be wanting ! So prays your truly sincere and affectionate Radstock." Similar inscriptions accompanied a copy of Watson's " Apology for the Bible," Bishop Wilson's " Maxims of Piety and Christianity," and other works of a corresponding character.

Soon after his arrival in London Lord Radstock took Clare to see Mrs. Emmerson, who had already been in

correspondence with him, and thus commenced a friendship the ardour and constancy of which knew no abate-
ment until poor Clare was no longer able to hold rational
intercourse with his fellow-creatures. Mrs. Emmerson
was the wife of Mr. Thomas Emmerson, of Berners-
street, Oxford-street, and afterwards of Stratford-place.
She was a lady in easy circumstances, and occupied a
good social position.* Being of refined and elegant
tastes, and singularly generous disposition, she associated
herself with young aspirants for fame in poetry, painting,
and sculpture, and to the utmost of her power en-
deavoured to procure for them public notice and patronage. She was herself a frequent writer of graceful verses,
and her letters disclose a sensitive, poetic mind, a habit
of self-denial when the happiness of her friends was
concerned, and a delicate physical organization liable to
prostrating attacks of various nervous disorders. Clare
preserved nearly three hundred of her letters, the dates
ranging from February, 1820, to July, 1837, or an average
of one letter in about every three weeks ; and the Editor,
having read the whole of them, feels constrained, a
different version of the relationship having been given,
to state his conviction that no poor struggling genius
was ever blessed with a tenderer or a truer friend. No
man of feeling could rise from the perusal of them without the deepest respect and admiration for the writer.
The style is effusive, and the language in which the
lady writes of Clare's poetry is occasionally eulogistic

* Mr. S. C. Hall kindly informs me that Mrs. Emmerson " was a handsome, graceful, and accomplished lady." Her letters show that she was Clare's
senior by eleven or twelve years. —ED.

to the point of extravagance, and was to that extent
injudicious; but all blemishes are forgotten in the presence
of overwhelming evidences of pure and disinterested
friendship. Although by no means insensible to the
reception given to her own verses, Clare's literary reputation lay much nearer to her heart. She firmly believed
that he was a great genius, and she insisted upon all
her friends believing so too, and buying his books. She
very soon began to feel an interest in his domestic affairs,
and to send him valuable presents. She was godmother
to his second child, which was named after her, Eliza
Louisa, and for years the coach brought regularly, a day
or two before Christmas, two sovereigns "to pay for little
Eliza's schooling," another sovereign for the Christmas
dinner, and a waistcoat-piece and two India silk necker-
chiefs "for my dear Clare" with many kind wishes "for
all in his humble cot." At another time Patty's eyes
were gladdened by the present of a dozen silver teaspoons
and a pair of sugar tongs. These were followed by a
silver seal, engraved for Clare in Paris and mounted in
ivory, while under the pretext that he must find postage
expensive she several times sent him a sovereign "under
the wax." At one time she would appear to have given
him sufficient clothing to equip the entire family, and
when in 1832 Clare made his venture as a cottage farmer
his thoughtful friend gave him £10 with which to buy
a cow, stipulating only (for the kind-hearted little woman
must be sentimental) that it should be christened "May."
After that, she strove hard to obtain for one of his boys
admission to Christ's Hospital, and in conjunction with

Mr. Taylor discharged a heavy account sent in by a local medical practitioner.

But in higher matters than these the genuineness of Mrs. Emmerson's friendship for Clare was demonstrated. The poet poured into her listening and patient ear the story of every trial and every annoyance which fell to his lot, not concealing from his friend those mental sufferings which were caused solely by his own indiscretion and folly. Under these latter circumstances she rebuked him with affectionate solicitude and fidelity. In perplexities arising out of matters of business she gave him the best advice in her power, and when her knowledge of affairs failed her appealed to her husband, who was always ready to do anything for "dear Johnny," as Clare came to be called in Stratford-place. When he complained of being distressed by wild fancies and haunted by gloomy forebodings, as he did many years before his reason gave way, she first rallied him, though often herself suffering acutely, and then entreated him to dispel his melancholy by communing afresh with Nature and by meditations on the Divine greatness and goodness.

Within a few weeks of the appearance of " Poems Descriptive of Rural Life and Scenery," a private subscription was set on foot by Lord Radstock for the benefit of Clare and his family. Messrs. Taylor and Hessey headed the list with the handsome donation of £100. Earl Fitzwilliam followed with a corresponding amount; The Duke of Bedford and the Duke of Devonshire gave £20 each; Prince Leopold of Saxe-Coburg (afterwards King of the Belgians), the Duke of Northumberland, the Earl of Cardigan, Lord John Russell, Sir Thomas Baring, Lord Kenyon, and several other noblemen and gentlemen, £10 each, making with numerous smaller subscriptions a total of £420 12 0. This sum was invested, in the name of trustees, in Navy Five per Cents., and yielded, until the conversion of that security to a lower denomination, about £20 a year.

About the same time the attention of Earl Spencer was called to Clare's circumstances by Mr. J. S. Bell, a Stamford surgeon, and his lordship signified to Mr. Bell his intention to settle upon the poet an annuity of £10 for life. These various benefactions, with the Marquis of Exeter's annuity of £15, put Clare in the possession of £45 a-year, and his friends were profuse in their congratulations on his good fortune. As he had now a fixed income greater than that he had ever derived from labour, it was thought that by occasional farm work and by the profit resulting from the sale of his poems he would be relieved from anxiety about domestic affairs, and be enabled to devote at least one half of his time to the cultivation of his poetic faculties. The expectation appears to have been a reasonable one, but as will be seen hereafter it was only imperfectly realized.

The first volume of poems passed rapidly through three editions, and a fourth was printed. Several of Clare's influential friends took exception to a few passages in the first issue on the ground that they were rather too outspoken in their rusticity, and Lord Radstock strongly urged the omission in subsequent editions of several lines which he characterized as " Radical slang." Mr. Taylor contested both points for some time, but Lord Radstock threatened to disown Clare if he declined to oblige his patrons, and the poet at length made the desired concessions. The following were the passages over which his lordship exercised censorship :—

Accursed Wealth ! o'erbounding human laws,
Of every evil thou remain'st the cause.

    *   *   *   *

Sweet rest and peace, ye dear, departed charms,
Which industry once cherished in her arms,
When ease and plenty, known but now to few,
Were known to all, and labour had its due.

    *   *   *   *

The rough, rude ploughman, off his fallow-grounds,
(That necessary tool of wealth and pride)—

Being strongly urged thereto by Mr. Taylor, Clare sent to London a large bundle of manuscripts with permission to his editor to make a selection therefrom for a new work. The correspondence connected with this project extended over several months, and in the autumn of 1821 the " Village Minstrel and other Poems" made its appearance in two volumes, with a portrait after Hilton and a view of the poet's cottage. In the course of the correspondence there occurs the following passage, which has an interest of its own, in a letter from Mr. Taylor :—
" Keats, you know, broke a blood-vessel, and has been

41

very ill. He is now recovering, and it is necessary for his getting through the winter that he should go to Italy. Rome is the place recommended. You are now a richer man than poor K., and how much more fortunate! We have some trouble to get through 500 copies of his work, though it is highly spoken of in the periodical works, but what is most against him it has been thought necessary in the leading review, the "Quarterly," to damn his fame on account of his political opinions. D——n them, I say, who could act in so cruel a way to a young man of undoubted genius." And again (March 26, 1821):—
"The life of poor Keats is ended at last: he died at the age of twenty-five. He used to say he should effect nothing which he would rest his fame upon until he was thirty, and all hopes are over at twenty-five. But he has left enough, though he did not think so, and if his biographer cannot do him justice the advocate is in fault, and not the cause. Poor fellow! Perhaps your feeling will produce some lines to his memory. One of the very few poets of this day is gone. Let another beware of Stamford. I wish you may keep to your resolution of shunning that place, for it will do you immense injury if you do not. You know what I would say. Farewell." There is little doubt that by the closing hint Mr. Taylor desired to put Clare on his guard against the indiscreet hospitality of well-to-do friends at Stamford.

While the "Village Minstrel" was in course of preparation the "London Magazine" passed into the possession of Messrs. Taylor & Hessey, and they at once invited Clare to contribute, offering payment at the rate of one guinea per page, with the right to re-publish at any time on the original terms of half profits. Clare accepted the offer, and as he contributed almost regularly for some time, a substantial addition was made to his income. Among Clare's fellow-contributors in 1821 were Charles Lamb and De Quincey, the former with " Essays of Elia," and the latter with " Confessions of an English Opium-Eater."

Two thousand copies of the " Village Minstrel " were printed, and by the beginning of December 800 had been sold. This was a very modified success, but a number of circumstances combined to make the season an unfavourable one for the publication of such a work. That the poetry of the " Village Minstrel " is far superior both in conception and execution to much contained in Clare's first book was undisputed, and indeed it may be said at once that every successive work which he published was an improvement upon its predecessor, until in the " Rural Muse " a vigour of conception and polish of diction are displayed which the most ardent admirers of Clare in his younger days— (Mrs. Emmerson always excepted, who believed him to be at least Shakespeare's equal)—would not have ventured to predict. The " Village Minstrel " was so named after the principal poem, which contains one hundred and nineteen Spenserian stanzas, and is to a considerable extent autobiographical. It was composed in 1819, at which time Clare was wretchedly poor, and this will no doubt account for the repining tone of a few of the

verses. It abounds, however, in poetical beauties, of
which the following stanzas may be taken as examples :—

O who can tell the sweets of May-day's morn,
To waken rapture in a feeling mind,
When the gilt East unveils her dappled dawn,
And the gay wood-lark has its nest resigned,
As slow the sun creeps up the hill behind ;
Moon reddening round, and daylight's spotless hue,
As seemingly with rose and lily lined ;
While all the prospect round beams fair to view,
Like a sweet Spring flower with its unsullied dew.

Ah, often, brushing through the dripping grass,
Has he been seen to catch this early charm,
List'ning to the " love song " of the healthy lass
Passing with milk-pail on her well-turned arm,
Or meeting objects from the rousing farm—
The jingling plough-teams driving down the steep
Waggon and cart, and shepherd dog's alarm,
Raising the bleatings of unfolding sheep,
As o'er the mountain top the red sun 'gins to peep.

The first volume contains also a poem entitled " William
and Robin," of which Mr. Taylor says in his " Introduction : "—" The pastoral, ' William and Robin,' one of
Clare's earliest efforts, exhibits a degree of refinement and
elegant sensibility which many persons can hardly believe
a poor uneducated clown could have possessed : the
delicacy of one of the lovers towards the object of his
attachment is as perfectly inborn and unaffected as if he
were a Philip Sidney."

Among the minor pieces of the " Village Minstrel "
are the following, which are given as additional illustrations—the first of Clare's descriptive and the latter
of his amatory manner :—

THE EVENING HOURS.

The sultry day it wears away,
    And o'er the distant leas
The mist again, in purple stain,
    Falls moist on flower and trees :
His home to find, the weary hind
    Glad leaves his carts and ploughs ;
While maidens fair, with bosoms bare,
    Go coolly to their cows.

The red round sun his work has done,
    And dropp'd into his bed ;
And sweetly shin'd the oaks behind
    His curtains fringed with red :
And step by step the night has crept,
    And day, as loth, retires ;
But clouds, more dark, night's entrance mark,
    Till day's last spark expires.

Pride of the vales, the nightingales
    Now charm the oaken grove ;
And loud and long, with amorous tongue,
    They try to please their love :
And where the rose reviving blows
    Upon the swelter'd bower,
I'll take my seat, my love to meet,
    And wait th' appointed hour,

And like the bird, whose joy is heard
    Now he his love can join,
Who hails so loud the even's shroud,
    I'll wait as glad for mine :
As weary bees o'er parched leas
    Now meet reviving flowers,
So on her breast I'll sink to rest,
    And bless the evening hours.

I LOVE THEE, SWEET MARY.

I love thee, sweet Mary, but love thee in fear ;
    Were I but the morning breeze, healthful and airy,
As thou goest a-walking I'd breathe in thine ear,
    And whisper and sigh, how I love thee, my Mary !

I wish but to touch thee, but wish it in vain ;
    Wert thou but a streamlet, a-winding so clearly,
And I little globules of soft dropping rain,
    How fond would I press thy white bosom, my Mary !

I would steal a kiss, but I dare not presume ;
    Wert thou but a rose in thy garden, sweet fairy,
And I a bold bee for to rifle its bloom,
    A whole Summer's day would I kiss thee, my Mary !

I long to be with thee, but cannot tell how ;
    Wert thou but the elder that grows by thy dairy,
And I the blest woodbine to twine on the bough,
    I'd embrace thee and cling to thee ever, my Mary !

Mr. Taylor called at Helpstone in October, 1821, on his way from Retford to London, and published, in the "London Magazine" for the following month, an interesting and genial account of his visit to Clare. While at Helpstone he urged Clare to accept an oft-repeated invitation to come to London and prolong his stay to a few weeks, but about this time the poet, always yearning after independence, became possessed with a longing to acquire a small freehold of about seven acres, which belonged to friends of his own who had mortgaged it to the amount of £200, and being unable to meet the interest thereupon were threatened with a foreclosure. The owners offered the property to Clare, who at once applied to his friends in London to sell out sufficient of the funded property to enable him to acquire it. His disappointment and mortification appear to have been very keen on learning that the funded property was vested in trustees who were restricted to paying the interest to him.

This resource having failed him, he offered to sell his writings to his publishers for five years for £200. To this proposal Mr. Taylor replied on the 4th of February, 1822 :—" It will not be honourable in us to buy the interest in your poems for five years for £200. It may be worth more than that, which would be an injury to you, and a discredit to us; or less, which would be a loss to us. Besides, if the original mortgage was for £200, it is not that sum which would redeem it now. Many expenses have been created by these money-lenders, all which must be satisfied before the writings would be given up. It is meddling with a wasp's nest to interfere rashly. I am happy that Lord Milton has taken the writings, to look them over. He may be able to do some good, and to keep your friends the Billingses in their little estate, but I fear it is not possible for you to do it without incurring fresh risks, and encountering such dangers from the want of sufficient legal advice as would be more than you would get through." Clare had set his heart upon accomplishing this little scheme ; his failure to compass it weighed upon his mind, and for a time he sought an alleviation of his unhappiness in the society of the Blue Bell and among hilarious friends at Stamford.

Clare paid a second visit to London in May, 1822, and was again hospitably entertained by his publishers, at whose house he met several literary men of note, whose friendship he afterwards enjoyed for years. Among these were Charles Lamb, Thomas Hood. H. F. Cary, Allan Cunningham, George Darley, and others ; but his most frequent companion in town would appear to have been Rippingille, the painter, to whom he was introduced at the house of Mrs. Emmerson. Clare was assured by that lady that he would find Mr. Rippingille an excellent and discreet young man, but there is reason to suspect that "friend Rip," as he was called by his intimates, had carefully concealed some of his foibles from Mrs. Emmerson, for he and Clare had several not very creditable drinking bouts, and were not particular in the class of entertainments which they patronized.

" Lord, what fools these mortals be !"

After Clare had returned to Helpstone and Rippingille to Bristol, where he lived for several years, the latter repeatedly urged his poet-friend to visit him, and this is the way in which the amusing rattlepate wrote :—

"My dear Johnny Clare,—I am perfectly sure that I sha'nt be able to write one word of sense, or spin out one decent thought. If the old Devil and the most romping of his imps had been dancing, and jostling, and running stark mad amongst the delicate threads and fibres of my brain, it could not be in a worse condition, but I am resolved to write in spite of the Devil, my stars, and want of brains, for all of which I have most excellent pre-cedents and examples, and sound orthodox authority, so here goes. To-night ; but what is to-night ? 'Twas last night, my dear Johnny. I was up till past five this morning, during which time I was stupid enough to imbibe certain potions of porter, punch, moselle, and madeira, that have been all day long uniting their forces in fermenting and fuming, and bubbling and humming.

  *   *   *   Are you coming, Clare, or are you going to remain until all the fine weather is gone, and then come and see nothing ? Or do you mean to come at all ? Now is your time, if you do. You will just be in time for the fair, which begins on the 1st of September and lasts ten days. And most glorious fun it is, I can tell you. Crowds, tribes, shoals, and natives of all sorts ! I looked at the standings the other night, and thought of you. Will he come, said I ? D—n the fellow ! Nothing can move him. There he sticks, and there he

will stick. Will none but a draggle-tailed muse suit him ?

> His evening devotions and matins
> Both addressed to a muse that wears pattens :
> A poet that kneels in the bogs,
> Where his muse can't go out without clogs,
> Or stir without crushing the frogs !
> —*Old Play.*

> Where toads die of vapours and hip,
> And tadpoles of ague and pip.
> —*Old Play.*

> Give 'em all, my dear Johnny, the slip,
> And at once take to Bristol a trip.
> By G—, you should come, and you must.
> Do you mean I should finish your bust ?
> If you don't, stay away and be cussed !

My muse is taken a little qualmish, therefore pray excuse her. She is a well-meaning jade, and if it was not for the wild treatment she received last night would, I have no doubt, have given you a very polite invitation, but I fear, Johnny, nothing will move you. Your heart is as hard as an overseer's. I dined at Elton's two days ago. We talked about you, wondered if you would come, feared not, regretted it, and the loss of the fine weather, and the fine scenery, and the other fine things : in fine, we lamented finely. Come and cheer our hearts. Bring Patty and all the little bardettes, if you will. We will find room for them somewhere. I have read only my introductory lecture yet, so that you may hear 'em or read 'em all, if you like. Having thrown my bread upon the waters, where I hope it will be found after many days, I take my leave, my dear Clare, in the full hope I shall see you by the 1st of September. Write to me by return, saying what day you will be here.

"Yours for ever and after,

"E. V. RIPPINGILLE."

Clare visited Charles Lamb, and received from him the following characteristic letter after his return to Helpstone :—

"India House, 31st Aug., 1822.

"Dear Clare,—I thank you heartily for your present. I am an inveterate old Londoner, but while I am among your choice collections I seem to be native to them and free of the country. The quantity of your observation has astonished me. What have most pleased me have been 'Recollections after a Ramble,' and those 'Grongar Hill' kind of pieces in eight-syllable lines, my favourite measure, such as 'Cowper Hill' and 'Solitude.' In some of your story-telling ballads the provincial phrases sometimes startle me. I think you are too profuse with them. In poetry, *slang* of every kind is to be avoided. There is a rustick Cockneyism as little pleasing as ours of London. Transplant Arcadia to Helpstone. The true rustic style, the Arcadian English, I think is to be found in Shenstone. Would his 'Schoolmistress,' the prettiest of poems, have been better if he had used quite the Goody's own language? Now and then a home rusticism is fresh and startling, but where nothing is gained in expression it is out of tenor. It may make folks smile and stare, but the ungenial coalition of barbarous with refined phrases will prevent you in the end from being so generally tasted as you deserve to be. Excuse my freedom, and take the same liberty with my *puns.*

"I send you two little volumes of my spare hours. They are of all sorts. There's a Methodist hymn for Sundays, and a farce for Saturday night. Pray give them a place on your shelf, and accept a little volume of which I have duplicate, that I may return in equal number to your welcome present.

"I think I am indebted to you for a sonnet in the 'London' for August.

"Since I saw you I have been in France and have eaten frogs. The nicest little rabbity things you ever tasted. Do look about for them. Make Mrs. Clare pick off the hind quarters; boil them plain with parsley and butter. The fore quarters are not so good. She may let them hop off by themselves.

"Yours sincerely,

"CHAS. LAMB."

During his second visit to London, Clare became for a few days the guest of Mr. Cary, at Chiswick. Here, it is said, he wrote several amorous sonnets in praise of Cary's wife, and presented them to the lady, who passed them on to her husband. The learned translator of Dante requested an explanation, which Clare at once gave. The circumstance that Cary corresponded with Clare for at least ten years afterwards will enable the reader to form his own estimate of the importance of the incident. Among Cary's letters were the following :—

          " Chiswick, London,

              " Jany. 3rd, 1822.

" Many happy years to you, dear Clare.

    " Do not think because I have not written to you sooner that I have forgot you. I often think of you in that walk we took here together, and which I take almost every day, generally alone, sometimes musing of absent friends and at others putting into English those old French verses which I dare say sometimes occasion you to cry 'Pish!'—(I hope you vent your displeasure in such innocent terms)—when turning over the pages of the magazine. I was much pleased with a native strain of yours, signed, I remember, 'Percy Green.' Mr. Taylor can tell you that I enquired with much earnestness after the author of it (it was the first with that signature), not knowing it to be yours, and what pleasure it gave me to find it was so. I am glad to find a new 'Shepherd's Calendar' advertised with your name. You will no doubt bring before us many objects in Nature that we have often seen in her but never before in books, and that in verse of a very musical construction. There are two things, I mean description of natural objects taken from the life, and a sweet melodious versification, that particularly please me in poetry ; and these two you can command if you choose. Of sentiment I do not reck so much. Your admiration of poets I felt most strongly earlier in life, and have still a good deal of it left, but time deadens that as

well as many of our other pleasantest feelings. Still, I had
rather pass my time in such company than in any other,
and the poetical part of my library is increasing above all
proportion above the rest. This you may think a strange
confession for me in my way of life to make, but whatever
one feels strongly impelled to, provided it be not wrong
in itself and can administer any benefit or pleasure to
others, I am inclined to think is the task allotted to one,
and thus I quiet my conscience about the matter. I did'nt
intend to make you my father confessor when I set out,
but now it is done I hope you will grant me absolution.

" Believe me, dear Clare,

" Ever sincerely yours,

" H. F. CARY."

" Chiswick, April 12th, 1823.

" Dear Clare,—   *   *   *

" Have you visited the haunts of poor Cowper
which you were invited to see ? And if so, what accordance did you find between the places and his descriptions
of them ? What a glory it is for poetry that it can make
any piece of trumpery an object of curiosity and interest !
I had the pleasure of meeting last week with Mr. Wordsworth. He is no piece of trumpery, but has all the
appearance of being that noblest work, an honest man.
I think I scarcely ever met with any one eminent for
genius who had not also something very amiable and
engaging in his manners and character. In Mr. Wordsworth I found much frankness and fervour. The first
impression his countenance gave me was one which I

did not receive from Chantrey's bust of him—that of his being a very benevolent man. Have you seen Barry Cornwall's new volume? He is one of the best writers of blank verse we have, but I think blank verse is not much in favour with you. The rhyme that is now in fashion runs rather too wild to please me. It seems to want pruning and nailing up. A sonnet, like a rose tree may be allowed to grow straggling, but a long poem should be trained into some order.   *   *   *

I hope you and your family have got well through this hard winter. Mrs. Cary, who has hitherto almost uniformly enjoyed good health, has suffered much from it. She and the rest of my family join in kind remembrances to you with, dear Clare,

" Yours sincerely,

" H. F. Cary."

" Chiswick, London, February 19th, 1825.

" My dear Clare,

          " I have been reproaching myself some time for not answering your last letter sooner, and as I am telling my congregation this Lent that it is no use to reproach oneself for one's sins if one does not amend them, I will mend this. I will freely own I should not have felt the same compunction if you had been in health and spirits, but when I find you so grievously complaining of the want of both, I cannot leave you any longer without such poor comfort as a line or two from me can give. I wish I were a doctor, and a skilful one, for your sake. I mean a doctor of medicine.

For though I were a doctor of divinity I doubt I could recommend to you no better prescription in that way than I can as plain Mister. Nay, it is one that any old woman in your parish could hit upon as readily as myself, and that is, patience and submission to a Will that is higher and wiser than our own. How often have I stood in need of it myself, and with what difficulty have I swallowed it, and how hard have I found it to keep on my stomach! May you, my friend, have better success! If you do not want it in one way you are sure to have occasion for it before long in some other. If you should be raised up from this sickness, as I trust you will, do not suppose but that you will have something else to try you. This, you will say, is not a very cheering prospect, but remember these lines in Crowe's poem, which you so justly admire :

> 'T is meet we jostle with the world, content,
> If by our Sovereign Master we be found
> At last not profitless.

What follows, I fear neither you nor I have philosophy enough to add with sincerity—

> For worldly meed,
> Given or withheld, I deem of it alike.

I will read the memoir of yourself which you purpose sending me, and not fail to tell you if I think you have spoken of others with more acrimony than you ought. There is no occasion for sending me with it your new publication. I shall get it as I have those before. I hope the last chapter of your memoir, if brought up to the present it me, will record your children's having got safely over the small pox, of which you express apprehensions in your last letter. We have got well through the winter hitherto. For want of better employment I have been teaching my youngest boy Dicky to write. Perhaps you will think me not over well qualified for so important an office, but I assure you when I have two parallel lines ruled at proper distances I can produce something like a copy. To teach others is no bad way to learn one's self. In spite of the floggings which I had at school, 1 could never learn that grammar for which you have so great an aversion, thoroughly, till I began to instruct my own son in it, but then I made a wonderful progress. I should not succeed so well in collecting ferns. A physician once recommended to me the study of botany for the good of my health, but he had published an edition of Linnæus. Another prescribed to me port wine, but, poor man, he soon fell a martyr to his own system. In such matters common sense and one's own inclination are the best guides. Mrs. C. and your other acquaintances here remember you kindly. I am, dear Clare, with best wishes for yourself and family,

" Your affectionate friend,

" H. F. CARY."

" British Museum, April 13th, 1830.

" Dear Clare,—I have waited some time to answer your letter, in hopes of being able to give you the information you require; but the information does not come, and I will wait no longer. I have not seen either Lamb or Wainwright since last summer, when the former spent one day with me here, and another day we all three met at the house of the latter, who now resides in a place he has inherited from a relative at Turnham Green. Lamb is settled at Endfield, about seven miles from London, with his sister, who I fear is in a very indifferent state of health ; so his friends see very little of him. * * *

In this grand age of utility, I suppose it will soon be discovered that a piece of canvas is more advantageously employed as the door of a safe, where it will secure a joint of meat from the flies, than if it was covered with the finest hues that Titian or Rubens could lay upon it, and a piece of paper better disposed of in keeping the same meat from being burnt while it is roasting, than in preserving the idle fancies of a poet. No matter : if it is so we must swim with the stream. You can employ yourself in cultivating your cabbages and in handling the hay fork, and I not quite so pleasantly in making catalogues of books. We will not be out of fashion, but show ourselves as useful as the rest of the world. In the meantime we may smile at what is going forward, entertain ourselves with our own whims in private, and expect that the tide some day may turn. My family, whom you are so kind as to enquire about, are all well, and all following the order of the day, except one, who has set himself to perverting canvas from its proper use by smearing it over with certain colours, fair indeed to look upon, but quite void of utility. I ought indeed to have made another exception, which is, that they are multiplying much faster than Mr. Malthus would approve. Cowper says somewhere of those who make the world older than the Bible accounts of it, that they have found out that He who made it and revealed its age to Moses was mistaken in the date. May it not be said of the anti-populationers that they virtually accuse him of as great ignorance in the command to multiply and replenish the earth? Well, you and I, Clare, have kept to this text. May we observe all the rest as well! which is so good a conclusion for a parson that I will say no more than that I am ever

" Yours truly,

" H. F. CARY.

" Mrs. C. is at Chiswick, but I can assure you of her good wishes."

" Dear Clare,—   *   *   *   You ask me for literary news. I have very little of a kind likely to interest you. Have you seen in the 'Edinburgh Review' an account of some poems by Elliot, a Sheffield workman? In his rhymes on the Corn Trade are not 'words that burn,' but words that scald. In his 'Love' there is a story told in a very affecting manner. In short they are the only new things I have been struck with for some time, and that before I knew who the writer was. I heard lately that our friend Mr. Lamb was very well, and his sister just recovered from one of those illnesses which she is often afflicted with. I have just sent to the press a translation of an old Greek poet. I do not expect he will please you much, as he treats of little but charioteering, boxing, running, and some old heathenish stories. But I will send you a copy, not requiring you to

read it.   Mrs. C., if she were at my elbow, would, I am
sure, desire to be kindly remembered to you.

> " Believe me, dear Clare,
>> " Sincerely yours,
>>> " H. F. CARY.

" British Museum, Octr. 30th, 1832."

Clare remained in London for several weeks, at the
end of which time he was suddenly recalled to Helpstone
by alarming reports of the state of his wife's health.   It
is to be feared that in more respects than one this second
visit to the metropolis had an unhealthy influence upon the
poet's mind and habits.   At this time he appears to have
made very little effort to resist the pressing hospitality of
his friends, and to have complied only too readily with
the convivial customs of the time.   He returned to
Helpstone moody and discontented, and in his letters to
Mrs. Emmerson he complained fretfully of the hardship
of his lot in being compelled to spend his days without
any literary companionship whatsoever.   About this time
that lady wrote to him two letters, which as illustrations
of the style of her correspondence are here given :—

> " 20, Stratford Place, 17th June, /22.

" My very dear Clare,—

> " Your letter reached me this morning, and
from the nature of its contents it leaves me nothing to
express in reply but my sincere regrets that any necessity
should have occurred to hasten your departure from
London without our again seeing each other.   I wish, my

dear friend, you had expressed more fully the real cause
of this sudden measure, for you leave me with many
painful fears upon my mind for the safety of your dear
wife, who I hope, ere this, has blessed you with a little
namesake, and that she is doing well with the dear babe.
I have also my own fears about yourself, your own health,
your state of mind, your worldly interests, &c., but
perhaps I am wrong to indulge in all these anxieties.
Mr. Emmerson and myself had looked for days past with
great solicitude for your return to us, and we had planned
many little schemes for our mutual enjoyment while you
were with us, but these, with many other matters with
which my mind and heart were full, are now at an end,
and God only knows when, or if ever, we may meet
again; but of this be assured, as long as my friendship
and correspondence are of value to you, you may command them. In our, alas, too short interviews we had
some interesting conversations. These will not be
forgotten by me, and I will hope on your return to your
own dear cot you will take the earliest opportunity to
write to your friend 'Emma.' Tell her all that affects
your happiness, and may you, my dear Clare, when
restored to the calm delights of retirement, experience
also the restoration of mental peace and every domestic
blessing! Mr. E. desires his kindest regards to you, and
his sincere regrets you could not spend a few days with
him ere you quitted London. Our noble and dear friend
[Lord Radstock] will also feel much disappointment at not
seeing you again. This is not what we had hoped for
and expected from your visit to Town. Yet let me not

reproach you with unkindness, though I feel much, very much, at this moment. Mr. Rippingille spent last evening with us and took his final leave. He goes off for Bristol this afternoon. I have sent your silk handkerchief, with another for you, my dear Clare, as a trifling remembrance of your very sincere and attached friend,

"Eliza L. Emmerson.

"P. S. Please let me know as soon as you reach home of your safe arrival, and if the little stranger has entered this world of woe, and if she bears the name of E. L. Lord R. has just left me, and sends his kind regards, and regrets at not having the opportunity to see you in Portland-place. Farewell.

"'Emma.'"

"Stratford Place, 26th June, 1822.

"My very dear Friend,—If it is necessary to make an apology for writing to you again so soon, the only one I shall attempt to make is that of offering you my sincere congratulations upon the birth of your sweet girl, Eliza Louisa, if I did not misunderstand you when you were in Town, and the certainty of which I wish to know in your next letter; also, if I may be allowed to stand godmother to my little namesake, and likewise if you have accepted the kind offer of Lord R. to become her noble godfather. You mention your dear wife in language that alarms and distresses me much for her safety. I hope in God, for your sake, and for the sake of your dear children, that all danger is over, and that she is now in a fair way to be speedily restored to you. Pardon me, my dear Clare, when I entreat you to do all in your power to comfort and compose her mind under her present delicate situation. Recollect if she is now a faded flower she has become so under your influence, and well may you be loth to lose the object who has shed her brightest hues on you, and who in giving birth to your sweet offspring may chance to fade almost to nothingness herself. But this should serve to bind your affections still stronger to her. Forgive me for talking thus to you, my dear Clare. I have no other motive than your domestic happiness, which I anxiously pray may be undisturbed by any event. I lament to learn by your letter that to stifle recollections of the past, &c., you should have fled to such resources on your journey home. Now you become the sufferer by such means. Why not exert your philosophy, instead of seeking that which serves to destroy your health and peace? You know, my dear Clare, that you are injuring yourself in the deepest sense by such habits. For God's sake, then, for your own dear children's sake, arm yourself with a determination, a fortitude, which would do honour to your excellent heart and good understanding, to fly from such a mode of consolation as from a poison that will quickly destroy you. Remember poor Burns! Let the solemn and affectionate warnings of your friend 'Emma' dissuade you, my dear Clare, from habits of inebriety. Independent of the loss of your health and mental powers, your moral character will be seriously injured by such means. You will charge me with preaching a sermon, I fear, and will be inclined to commit my good wishes to the flames, but you must not hate me for my counsel. I can readily suppose how the 'good Quaker' would be shocked at your 'disguise,' and I heartily regret the event, altho' I honour your liberality and candour in telling me of it. I have not heard from our friend Rippingille, but expect to do so daily. When I write to him I will make known your wishes to correspond with him.   *   *   *   You tell me you 'have many things to say to me in future about your journey, &c., &c.' Pray do not be long, my dear Clare, ere you make such communications, with all else that concerns you, for I shall be most anxious to hear good accounts of your dear wife and the sweet babe. Mr. E. desires me to say everything that is kind to you for him, as does our noble and dear friend. Heaven bless you, my dear Clare.

" Ever sincerely yours,

" ' EMMA.' "

In 1823, Clare suffered from a long and serious illness ; brought on, in all probability, by an insufficiency of food, and by mental anxiety caused by his inability to free himself from the importunity of creditors. During his illness he was visited by Mr. Taylor, who had come down to Stamford to attend the funeral of Mr. Gilchrist, and Mr. Taylor, shocked at the poet's appearance, procured for him at once the services of the principal physician in Peterborough.

Clare had also an excellent and warm-hearted friend in Mrs. Marsh, wife of the Bishop of Peterborough, who corresponded with him frequently, in a familiar and almost motherly manner, from 1821 to 1837. When Clare complained of indisposition, a messenger would be dispatched from "The Palace," with medicines or plaisters, camphor lozenges, or "a pound of our own tea," with sensible advice as to personal habits and diet. At another time hot-house grapes are sent, or the messenger bears toys for the children, or a magnifying glass to assist Clare in his observations in entomolgy, or books, or "three numbers of Cobbett's penny trash, which Mr. Clare may keep." One day Mrs. Marsh writes—" To show you how I wish to cheer you I am sending you cakes, as one does to children : they are harmless, so pray enjoy them, and write to tell me how you are." Engravings of the new chain pier are sent from Brighton, and on one occasion (in 1829) a steel pen was enclosed in a letter, as a great curiosity. Clare was on several occasions a visitor at the Bishop's Palace, and in July, 1831, Mrs. Marsh wrote the following note, which confirms the impression received from the perusal of other letters, that about that time Clare's mind had been much exercised with respect to his soul's health :—" My dear Mr. Clare,—I must take my leave, and in doing so must add that in thinking of you it is my greatest comfort to know that you fix your trust where our only and never-failing trust rests." Lady Milton also frequently sent her humble neighbour presents suitable to his invalid condition.

Clare had not entirely recovered from this illness, when in May, 1824. he once more accepted the invitation of his publishers to visit London. They were desirous that he should have the benefit of the advice of Dr. Darling, the kind-hearted physician already mentioned. On seeing him in Fleet-street Dr. Darling ordered that he should be kept perfectly free from excitement of all kinds, but at the end of two or three weeks he was permitted to meet a literary party composed chiefly of contributors to the "London Magazine." Among the guests were Coleridge, Lamb, De Quincey, Hazlitt, and Allan Cunningham. In the manuscript memoir to which reference has already been made, Clare noted down his impressions of Coleridge and others, and they are embodied in Mr. Martin's account of this visit. He was a frequent visitor to Mrs. Emmerson, and a few days before he left London was once more thrown into the society of Rippingille, who declared that he had left Bristol solely for the purpose of meeting his friend. Clare, obeying implicitly the injunctions of Dr. Darling, declined all invitations to revelry, and therefore the companionship was less prejudicial to his health and spirits than on the occasion of his former visit. At his publishers', Clare made the acquaintance of Mr. (afterwards Sir Charles) Elton, brother-in-law of Hallam, the historian, and uncle to the subject of "In Memoriam." Mr. Elton, who was a friend and patron of Rippingille, was much pleased with Clare, and while he was yet in London sent him from Clifton the following metrical epistle, which afterwards appeared in the "London

Magazine." It contains several interesting touches of
portraiture :—

> So loth, friend John, to quit the town !
> 'T was in the dales thou won'st renown ;
> I would not, John, for half a crown,
>> Have left thee there,
> Taking my lonely journey down
>> To rural air.
>
> The pavement flat of endless street
> Is all unsuited to thy feet,
> The fog-wet smoke is all unmeet
>> For such as thou,
> Who thought'st the meadow verdure sweet,
>> But think'st not now.
>
> "Time's hoarse unfeather'd nightingales " *
> Inspire not like the birds of vales :
> I know their haunts in river dales,
>> On many a tree,
> And they reserve their sweetest tales,
>> John Clare, for thee.
>
> I would not have thee come to sing
> Long odes to that eternal spring
> On which young bards their changes ring,
>> With buds and flowers :
> I look for many a better thing
>> Than brooks and bowers.

* Coleridge's definition of watchmen.

'T is true thou paintest to the eye
The straw-thatched roof with elm trees high,
But thou hast wisdom to descry
    What lurks below—
The springing tear, the melting sigh,
    The cheek's heart-glow.

The poets all, alive and dead,
Up, Clare, and drive them from thy head !
Forget whatever thou hast read
    Of phrase or rhyme,
For he must lead and not be led
    Who lives through time.

What thou hast been the world may see,
But guess not what thou still may'st be :
Some in thy lines a Goldsmith see,
    Or Dyer's tone :
They praise thy worst ; the best of thee
    Is still unknown.

Some grievously suspect thee, Clare :
They want to know thy form of prayer :
Thou dost not cant, and so they stare,
    And hint free-thinking :
They bid thee of the devil beware,
    And vote thee sinking.

With smile sedate and patient eye,
Thou mark'st the zealots pass thee by
To rave and raise a hue and cry
    Against each other :
Thou see'st a Father up on high ;
    In man a brother.

I would not have a mind like thine
Its artless childhood tastes resign,
Jostle in mobs, or sup and dine
    Its powers away,
And after noisy pleasures pine
    Some distant day.

And, John, though you may mildly scoff,
That hard, afflicting churchyard cough
Gives pretty plain advice, " Be off,
    While yet you can."
It is not time yet, John, to doff
    Your outward man.

Drugs ! can the balm of Gilead yield
Health like the cowslip-yellow'd field ?
Come, sail down Avon and be heal'd,
    Thou Cockney Clare.
My recipe is soon reveal'd—
    Sun, sea, and air.

What glue has fastened thus thy brains
To kennel odours and brick lanes?
Or is it intellect detains?
    For, faith, I'll own
The provinces must take some pains
    To match the town.

Does *Agnus* [1] fling his crotchets wild—
" In wit a man," in heart a child?
Has *Lepus'* [2] sense thine ear beguiled
    With easy strain?
Or hast thou nodded blithe, and smiled
    At *Janus'* [3] vein?

Does *Nalla,* [4] that mild giant, bow
His dark and melancholy brow?
Or are his lips distending now
    With roaring glee
That tells the heart is in a glow—
    The spirit free?

Or does the *Opium-eater* [5] quell
Thy wondering sprite with witching spell?
Read'st thou the dreams of murkiest hell
    In that mild mien?
Or dost thou doubt yet fear to tell
    Such e'er have been?

And while around thy board the wine
Lights up the glancing eyeballs' shine,
Seest thou in elbow'd thought recline
    The *Poet true* [6]
Who in " Colonna " seems divine
    To me and you ?

But, Clare, the birds will soon be flown :
Our Cambridge wit resumes his gown :
Our *English Petrarch* [7] trundles down
    To Devon's valley :
Why, when our Maga 's out of town,
    Stand shilly-shally ?

The table-talk of London still
Shall serve for chat by rock and rill,
And you again may have your fill
    Of season'd mirth,
But not if spade your chamber drill
    Six feet in earth.

Come, then ! Thou never saw'st an oak
Much bigger than a waggon spoke :
Thou only could'st the Muse invoke
    On treeless fen :
Then come and aim a higher stroke,
    My man of men.

The wheel and oar, by gurgling steam,
Shall waft thee down the wood-brow'd stream,
And the red channel's broadening gleam
    Dilate thy gaze,
And thou shalt conjure up a theme
    For future lays.

And thou shalt have a jocund cup
To wind thy spirits gently up—
A stoup of hock or claret cup
    Once in a way,
And we 'll take notes from *Mistress Gupp* [8]
    That same glad day.

And *Rip Van Winkle* [9] shall awake
From his loved idlesse for thy sake,
In earnest stretch himself, and take
    Pallet on thumb,
Nor now his brains for subjects rake—
    John Clare is come !

His touch will, hue by hue, combine
Thy thoughtful eyes, that steady shine,
The temples of Shakesperian line,
    The quiet smile,
The sense and shrewdness which are thine,
    Withouten guile.

Key to the Rhyming Letter.

The following key accompanied the letter on its publication :—

1. *Agnus*—Charles Lamb.
2. *Lepus*—Julius Hare, author of "Guesses at Truth."
3. *Janus*—The writer in the "London Magazine" who signed himself Janus Weathercock.
4. *Nalla*—Allan Cunningham.
5. *Opium-eater*—De Quincey, author of "The Confessions of an English Opium-eater."
6. *The Poet true*—The writer who assumes the name of Barry Cornwall.
7. *The English Petrarch*—The Rev. Mr. Strong, translator of Italian sonnets.
8. *Mistress Gupp*—A lady immortalized by her invention to keep muffins warm on the lid of the tea-urn.
9. *Rip Van Winkle*—E. V. Rippingille, painter of the "Country Post Office," the "Portrait of a Bird," &c.

The friendship of Allan Cunningham was always highly prized by Clare, and shortly after his return from London he sent him an autograph of Bloomfield, the receipt of which Cunningham acknowledged in the following letter :—

"27, Belgrave-place, 23rd September, 1824.

"Dear Clare,—I thank you much for Bloomfield's note, and as much for your own kind letter. I agree with you in the praise you have given to his verse. That he has living life about his productions there can be little doubt.

He trusts too much to Nature and to truth to be a fleeting favourite, and he will be long in the highway where Fame dispenses her favours. I have often felt indignant at the insulting way his name has been introduced both by critics and poets. To scorn him because of the humility of his origin is ridiculous anywhere, and most of all here, where so many of our gentles and nobles have come from the clods of the valley. Learned men make many mistakes about the value of learning. I conceive it is chiefly valuable to a man's genius in enabling him to wield his energies with greater readiness or with better effect. But learning, though a polisher and a refiner, is not the creator. It may be the mould out of which genius stamps its coin, but it is not the gold itself.   *   *   *   I am glad to hear that you are a little better. Keep up your heart and sing only when you feel the internal impulse, and you will add something to our poetry more lasting than any of the peasant bards of old England have done yet.

"I remain, dear Clare, your very faithful friend,

"ALLAN CUNNINGHAM."

George Darley, another member of the "London" brotherhood, conceived a sincere regard for Clare, and frequently wrote to him. He was author of several dramatic poems, and of numerous works on mathematics, and was besides a candidate for the Professorship of English Literature at the founding of the London University.

The following are among the more entertaining of the letters which he addressed to the poet :—

"Friday, March 2—27,

"5, Upper Eaton-st, Grosvenor-place.

"My dear Clare,—You see in what a brotherly way I commence my letter: not with the frigid ' Sir,' as if I were addressing one of a totally unkindred clay, one of the drossy children of earth, with whom I have no relationship, and feel I could never have any familiarity. * * * Have you ever felt that the presence of a man without feeling made you a fool ? I am always dumb, or pusillanimous, or (if I speak) ridiculous, in the company of such a person. I love a reasoner, and do not by any means wish to be flashing lightning, cloud-riding, or playing with stars. But a marble-hearted companion, who, if you should by chance give way to an impetuous fancy, or an extravagant imagination, looks at you with a dead fish's eye, and asks you to write the name under your picture—I would as soon ride in a post chaise with a lunatic, or sleep with a corse. Never let me see the sign of such a man over an alehouse ! It would fright me away sooner than the report of a mad dog or a scolding landlady. I would as soon enter the house if it hung out a pestle and mortar. The fear of a drug in my posset would not repel me so inevitably as the horror with which I should contemplate the frost-bitten face of a portrait such as I have described. But perhaps with all *your* feeling you will think my heart somewhat less sound than a ripe medlar, if it be so unhealthily sensitive as what I have said appears to indicate. There is, I grant, as in all other things, a mean which ought to be observed. Recollect, however, I am not an Englishman. [Darley was an Irishman.] I should have answered your letter long since, without waiting for your poems, in order to say something handsome upon them, but have been so occupied with a myriad of affairs that I have scarcely had a moment to sleep in. It is now long, long past midnight, and all is as silent around my habitation as if it were in the midst of a forest, or the plague had depopulated London. After a day's hard labour at mathematical operations and corrections I sit down to write to you these hasty and, I fear, almost unreadable lines. Will you excuse them for the promise of something better when I have more leisure to be *point-device?* Your opinion of my geometry was very grateful, chiefly as it confirmed my own—that there has been a great deal too much baby-making of the English people by those who pretend to instruct them in science. These persons write upon the Goody-two-shoes plan, and seem to look upon their readers as infants who have not yet done drivelling. To improve the reason is quite beside their purpose; they merely design to titillate the fancy or provide talking matter for village oracles. In not one of their systems do I perceive a regular progression of reasoning whereby the mind may be led, from truth to truth, to knowledge, as we ride step by step up to a fair temple on a goodly hill of prospect. They jumble together heaps of facts, the most wonder-striking they can get, which may indeed be said to confound the imagination by their variety;

but there is no ratiocinative dependence between them, nor are they referred to demonstrative principles, which would render people knowledgible, as well as knowing, of them. Each is a syllabus indeed, but not a science. It tells many things but teaches none. There is little merit due to me for perceiving this error, and none for avoiding it.   *   *   *   Algebra is the only true arithmetic. The latter is founded on the former in almost all its rules, and one is just as easily learned as the other.   *   *   *   If arithmetic be to be taught rationally it must be taught algebraically. With half the pains that a learner takes to make himself master of the rule of three and fractions, he would acquire as much algebra as would render every rule in arithmetic as easy as chalking to an inn-keeper. I am apt to speak in the King Cambyses' vein, but you understand what I wish to convey. As to the continuation of the " Lives of the Poets," it is a work sadly wanting, but I am not the person to supply the desideratum, even were my power equal to the deed. Criticism is abomination in my sight. It is fit only for the headsmen and hangmen of literature, fellows who live by the agonies and death of others. You will say this is not the criticism you mean, and that there is a different species (the only genuine and estimable species) which has an eye to beauty rather than defect, and which delights in glorifying true poetry rather than debating it. Aye, but have you ever considered how much harder it is to praise than to censure piquantly ?   I should ever be running into the contemptuous or abusive style, as I did in the " Letters to Dramatists." Besides, even in the best of poets, Shakspeare and Milton, how much is there justly condemnable? On the inferior luminaries. I should have to be continually pointing out spots and blemishes. In short, as a vocation I detest criticism. It is a species of fratricide with me, for I never can help cutting, slashing, pinking, and carbonadoing—a most unnatural office for one of the brotherhood, one who presumes to enrol himself among those whom he conspires with the Jeffreys and Jerdans to mangle and destroy. It is a Cain-like profession, and I deserve to be branded, and condemned to wander houseless over the world, if ever I indulge the murderous propensity to criticism. I was sorry to hear from Taylor yesterday that you were not in good health. What *can* be the matter with you, so healthfully situated and employed? Methinks you should live the life of an oak-tree or a sturdy elm, that groans in a storm, but only for pleasure. Do you meditate too much or sit too immovably?   *   *

*   *   *   Poetry, I mean the composition of it, does not always sweeten the mind as much as the reading of it. There is always an anxiety, a fervour, an impatience, a vaingloriousness attending it which untranquillizes even in the sweetest-seeming moods of the poet. Like the bee, he is restless and uneasy even in collecting his sweets.   *   *   *

"Farewell, my dear Clare, and when you have leisure and inclination write to me again.

*   *   *   *

"Sincerely yours,

"GEORGE DARLEY."

Letters from George Darley.

" London, 5 Upper Eaton-st., Grosvenor-place,
" March 14th, 1829.

" My dear Clare,—You have been reproaching me,
I dare say, for my long neglect of your last letter, but
you might have saved yourself that trouble, as my own
conscience has scourged me repeatedly these two months
about it. The truth is I have been a good deal harassed
in several ways, and now sit down, in the midst of a
headache, to write, when I can hardly tell which end of
my pen is paper-wards. I will attempt, however, to
return your questions legible if not intelligible answers.
There have been so many ' Pleasures ' of so-and-so that
I should almost counsel you against baptizing your poem
on Spring the ' Pleasures ' of anything. Besides, when
a poem is so designated it is almost assuredly prejudged
as deficient in action (about which you appear solicitous).
' The Pleasures of Spring,' from you, identified as you
are with descriptive poesy, would almost without doubt
sound in the public ear as an announcement of a series of
literary scene paintings. Beautiful as these may be, and
certainly would be from your pencil, there is a deadness
about them which tends to chill the reader : he must be
animated with something of a livelier prospect, or, as
Hamlet says of Polonius, ' he sleeps. ' It may be
affirmed without hesitation that, however independent of
description a drama may be, no descriptive poem is
independent of something like dramatic spirit to give it
interest with human beings. How dull a thing would
even the great descriptive poem of the Creation be
without Adam and Eve, their history and hapless fall, to

enliven it! But I cannot see why you should not infuse a dramatic spirit into your poem on Spring, which is only the development of the living principle in Nature. See how full of life those descriptive scenes in the 'Midsummer Night's Dream' and the 'Winter's Tale' are. Characters may describe the beauties or qualities of Spring just as well as the author, and nothing prevents a story going through the season, so as to gather up flowers and point out every beautiful feature in the landscape on its way. Thomson has a little of this, but not enough. Imagine his 'Lavinia' spread out into a longer story, incidents and descriptions perpetually relieving each other! Imagine this, and you have a model for your poem. Allan Ramsay's 'Gentle Shepherd' would be still better, only that his poem *is* cast into actual dramatic characters. Besides, though with plenty of feeling and a good deal of homestead poetry, he wants imagination, elegance, and a certain scorn of mere earth, which is essential to the constitution of a true poet. You want none of these, but you want his vivacity, character, and action : I mean to say you have not *as yet* exhibited these qualities. The hooks with which you have fished for praise in the ocean of literature have not been garnished with live bait, and none of us can get a bite without it. How few read 'Comus' who have the 'Corsair' by heart! Why? Because the former, which is almost dark with the excessive bright of its own glory, is deficient in human passions and emotions, while the latter possesses these although little else.

" Your sincere friend and brother poet,

" GEORGE DARLEY."

Clare's Diary.

It was on the occasion of his third visit to London that Dr. Darling exacted from Clare the promise, already referred to, that he would observe the strictest moderation in drinking, and if possible abstain altogether. Clare kept his word, but his domestic difficulties remaining unabated he suffered much, not only from physical weakness but from melancholy forebodings which were destined to be only too completely realized. He made many ineffectual attempts to obtain employment in the neighbourhood of Helpstone, and it is especially to be regretted that his applications, first to the Marquis of Exeter's steward and then to Earl Fitzwilliam's, for the situation of gardener were unsuccessful, because the employment would have been congenial to his tastes, and the wages, added to his annuities, would have been to him a competence.

During the years 1824–25 Clare kept a diary, which, for those who desire to know the man as well as the poet, is full of interest, on account of the side-lights which it throws upon his character, and also upon his pursuits during this period of involuntary leisure. The following extracts are selected :—

September 7, 1824.—I have read "Foxe's Book of Martyrs" and finished it to-day, and the sum of my opinion is, that tyranny and cruelty appear to be the inseparable companions of religious power, and the aphorism is not far from truth that says "all priests are the same."

September 11.—Wrote an essay to-day on the sexual system of plants, and began one on the fungus tribe, and on mildew, blight, &c., intended for " A Natural History of Helpstone," in a series of letters to Hessey, who will publish it when finished. Received a kind letter from C. A. Elton.

September 12.—Finished another page of my life. I have read the first chapter of Genesis, the beginning of which is very fine, but the sacred historian took a great deal upon credit for this world when he imagined that God created the sun, moon, and stars, those mysterious hosts of heaven, for no other purpose than its use. It is a harmless and universal propensity to magnify consequences that pertain to ourselves, and it would be a foolish thing to test Scripture upon these groundless assertions, for it contains the best poetry and the best morality in the world.

September 19.—Read snatches of several poets and the Song of Solomon : thought the supposed allusions in that luscious poem to our Saviour very overstrained, far-fetched, and conjectural. It appears to me an Eastern love poem, and nothing further, but an over-heated religious fancy is strong enough to fancy anything. I think the Bible is not illustrated by that supposition : though it is a very beautiful poem it seems nothing like a prophetic one, as it is represented to be.

September 22.—Very ill, and did nothing but ponder over a future existence, and often brought up the lines to my memory said to have been uttered by an unfortunate nobleman when on the brink of it, ready to take the plunge—

> "In doubt I lived, in doubt I die,
> Nor shrink the dark abyss to try,
> But undismayed I meet eternity."

The first line is natural enough, but the rest is a rash courage in such a situation.

September 23.—A wet day: did nothing but nurse my illness: could not have walked out had it been fine. Very disturbed in conscience about the troubles of being forced to endure life and die by inches, and the anguish of leaving my children, and the dark porch of eternity, whence none return to tell the tale of their reception.

September 24.—Tried to walk out and could not: have read nothing this week, my mind almost over-weighting me with its upbraidings and miseries: my children very ill, night and morning, with a fever, makes me disconsolate, and yet how happy must be the death of a child! It bears its sufferings with an innocent patience that maketh man ashamed, and with it the future is nothing but returning to sleep, with the thought, no doubt, of waking to be with its playthings again.

September 29.—Took a walk in the fields: saw an old wood stile taken away from a familiar spot which it had occupied all my life. The posts were overgrown with ivy, and it seemed akin to nature and the spot where it stood, as though it had taken it on lease for an undisturbed existence. It hurt me to see it was gone, for my affections claim a friendship with such things; but nothing is lasting in this world. Last year Langley Bush was destroyed—an old white-thorn that had stood for more than a century, full of fame. The gipsies, shepherds, and herdsmen all had their tales of its history, and it will be long ere its memory is forgotten.

October 8.—Very ill to-day and very unhappy. My three children are all unwell. Had a dismal dream of being in hell: this is the third time I have had such a dream. As I am more than ever convinced that I cannot recover I will make a memorandum of my temporal concerns, for next to the spiritual they ought to be attended to for the sake of those left behind. I will insert them in No. 5 in the Appendix.

October 9.—Patty has been to Stamford, and brought me a letter from Ned Drury, who came from Lincoln to the mayor's feast on Thursday. It revives old recollections. Poor fellow: he is an odd one, but still my recollections are inclined in his favour. What a long way to come to the mayor's feast! I would not go one mile after it to hear the din of knives and forks, and to see a throng of blank faces about me, chattering and stuffing, " that boast no more expression than a muffin."

October 12.—Began to teach a poor lame boy the common rules of arithmetic, and find him very apt and willing to learn.

October 16.—Wrote two more pages of my life : find it not so easy as I at first imagined, as I am anxious to give an undisguised narrative of facts, good and bad. In

the last sketch which I wrote for Taylor I had little
vanities about me to gloss over failings which I shall now
take care to lay bare, and readers, if they ever are
published, to comment upon as they please. In my last
four years I shall give my likes and dislikes of friends and
acquaintances as free as I do of myself.

December 25.—Christmas Day : gathered a handful
of daisies in full bloom : saw a woodbine and dogrose in
the woods putting out in full leaf, and a primrose root full
of ripe flowers. What a day this used to be when I was
a boy ! How eager I used to be to attend the church to
see it stuck with evergreens (emblems of eternity), and
the cottage windows, and the picture ballads on the wall,
all stuck with ivy, holly, box, and yew ! Such feelings are
past, and "all this world is proud of."

January 7, 1825.—Bought some cakes of colours with
the intention of trying to make sketches of curious snail
horns, butterflies, moths, sphinxes, wild flowers, and
whatever my wanderings may meet with that are not too
common.

January 19.—Just completed the 9th chapter of my
life. Corrected the poem on the "Vanities of the
World," which I have written in imitation of the old
poets, on whom I mean to father it, and send it to
Montgomery's paper "The Iris," or the "Literary
Chronicle," under that character.

February 26.—Received a letter in rhyme from a John
Pooley, who ran me tenpence further in debt, as I had not
money to pay the postage.

March 6.—Parish officers are modern savages, as the following fact will testify :—" Crowland Abbey.—Certain surveyors have lately dug up several foundation stones of the Abbey, and also a great quantity of stone coffins, for the purpose of repairing the parish roads."—*Stamford Mercury*.

March 9.—I had a very odd dream last night, and take it as an ill omen, for I don't expect that the book will meet a better fate. I thought I had one of the proofs of the new poems from London, and after looking at it awhile it shrank through my hands like sand, and crumbled into dust. The birds were singing in Oxey Wood at six o'clock this evening as loud and various as in May.

March 31.—Artis and Henderson came to see me, and we went to see the Roman station agen Oxey Wood, which he says is plainly Roman.

April 16.—Took a walk in the fields, bird-nesting and botanizing, and had like to have been taken up as a poacher in Hilly Wood, by a meddlesome, conceited gamekeeper belonging to Sir John Trollope. He swore that he had seen me in the act, more than once, of shooting game, when I never shot even so much as a sparrow in my life. What terrifying rascals these wood-keepers and gamekeepers are! They make a prison of the forest, and are its gaolers.

April 18.—Resumed my letters on Natural History in good earnest, and intend to get them finished with this year, if I can get out into the fields, for I will insert nothing but what has come under my notice.

May 13.—Met with an extraordinary incident to-day, while walking in Openwood. I popt unawares on an old fox and her four young cubs that were playing about. She saw me, and instantly approached towards me growling like an angry dog. I had no stick, and tried all I could to fright her by imitating the bark of a fox-hound, which only irritated her the more, and if I had not retreated a few paces back she would have seized me : when I set up an haloo she started.

May 25.—I watched a bluecap or blue titmouse feeding her young, whose nest was in a wall close to an orchard. She got caterpillars out of the blossoms of the apple trees and leaves of the plum. She fetched 120 caterpillars in half an hour. Now suppose she only feeds them four times a day, a quarter of an hour each time, she fetched no less than 480 caterpillars.

May 28.—Found the old frog in my garden that has been there four years. I know it by a mark which it received from my spade four years ago. I thought it would die of the wound, so I turned it up on a bed of flowers at the end of the garden, which is thickly covered with ferns and bluebells. I am glad to see it has recovered.

June 3.—Finished planting my auriculas: went a-botanizing after ferns and orchises, and caught a cold in the wet grass, which has made me as bad as ever. Got the tune of "Highland Mary" from Wisdom Smith, a gipsy, and pricked another sweet tune without name as he fiddled it.

June 4.—Saw three fellows at the end of Royce Wood, who I found were laying out the plan for an iron railway from Manchester to London. It is to cross over Round Oak spring by Royce Wood corner for Woodcroft Castle. I little thought that fresh intrusions would interrupt and spoil my solitudes. After the enclosure they will despoil a boggy place that is famous for orchises at Royce Wood end.

June 23.—Wrote to Mrs. Emmerson and sent a letter to "Hone's Every-day Book," with a poem which I fathered on Andrew Marvell.

July 12.—Went to-day to see Artis: found him busy over his antiquities and fossils. He told me a curious thing about the manner in which the golden-crested wren builds her nest: he says it is the only English bird that suspends its nest, which it hangs on three twigs of the fir branch, and it glues the eggs at the bottom of the nest, with the gum out of the tree, to keep them from being thrown out by the wind, which often turns them upside down without injury.

August 21.—Received a letter from Mr. Emmerson which tells me that Lord Radstock died yesterday. He was the best friend I have met with. Though he possessed too much simple-heartedness to be a fashionable friend or hypocrite, yet it often led him to take hypocrites for honest friends and to take an honest man for a hypocrite.

September 11. — Went to meet Mr. and Mrs. Emmerson at the New Inn at Deeping, and spent three days with them.

From "No. 5 in the Appendix."—I will set down before I forget it a memorandum to say that I desire Mrs. Emmerson will do just as she pleases with any MSS. of mine which she may have in her possession, to publish them or not as she chooses; but I desire that any living names mentioned in my letters may be filled up by * * and all objectionable passages omitted— a wish which I hope will be invariably complied with by all. I also intend to make Mr. Emmerson one of the new executors in my new will. I wish to lie on the north side of the churchyard, about the middle of the ground, where the morning and evening sun can linger the longest on my grave. I wish to have a rough unhewn stone, something in the form of a mile stone, [sketched in the margin] so that the playing boys may not break it in their heedless pastimes, with nothing more on it than this inscription :—"Here rest the hopes and ashes of John Clare." I desire that no date be inserted thereon, as I wish it to live or die with my poems and other writings, which if they have merit with posterity it will, and if they have not it is not worth preserving. October 8th, 1824. "Vanity of vanities, all is vanity."

The "Artis" and "Henderson" referred to in the Diary were respectively butler and head gardener at Milton Park. Artis made a name for himself as the discoverer of extensive Roman remains at Castor, the ancient Durobrivæ, of which he published a description, and Henderson was an accomplished botanist and entomologist. Their uniform kindness to the poor poet did them great honour.

While Clare was amusing himself by rhyming in the manner of the poets of the seventeenth century, he had the following correspondence with James Montgomery :—

"Helpstone, January 5, 1825.

"My dear Sir,—I copied the following verses from a MS. on the fly-leaves of an old book entitled 'The World's Best Wealth, a Collection of Choice Counsels in Verse and Prose, printed for A. Bettesworth, at the Red Lion in Paternoster Row, 1720 :' they seem to have been written after the perusal of the book, and are in the manner of the company in which I found [them]. I think they are as good as many old poems that have been preserved with more care ; and, under that feeling, I was tempted to send them, thinking they might find a corner from oblivion in your entertaining literary paper, the 'Iris;' but if my judgment has misled me to overrate their merit, you will excuse the freedom I have taken, and the trouble I have given you in the perusal ; for, after all, it is but an erring opinion, that may have little less than the love of poesy to recommend it.

"I am yours sincerely,

"JOHN CLARE.

"James Montgomery, Esq., Sheffield."

To this letter Montgomery replied in the following terms :—

"Dear Sir,—Some time ago I received from you certain verses said to be copied from the fly-leaves of an old printed book on which they were written. The title was 'The Vanity of Life,' and the book's title 'The

---

World's Best Wealth,' &c. Now though I suspected,
from a little ambiguity in the wording of your letter, that
these verses were not quite so old as they professed to be,
and that you yourself perhaps had written them to
exercise your own genius, and sent them to exercise my
critical acuteness, I thought that the glorious offence
carried its own redemption in itself, and I would not only
forgive but rejoice to see such faults committed every day
for the sake of such merits. It is, however, now of some
importance to me to know whether they are of the date
which they affect, or whether they are of your own production. The supposition of your being capable of such
a thing is so highly in your favour, that you will forgive
the wrong, if there be any, implied in my enquiry. But I
am making a chronological collection of ' Christian Poetry,'
from the earliest times to the latest dead of our contemporaries who have occasionally tried their talents on
consecrated themes, and if these stanzas were really the
work of some anonymous author of the last century I
shall be glad to give them the place and the honour due,
but if they are the ' happy miracle' of your ' rare birth'
then, however reluctantly, I must forego the use of them.
Perhaps the volume itself contains some valuable pieces
which I have not seen, and which might suit my purpose.
The title tempts me to think that this may be the case,
and as I am in search of such jewels as certainly
constitute ' the world's best wealth,' I hope to find a
few in this old-fashioned casket, especially after the
specimen you have sent, and which I take for granted to
be a genuine specimen of the quality (whatever be its

antiquity) of the hidden treasures. If you will oblige me by sending the volume itself by coach I will take great care of it, and thankfully return it in due time free of expense. Or if you are unwilling to trust so precious a deposit out of your own hands, will you furnish me with a list of those of its contents (with the authors' names, where these are attached) which you think are most likely to meet my views, namely, such as have direct religious subjects and are executed with vigour or pathos? I can then see whether there be any pieces which I have not already, and if there be, I dare say you will not grudge the labour of transcribing two or three hundred lines to serve, not a brother poet only, but the Christian public. At any rate, an early reply to this application will be greatly esteemed, and may you never ask in vain for anything which it is honest or honourable to ask for. I need not add that this letter comes from one who sincerely respects your talents and rejoices in the success which has so conspicuously crowned them, when hundreds of our fraternity can get neither fame nor profit—no, nor even a hearing—and a threshing for all their pains.

" I am truly your friend and servant,

" J. MONTGOMERY.

" Sheffield, May, 5, 1826."

Clare was a great admirer of Chatterton, and the melancholy fate of "the marvellous boy" was frequently referred to by him in his correspondence. The idea of imitating the older poets was no doubt suggested to him by Chatterton's successful efforts, but he possessed neither the special faculty nor the consummate artifice of his model, and therefore we are not surprised to find him confessing at once to the trick he had attempted. He replied to Montgomery :—

" Helpstone, May 8, 1826.

" My dear Sir,—I will lose no time in answering your letter, for I was highly delighted to meet so kind a notice from a poet so distinguished as yourself; and if it be vanity to acknowledge it, it is, I hope, a vanity of too honest a nature to be ashamed of—at least I think so, and always shall. But your question almost makes me feel ashamed to own to the extent of the falsehood I committed ; and yet I will not double it by adding a repetition of the offence. I must confess to you that the poem is mine, and that the book from whence it was pretended to have been transcribed has no existence (that I know of) but in my invention of the title. And now that I have confessed to the crime, I will give you the reasons for committing it. I have long had a fondness for the poetry of the time of Elizabeth, though I have never had any means of meeting with it, farther than in the confined channels of Ritson's 'English Songs,' Ellis's 'Specimens,' and Walton's 'Angler;' and the winter before last, though amidst a severe illness, I set about writing a series of verses, in their manner, as well as I could, which I intended to pass off under their names, though some whom I professed to imitate I had never seen. As I am no judge of my own verses, whether they are good or bad, I wished to have the opinion of some one on whom I could rely ; and as I was told you were the editor

of the ' Iris,' I ventured to send the first thing to you,
with many 'doubts and fears.' I was happily astonished
to see its favourable reception. Since then I have written
several others in the same style, some of which have been
published ; one in Hone's ' Every-day Book,' on ' Death,'
under the name of Marvell, and some others in the
' European Magazine ;' 'Thoughts in a Churchyard,' the
' Gipsy's Song,' and a ' Farewell to Love.' The first was
intended for Sir Henry Wootton ; the next for Tom
Davies ; the last for Sir John Harrington. The last
thing I did in these forgeries was an ' Address to Milton,'
the poet, under the name of Davenant. And as your kind
opinion was the first and the last I ever met with from a
poet to pursue these vagaries or shadows of other days, I
will venture to transcribe them here for the ' Iris,' should
they be deemed as worthy of it as the first were by your
judgment, for my own is nothing : I should have
acknowledged their kind reception [sooner] had I not
waited for the publication of my new poems, 'The Shepherd's Calendar,' which was in the press then, where it
has been ever since, as I wish, at its coming, to beg your
acceptance of a copy, with the other volumes already
published, as I am emboldened now to think they will be
kindly received, and not be deemed intrusive, as one
commonly fears while offering such trifles to strangers.
I shall also be very glad of the opportunity in proving
myself ready to serve you in your present undertaking ;
and could I light on an old poem that would be worth
your attention, 300 or even 1,000 lines would be no
objection against my writing it out ; but I do assure you I

would not make a forgery for such a thing, though I suppose now you would suspect me ; for I consider in such company it would be a crime, where blossoms are collected to decorate the ' Fountain of Truth.' But I will end, for I get very sleepy and very unintelligible.

> " I am, my dear Sir,
>> " Yours very sincerely and affectionately,
>>> " JOHN CLARE.
> " Mr. Montgomery, Sheffield."

At intervals during the years 1825–26 Clare was occupied in supplying his publishers with poems for his next volume—" The Shepherd's Calendar," which was brought out in May, 1827, with a frontispiece by De Wint. The descriptive poem which gives the title to the volume consists of twelve cantos, of various measures, and is followed by " Village Stories " and other compositions. Of the stories, that entitled " Jockey and Jenny ; or, the Progress of Love," appears to have made the most favourable impression upon Clare's contemporaries. In this poem will be found the following bold and original apostrophe to Night :—

Ah, powerful Night ! Were but thy chances mine !
Had I but ways to come at joys like thine !
Spite of thy wizard look and sable skin,
The ready road to bliss 't is thine to win.
All nature owns of beautiful and sweet
In thy embraces now unconscious meet :
Young Jenny, ripening into womanhood,
That hides from day, like lilies while in bud,

To thy grim visage blooms in all her charms,
And comes, like Eve, unblushing to thy arms.
Of thy black mantle could I be possest,
How would I pillow on her panting breast,
And try those lips where trial rude beseems,
Breathing my spirit in her very dreams,
That ne'er a thought might wander from her heart,
But I possessed it, or ensured a part!
Of all the blessings that belong to thee,
Had I this one how happy should I be!

In "The Dream," which appeared in the same volume, Clare's muse took a still more ambitious flight—with what success the reader has here an opportunity to judge for himself. The obscurities in the composition must find their excuse in the nature of the subject:—

THE DREAM.

Thou scarest me with dreams.—JOB.

When Night's last hours, like haunting spirits, creep
With listening terrors round the couch of sleep,
And Midnight, brooding in its deepest dye,
Seizes on Fear with dismal sympathy,
"I dreamed a dream" something akin to fate,
Which Superstition's blackest thoughts create—
Something half natural to the grave that seems,
Which Death's long trance of slumber haply dreams;
A dream of staggering horrors and of dread,
Whose shadows fled not when the vision fled,
But clung to Memory with their gloomy view,
Till Doubt and Fancy half believed it true.

That time was come, or seem'd as it was come,
When Death no longer makes the grave his home;
When waking spirits leave their earthly rest
To mix for ever with the damn'd or blest;
When years, in drowsy thousands counted by,
Are hung on minutes with their destiny:
When Time in terror drops his draining glass,
And all things mortal, like to shadows, pass,
As 'neath approaching tempests sinks the sun—
When Time shall leave Eternity begun.
Life swoon'd in terror at that hour's dread birth;
As in an ague, shook the fearful Earth;
And shuddering Nature seemed herself to shun,
Whilst trembling Conscience felt the deed was done.
A gloomy sadness round the sky was cast,
Where clouds seem'd hurrying with unusual haste;
Winds urged them onward, like to restless ships;
And light dim faded in its last eclipse;
And Agitation turn'd a straining eye;
And Hope stood watching like a bird to fly,
While suppliant Nature, like a child in dread,
Clung to her fading garments till she fled.
Then awful sights began to be reveal'd,
Which Death's dark dungeons had so long conceal'd;
Each grave its doomsday prisoner resign'd,
Bursting in noises like a hollow wind;
And spirits, mingling with the living then,
Thrill'd fearful voices with the cries of men.
All flying furious, grinning deep despair,
Shaped dismal shadows on the troubled air:

Red lightning shot its flashes as they came,
And passing clouds seem'd kindling into flame;
And strong and stronger came the sulphury smell,
With demons following in the breath of hell,
Laughing in mockery as the doom'd complain'd,
Losing their pains iu seeing others pain'd.

   Fierce raged Destruction, sweeping o'er the land,
And the last counted moment seem'd at hand:
As scales near equal hang in earnest eyes
In doubtful balance, which shall fall or rise,
So, in the moment of that crushing blast,
Eyes, hearts, and hopes paused trembling for the last.
Loud burst the thunder's clap and yawning rents
Gash'd the frail garments of the elements;
Then sudden whirlwinds, wing'd with purple flame
And lightning's flash, in stronger terrors came,
Burning all life and Nature where they fell,
And leaving earth as desolate as hell.
The pleasant hues of woods and fields were past,
And Nature's beauties had enjoyed their last:
The colour'd flower, the green of field and tree,
What they had been for ever ceased to be:
Clouds, raining fire, scorched up the hissing dews;
Grass shrivell'd brown in miserable hues;
Leaves fell to ashes in the air's hot breath,
And all awaited universal Death.
The sleepy birds, scared from their mossy nest,
Beat through the evil air in vain for rest;
And many a one, the withering shades among,

Waken'd to perish o'er its brooded young.
The cattle, startled with the sudden fright,
Sicken'd from food, and madden'd into flight ;
And steed and beast in plunging speed pursued
The desperate struggle of the multitude.
The faithful dogs yet knew their owners' face,
And cringing follow'd with a fearful pace,
Joining the piteous yell with panting breath,
While blasting lightnings follow'd fast with death ;
Then, as Destruction stopt the vain retreat,
They dropp'd, and dying lick'd their masters' feet.
When sudden thunders paus'd, loud went the shriek,
And groaning agonies, too much to speak,
From hurrying mortals, who with ceaseless fears
Recall'd the errors of their vanish'd years ;
Flying in all directions, hope bereft,
Followed by dangers that would not be left ;
Offering wild vows, and begging loud for aid,
Where none was nigh to help them when they pray'd.
None stood to listen, or to soothe a friend,
But all complained, and sorrow had no end :
Sons from their fathers, fathers sons did fly,
The strongest fled, and left the weak to die ;—
Pity was dead :—none heeded for another,—
Brother left brother, and the frantic mother
For fruitless safety hurried east and west,
And dropp'd the babe to perish from her breast ;
All howling prayers that would be noticed never,
And craving mercy that was fled for ever ;
While earth, in motion like a troubled sea,

Open'd in gulfs of dread immensity
Amid the wild confusions of despair,
And buried deep the howling and the prayer
Of countless multitudes, and closed—and then
Open'd and swallow'd multitudes again.
Stars, drunk with dread, roll'd giddy from the heaven,
And staggering worlds like wrecks in storms were
    driven ;
The pallid moon hung fluttering on the sight,
As startled bird whose wings are stretch'd for flight ;
And o'er the East a fearful light begun
To show the sun rise—not the morning sun,
But one in wild confusion, doom'd to rise
And drop again in horror from the skies.
To heaven's midway it reel'd, and changed to blood,
Then dropp'd, and light rushed after like a flood,
The heaven's blue curtains rent and shrank away,
And heaven itself seem'd threaten'd with decay ;
While hopeless distance, with a boundless stretch,
Flash'd on Despair the joy it could not reach,
A moment's mockery—ere the last dim light
Vanish'd, and left an everlasting Night ;
And with that light Hope fled and shriek'd farewell,
And Hell in yawning echoes mock'd that yell.
Now Night resumed her uncreated vest,
And Chaos came again, but not its rest ;
The melting glooms that spread perpetual stains,
Kept whirling on in endless hurricanes ;
And tearing noises, like a troubled sea,
Broke up that silence which no more would be.

The reeling earth sank loosen'd from its stay,
And Nature's wrecks all felt their last decay.
The yielding, burning soil, that fled my feet,
I seem'd to feel and struggled to retreat ;
And 'midst the dread of horror's mad extreme
I lost all notion that it was a dream :
Sinking I fell through depths that seem'd to be
As far from fathom as eternity ;
While dismal faces on the darkness came
With wings of dragons and with fangs of flame,
Writhing in agonies of wild despairs,
And giving tidings of a doom like theirs.
I felt all terrors of the damn'd, and fell
With conscious horror that my doom was hell :
And Memory mock'd me, like a haunting ghost,
With light and life and pleasures that were lost ;
As dreams turn night to day, and day to night,
So Memory flash'd her shadows of that light
That once bade morning suns in glory rise,
To bless green fields and trees, and purple skies,
And waken'd life its pleasures to behold ;—
That light flash'd on me like a story told ;
And days mis-spent with friends and fellow-men,
And sins committed,—all were with me then.
The boundless hell, whose demons never tire,
Glimmer'd beneath me like a world on fire :
That soul of fire, like to its souls entomb'd,
Consuming on, and ne'er to be consum'd,
Seem'd nigh at hand, where oft the sulphury damps
O'er-aw'd its light, as glimmer dying lamps,

Spreading a horrid gloom from side to side,
A twilight scene of terrors half descried.
Sad boil'd the billows of that burning sea,
And Fate's sad yellings dismal seem'd to be ;
Blue roll'd its waves with horrors uncontrolled,
And its live wrecks of souls dash'd howlings as they
    roll'd.
Again I struggled, and the spell was broke,
And 'midst the laugh of mocking ghosts I woke ;
My eyes were open'd on an unhoped sight—
The early morning and its welcome light,
And, as I ponder'd o'er the past profound,
I heard the cock crow, and I blest the sound.

"The Shepherd's Calendar" sold very slowly, for several months after its publication Mr. Taylor wrote to Clare—"The season has been a very bad one for new books, and I am afraid the time has passed away in which poetry will answer. With that beautiful frontispiece of De Wint's to attract attention, and so much excellent verse inside the volume, the 'Shepherd's Calendar' has had comparatively no sale. It will be a long time, I doubt, before it pays me my expenses, but ours is the common lot.   *   *   *   I am almost hopeless of the sale of the books reimbursing me. Of profit I am certain we have not had any, but that I should not care for : it is to be considerably out of pocket that annoys me, and by the new works my loss will probably be heavy." And again, after the lapse of four or five months—"The poems have not yet sold much, but I

cannot say how many are disposed of. All the old
poetry-buyers seem to be dead, and the new ones have no
taste for it."

And now for a time Clare eked out his scanty income
by writing poems for the annuals, the silk-bound illustrated favourites of fashion, which for ten or twelve years
almost sufficed to satisfy the languid appetite of the
English public for poetry. Clare was sought after by
several editors; among the rest, Allan Cunningham,
editor of the " Anniversary;" Mr. and Mrs. S. C. Hall,
who severally conducted the " Amulet" and the
" Juvenile Forget-me-not ;" Alaric A. Watts, editor of the
" Literary Souvenir;" Thomas Hood, and others. " The
Rural Muse," the last volume which Clare published, was
composed almost entirely of poems which had appeared
in the annuals, or other periodicals. The remuneration
which Clare received was respectable, if not munificent.
His kind-hearted Scotch friend, Allan Cunningham, was
certain to see that he was treated with liberality : Mrs.
Hall, on behalf of Messrs. Ackermann, sent him in
October, 1828, three guineas for "The Grasshopper,"
and in the following month Mr. Hall wrote " Enclosed
you will receive £5 for your contributions to the
'Amulet' and the 'Juvenile Forget-me-not.' I am however still £2 in your debt, £7 being the sum I have set
apart for you. How shall I forward you the remaining
£2 ?" Mr. Alaric Watts frequently importuned Clare
for contributions for the " Literary Souvenir " and the
" Literary Magnet," but he was exceedingly fastidious

and plain-spoken, and although he sent Clare presents of books he never said in his letters anything about payment. At length Clare hinted to him that some acknowledgment of that kind would be acceptable, and then Mr. Watts replied, "I have no objection to make you some pecuniary return if you send me any poem worthy of yourself, but really those you have sent me of late are so very inferior, with the exception of a little drinking song, which I shall probably print, that it would do you no service to insert them." This appears to have closed the correspondence.

A sketch of Clare's life would be incomplete which did not notice the subject of his relations with his publishers.

His first two works—"Poems descriptive of Rural Life and Scenery" and the "Village Minstrel"—were published conjointly by Messrs. Taylor and Hessey and Mr. Drury, of Stamford, on the understanding that Clare was to receive one half of the profits, and that the London and local publishers should divide the remaining half of the profits between them. Before the publication of the third work—the "Shepherd's Calendar"—an arrangement was come to by which Mr. Drury ceased to have any interest in Clare's books, and the London firm renewed the agreement which gave Clare one half of the profits. It was the practice of Taylor and Hessey to remit to Clare money on account, in sums of £10 or £20, and evidently at their own discretion—a discretion which, considering Clare's position and circumstances, appears to have been wisely and considerately exercised.

Added together, these remittances made, for a person in Clare's condition, a considerable sum of money, but the poet fretted and chafed under the want of confidence in his judgment which he thought was implied by this mode of treatment, and he repeatedly applied to Taylor and Hessey for a regular and business-like statement of account. During the time Mr. Drury had a pecuniary interest in the sale of Clare's books, the London publishers excused themselves from furnishing an account on the ground that it had been complicated by Mr. Drury's claims, but years passed away after the latter had been arranged with, and still the rendering of the account was postponed. This irritated Clare, and he frequently spoke and wrote of his publishers with a degree of bitterness which he afterwards regretted. His suspicions, for which there was no real foundation, were at one time encouraged rather than otherwise by influential friends in London, and therefore in February, 1828, he resolved to take another journey to Town, with the two-fold object of having a settlement with his publishers and consulting Dr. Darling respecting a distressing ailment with which he was then afflicted.

" My dear and suffering Clare,", wrote Mrs. Emmerson at this time, " your painful letter of to-day is no sooner read by me than I take up my pen, and an extra-sized sheet of paper, to pour out the regrets of my heart for your illness. God knows I am little able to give thee ' comfort,' for indeed, my Clare, thy friend is a beggar in philosophy, so heavily have the ills of humanity pressed upon her of late; but such 'comfort' as confiding and sympathizing souls can offer do I give in full to thee. Receive it, then, my poor Clare, and let the utterings of my pen (which instead of gloomy ink I would dip into the sweet balm of Gilead for thy afflictions) prove again and again thy ' physician.' Forget not what you told me in your former letter: 'your letters come over my melancholy musings like the dews of the morning. I am already better, and you are my physician.' * * * Now, my dear Clare, let me, instead of listening to, or rather acting upon your melancholy forebodings, entreat you to cheer up, and in the course of another week make up a little bundle of clothes, and set yourself quietly inside the Deeping coach for London. I will get your 'sky chamber' ready to receive you, or my niece Eliza shall yield to you her lower apartment, the blue room. We can then, ' in council met,' talk over wills, and new volumes of poems, and all other worldly matters relating to yourself, myself, and posterity." And again, on the 20th of February—" I was yesterday obliged to receive a whole family of foreigners to dinner. I now hasten, my dear Clare, to entreat you will not allow your kind resolves of coming to visit us to take an unfavourable change. * * * I would send down the money for your journey, but am fearful it might be lost. Let me merely say then, that I shall have the pleasure to give it you when we meet. I am sure you will benefit in your health by coming to see us. I have a most worthy friend, a physician, who will do everything, I am sure, to aid you. We shall have a thousand things to chat over when we meet, and it will require a calm head and a quiet heart to effect all we propose. Bring your MSS. with you, and I will do all in my power."

The cordiality of this invitation was irresistible, and Clare, a few days afterwards, presented himself in Stratford-place, where he was entertained during his stay in London, which extended over five weeks.

Shortly after his arrival he called upon Mr. Taylor, who told him that the sale of the "Shepherd's Calendar" had not been large, and that if he chose to sell his books himself in his own neighbourhood he might have a supply at cost price, or half-a-crown per volume. Clare consulted his intimate friends on this project: Allan Cunningham indignantly inveighed against Mr. Taylor for making a suggestion so derogatory to the dignity of a poet, and Mrs. Emmerson at first took a similar view, but afterwards changed her mind, on seeing Clare himself pretty confident that he could sell a sufficient number of copies not only to clear himself from debt but enable him to rent a small farm. After Clare had accepted the offer she wrote to him as follows :—" I am sincerely happy to hear from your last communications about Mr. Taylor that you can now become the merchant of your own gems, so get purchasers for them as fast as possible, and, as Shakspeare says, 'put money in thy purse.' I hope your long account with T. may shortly and satisfactorily be settled. 'T is well of you to do things gently and with kindly disposition, for indeed I think Mr. Taylor is a worthy man at heart."

The promised statement of account was furnished in August or September, 1829, but Clare disputed its accuracy and some of his corrections were accepted. Years elapsed before he could feel quite satisfied that he had been fairly treated, and in the meantime a rupture with his old friend and trustee, Mr. Taylor, was only averted by that gentleman's kindness and forbearance. Clare gave the pedlar project a fair trial, but it brought him little beyond fatigue, mortification, and disappointment. About this time his fifth child was born.

Not long after Clare's return from London, the Mayor of Boston invited him to visit that town. He accepted the invitation and was hospitably entertained. A number of young men of the town proposed a public supper in his honour, and gave him notice that he would have to reply to the toast of his own health. Clare shrank from this terrible ordeal and quitted Boston with scant ceremony. This he regretted on discovering that his warm-hearted friends and admirers had, unknown to him, put ten pounds into his travelling bag. His visit to Boston was followed by an attack of fever which assailed in turn every member of his family, and rendered necessary the frequent visits of a medical man for several months. For a long time Clare was quite unable to do any work in the fields, or sell any of his poems, and hence arose fresh embarrassments.

In the autumn of 1829 Clare once more made a farming venture on a small scale, and for about eighteen months he was fairly successful. This raised his spirits to an unwonted pitch, and his health greatly improved; but the gleam of sunshine passed away and poverty and sickness were again his portion. In 1831 his household consisted of ten persons, a sixth child having been born to him in the previous year. To support so large a family it was not sufficient that he frequently denied himself the commonest necessaries of life: this for years past he had been accustomed to do, but still he could not "keep the wolf from the door." In his distress he consulted his confidential friends, Artis and Henderson. While talking with Henderson one day at Milton Park, Clare had the good fortune to meet the noble owner, to whom he told all his troubles. His lordship listened attentively to the story, and when Clare had finished promised that a cottage and a small piece of land should be found for him. The promise was kept, for we find Mr. Emmerson writing on the 9th of November, 1831, "Why have you not, with your own good pen, informed me of the circumstance of your shortly becoming Farmer John? Yes, thanks to the generous Lord Milton, I am told in a letter from your kind friend, the Rev. Mr. Mossop (dated October 27th) that you have the offer of a most comfortable cottage, which will be fitted up for your reception about January the 1st, 1832, that it will have an acre of orchard and garden, inclusive of a common for two cows, with a meadow sufficient to produce fodder for the winter."

The cottage which Lord Milton set apart for Clare was situated at Northborough, a village three miles from Helpstone, and thus described by the author of " Rambles

Roundabout " :—" Northborough is a large village, not in the sense of its number of houses or its population, but of the space of ground which it covers. The houses are mostly cottages, half-hidden in orchards and luxuriant gardens, having a prodigality of ground. There is not an eminence loftier than a molehill throughout, yet the spacious roads and the wealth of trees and flowers make it a very picturesque and happy-looking locality. Clare's cottage stands in the midst of ample grounds." It has been generally supposed that the cottage was provided for Clare rent-free, but that this was not the case is shown by the fact that in one of his letters to Mrs. Emmerson he told her that he had had to sub-let the piece of common for less than he was himself paying for it. The rent was either £13 or £15 a-year, but whether the regular payment of that amount was insisted upon is very doubtful.

To the astonishment and even annoyance of many of Clare's friends, when he was informed that the cottage was ready for its new tenants, he showed the utmost reluctance to leave Helpstone. Mr. Martin gives the following account of what took place :—" Patty, radiant with joy to get away from the miserable little hut into a beautiful roomy cottage, a palace in comparison with the old dwelling, had all things ready for moving at the beginning of June, yet could not persuade her husband to give his consent to the final start. Day after day he postponed it, offering no excuse save that he could not bear to part from his old home. Day after day he kept walking through fields and woods among his old haunts,

with wild, haggard look, muttering incoherent language.
The people of the village began to whisper that he was
going mad. At Milton Park they heard of it, and Artis
and Henderson hurried to Helpstone to look after their
friend. They found him sitting on a moss-grown stone,
at the end of the village nearest the heath. Gently they
took him by the arm, and, leading him back to the hut,
told Mrs. Clare that it would be best to start at once to
Northborough, the Earl being dissatisfied that the removal
had not taken place. Patty's little caravan was soon
ready, and the poet, guided by his friends, followed in the
rear, walking mechanically, with eyes half shut, as if
in a dream. His look brightened for a moment when
entering his new dwelling place, a truly beautiful cottage,
with thatched roof, casemented windows, wild roses over
the porch, and flowery hedges all round. Yet before
many hours were over he fell back into deep melancholy,
from which he was relieved only by a new burst of song."
His feelings found vent in the touching verses beginning
" I've left my own old home of homes."

Shortly after removing to Northborough Clare made
another ineffectual attempt to induce his trustees to draw
out a portion of his fund money. Writing in connection
with this subject Mr. Emmerson says—" Mrs. Emmerson
and myself take a lively interest in your welfare, and we
shall be glad to know exactly how you stand in your
affairs, what debts you owe, and what stock you require
for your present pursuit : by stock, I mean a cow or cows,
pigs, &c. Pray give me an early reply to all these
particulars, that we may see if anything can be done here

to serve you." Clare replied at once, and in a few days
Mrs. Emmerson wrote as follows :—" We have consulted
with Mr. Taylor. Mr. Emmerson went to him yesterday
on the receipt of your letter, and informed him of its
contents, and it was concluded to set on foot a *private*
friendly subscription to help Farmer John in his concerns.
E. L. E. will give £10, which must be laid out in the
purchase of a cow, which she begs may be called by the
poetic name of Rose, or Blossom, or May. Mr. Taylor
will kindly give £5 to purchase two pigs, and I dare say
we shall succeed in getting another £5 to buy a butter
churn and a few useful tools for husbandry, so that you
may all set to work and begin to turn your labour to
account, and by instalments pay off the various little debts
which have accumulated in your own neighbourhood.
Your garden, and orchard, and dairy will soon release you
from these demands, I hope ; at any rate you will thus have
a beginning, and with the blessing of Providence, and
health on your side, and care and industry on the part of
your wife and children, I hope my dear Clare will sit
down happy ere long in his new abode, rather than have
cause to regret leaving his ' own old home of homes.' It
is a very natural and tender lament."

Clare had not lived long at Northborough when he
was waited upon by the editor of a London magazine
who wormed from him an account of his private affairs,
and having dressed up that account in what would now be
called a sensational style, published it to the world. The
article contained many unjust insinuations against Clare's
patrons and publishers, and Mr. Taylor commenced

actions, afterwards abandoned, against the magazine in which it originally appeared, the "Alfred," and also against a Stamford paper, into which the article was copied.   Clare indignantly protested against the use to which his conversation with his meddlesome visitor had been put, but it is impossible entirely to acquit him of blame.   Mr. Taylor remonstrated with him upon his indiscretion, but with a consideration for his inexperience which it is very pleasant to notice, refrained from a severity of rebuke to which Clare had no doubt exposed himself.   " I have been much hurt," he says, " at finding that my endeavours to do you service have ended no better than they have, but if you supposed that I had been benefited by it, or that I had withheld from you anything you were entitled to—any profit whatever on any of your works—you have been grievously mistaken." Mr. Taylor was constant to the end, for after this he promoted Clare's interests by every means in his power, conferring with Dr. Darling on his behalf, discharging in conjunction with Mrs. Emmerson a heavy account sent in by a local medical man, advising him in all his troubles, offering him a home whenever he chose to come to London to see Dr. Darling, editing his last volume of poems, although it was brought out by a house with which he had no connection, and, finally, contributing to his maintenance when it became necessary to send him to a private asylum.   Among the indications which Clare gave of the approaching loss of reason were frequent complaints that he was haunted by evil spirits, and that he and his family were bewitched.   Writing on this subject in February, 1833, Mr. Taylor said :—" As for evil spirits, depend upon it, my dear friend, that there are none, and that there is no such thing as witchcraft. But I am sure that our hearts naturally are full of evil thoughts, and that God has intended to set us free from the dominion of such thoughts by his good Spirit. You will not expect me to say much on this subject, knowing that I never press it upon my friends. I must, however, so far depart from my custom as to say, that I am perfectly certain a man may be happy even in this life if he will listen to the Word which came down from heaven, and be as a little child in his obedience and willingness to do what it requires of him. I am sure of this, that if we receive the Spirit of God in our hearts *we shall never die.* We shall go away from this scene, and our bodies will be consigned to the grave, but with less pain than we have often felt in life we shall be carried through what seem to be the pangs of death, and then we shall be with that holy and blessed company at once who have died fully believing in Christ, and who shall never again be separated from him and happiness. Farewell, my dear Clare.

" Believe me ever most sincerely yours,

" JOHN TAYLOR."

In 1832 Clare projected a new volume of poems, and with the assistance of his friends obtained in a few months two hundred subscribers. Mr. Taylor having represented that as publisher to the London University poetry was no longer in his line of business, Mr. Emmerson undertook the task of finding another publisher, and opened a correspondence with Mr. How, a gentleman connected with the house of Whittaker & Co. A large number of manuscript poems and of fugitive pieces from the annuals were submitted to Mr. How, who was requested by Mr. Emmerson to make the poet an offer. The negociation was successful, for on the 8th of March, 1834, Mr. Emmerson was enabled to write to Clare as follows :—

" My very dear Clare,—

" At length with great pleasure, although after great anxiety and trouble, I have brought your affair with Mr. How to a conclusion. I have enclosed a receipt for your signature, and if you will write your name at the bottom of it and return it enclosed in a letter to me, I shall have the £40 in ready money for you immediately. You will perceive by the receipt that I have sold only the copyright of the first edition, and that Mr. How stipulates shall consist of only 750 copies, or at the utmost 1000.   *   *   *   *
And now, with the license of a friend, I am about to talk to you about your affairs. This money has been hardly earned by your mental labour, and with difficulty obtained by me for you, only by great perseverance. We are therefore most anxious it should be the means of freeing you from all debt or incumbrance, in order that your mind may be once more at ease, and that you may revel with your muse at will, regardless of all hauntings save hers, and when she troubles you you can pay her off in her own coin.   *   *   *   *
The sum you stated some time since I think was £35

as sufficient to clear all your debts, and thus you will be able to start fairly with the world again." *

While the "Rural Muse" was in the press, Mr. How, one of the very few of Clare's earlier friends who are still living, suggested to him the advisableness of his applying to the committee of the Literary Fund for a grant, and promising to exert himself to the utmost to secure the success of the application. Clare applied for £50, and obtained it, whereupon Mrs. Emmerson, to whose heart there was no readier way than that of showing kindness to poor Clare, writes—"In my last, I told you I had written to Mr. How on the subject of the Literary Fund, &c. Yesterday morning the good little man came to communicate to me the favourable result of the application. The committee have nobly presented you with fifty pounds. *Blessings on them!* for giving you the means to do honour to every engagement, and leave you, I hope, a surplus to fly to when needed.   *   *   * Mr. How is just the sort of man for my own nature. He is willing to do his best for Clare. He has shown himself in the recent event as one of the few who perform what they promise. God bless him for his kindly exertions to emancipate you from your thraldom!"

The "Rural Muse" was published in July, 1835, and was cordially received by the "Athenæum," "Black-

---

* Mr. How's connection with the firm of Whittaker & Co. terminated before the appearance of the "Rural Muse," but he brought out the volume, through them, on his own account, and twenty years afterwards transferred the copyright to Mr. Taylor, who, in 1854, contemplated the re-issue of Clare's poems in a collected form.

wood's Magazine," the " Literary Gazette," and other leading periodicals. It was well printed and embellished with engravings of Northborough Church and the poet's cottage. It has been already intimated that the poems included within this volume, while retaining all the freshness and simplicity of Clare's earlier works, exhibit traces of the mental cultivation to which for years so large a portion of his time had been devoted. The circle of subjects is greatly expanded, the passages to which exception may be taken on the score of carelessness or obscurity are few, and the diction is often refined and elevated to a degree of which the poet had not before shown himself capable. The following extracts are made almost at random :—

Autumn.

Syren of sullen moods and fading hues,
Yet haply not incapable of joy,
    Sweet Autumn ! I thee hail
    With welcome all unfeigned ;

And oft as morning from her lattice peeps
To beckon up the sun, I seek with thee
    To drink the dewy breath
    Of fields left fragrant then,

In solitudes, where no frequented paths
But what thine own foot makes betray thine home,
    Stealing obtrusive there
    To meditate thy end ;

"The Rural Muse."

By overshadowed ponds, in woody nooks,
With ramping sallows lined, and crowding sedge,
    Which woo the winds to play,
    And with them dance for joy;

And meadow pools, torn wide by lawless floods,
Where waterlilies spread their oily leaves,
    On which, as wont, the fly
    Oft battens in the sun;

Where leans the mossy willow half way o'er,
On which the shepherd crawls astride to throw
    His angle, clear of weeds
    That crown the water's brim;

Or crispy hills and hollows scant of sward,
Where step by step the patient, lonely boy,
    Hath cut rude flights of stairs
    To climb their steepy sides;

   *   *   *   *   *   *

Now filtering winds thin winnow through the woods
With tremulous noise, that bids, at every breath,
    Some sickly cankered leaf
    Let go its hold and die.

And now the bickering storm, with sudden start,
In flirting fits of anger carps aloud,
    Thee urging to thine end,
    Sore wept by troubled skies.

And yet, sublime in grief, thy thoughts delight
To show me visions of most gorgeous dyes,
    Haply forgetting now
    They but prepare thy shroud;

Thy pencil dashing its excess of shades,
Improvident of wealth, till every bough
    Burns with thy mellow touch
    Disorderly divine.

Soon must I view thee as a pleasant dream
Droop faintly, and so reckon for thine end,
    As sad the winds sink low
    In dirges for their queen;

While in the moment of their weary pause,
To cheer thy bankrupt pomp, the willing lark
    Starts from his shielding clod,
    Snatching sweet scraps of song.

Thy life is waning now, and Silence tries
To mourn, but meets no sympathy in sounds,
    As stooping low she bends,
    Forming with leaves thy grave;

To sleep inglorious there mid tangled woods,
Till parch-lipped Summer pines in drought away;
    Then from thine ivied trance
    Awake to glories new.

MAY.

Now comes the bonny May, dancing and skipping
Across the stepping-stones of meadow streams,
Bearing no kin to April showers a-weeping,
But constant Sunshine as her servant seems.
Her heart is up—her sweetness, all a-maying,
Streams in her face, like gems on Beauty's breast;
The swains are sighing all, and well-a-daying,
Lovesick and gazing on their lovely guest.
The Sunday paths, to pleasant places leading,
Are graced by couples linking arm in arm,
Sweet smiles enjoying or some book a-reading,
Where Love and Beauty are the constant charm;
For while the bonny May is dancing by,
Beauty delights the ear, and Beauty fills the eye.

Birds sing and build, and Nature scorns alone
On May's young festival to be a widow;
The children, too, have pleasures all their own,
In gathering lady-smocks along the meadow.
The little brook sings loud among the pebbles,
So very loud, that water-flowers, which lie
Where many a silver curdle boils and dribbles,
Dance too with joy as it goes singing by.
Among the pasture mole-hills maidens stoop
To pluck the luscious marjoram for their bosoms;
The greensward 's littered o'er with buttercups,
And white-thorns, they are breaking down with
    blossoms.
'T is Nature's livery for the bonny May,
Who keeps her court, and all have holiday.

Princess of Months (so Nature's choice ordains,)
And Lady of the Summer still she reigns.
In spite of April's youth, who charms in tears,
And r osy June, who wins with blushing face ;
July, sweet shepherdess, who wreathes the shears
Of shepherds with her flowers of winning grace;
And sun-tanned August, with her swarthy charms,
The beautiful and rich ; and pastoral, gay
September, with her pomp of fields and farms;
And wild November's sybilline array ;—
In spite of Beauty's calendar, the Year
Garlands with Beauty's prize the bonny May.
Where' er she goes, fair Nature hath no peer,
And months do love their queen when she 's away.

MEMORY.

I would not that my memory all should die,
And pass away with every common lot:
I would not that my humble dust should lie
In quite a strange and unfrequented spot,
By all unheeded and by all forgot,
With nothing save the heedless winds to sigh,
And nothing but the dewy morn to weep
About my grave, far hid from the world's eye :
I fain would have some friend to wander nigh
And find a path to where my ashes sleep —
Not the cold heart that merely passes by,
To read who lies beneath, but such as keep
Past memories warm with deeds of other years,
And pay to friendship some few friendly tears.

"He waxes desperate with imagination."

The "Rural Muse" sold tolerably well for some months, and Mr. Whittaker told Mr. Emmerson that "he thought they would get off the first edition." But the time was rapidly approaching when literary fame or failure, the constancy or fickleness of friends, the pangs of poverty or the joys of competence were to be alike matters of indifference to John Clare. He began to write in a piteous strain to Mrs. Emmerson, Mr. Taylor, and Dr. Darling, all of whom assured him of their deep sympathy, and promised assistance. Mrs. Emmerson, although completely prostrated by repeated and serious attacks of illness, sent him cheering letters so long as she could hold her pen, while Mr. Taylor wrote—" If you think that you can now come here for the advice of Dr. Darling I shall be very happy to see you, and any one who may attend you." The attacks of melancholy from which he had suffered occasionally for many years became more frequent and more intense, his language grew wild and incoherent, and at length he failed to recognize his own wife and children and became the subject of all kinds of hallucinations. There were times when he was perfectly rational, and he returned to work in his garden or in his little study with a zest which filled his family and neighbours with eager anticipations of his recovery, but every succeeding attack of his mental malady was more severe than that which preceded it. Of all that followed little need be said, for it is too painful to be dwelt upon, and the story of Clare's life hurries therefore to its close.

His lunacy having been duly certified, Mr. Taylor and other of Clare's old friends in London charged themselves with the responsibility of removing him to the private asylum of Dr. Allen at High Beech, in Epping Forest. Mr. Taylor sending a trustworthy person to Northborough to accompany him to London and take care of him on the road. This was in June or July, 1837, and Clare remained under Dr. Allen's care for four years.

Allan Cunningham, Mr. S. C. Hall, and other of Clare's literary friends energetically appealed to the public on behalf of the unhappy bard. Mr. Hall in the " Book of Gems " for 1838 wrote—" It is not yet too late : although he has given indications of a brain breaking up, a very envied celebrity may be obtained by some wealthy and good Samaritan who would rescue him from the Cave of Despair," adding, " Strawberry Hill might be gladly sacrificed for the fame of having saved Chatterton."

This appeal brought Mr. Hall a letter from the Marquis of Northampton, whose name is now for the first time associated with that of the poet. The Marquis informed Mr. Hall that he was not one of Clare's exceeding admirers, but he was struck and shocked by what that gentleman had said about "our county poet," and thought it would be " a disgrace to the county," to which Clare was "a credit," if he were left in a state of poverty. The county was neither very wealthy nor very literary, but his lordship thought that a collection of Clare's poems might be published by subscription, and if that suggestion were adopted he would take ten or twenty copies, or he would give a donation of money, if direct assistance of that kind were preferred. Mr. Hall says in his "Memories,"—"The plan was not carried out, and if the Marquis gave any aid of any kind to the peasant-poet the world, and I verily believe the poet himself, remained in ignorance of the amount."

All that was possible was done for Clare at the house . of Dr. Allen, one of the early reformers of the treatment of lunatics. He was kept pretty constantly employed in the garden, and soon grew stout and robust. After a time he was allowed to stroll beyond the grounds of the asylum and to ramble about the forest. He was perfectly harmless, and would sometimes carry on a conversation in a rational manner, always, however, losing himself in the end in absolute nonsense. In March, 1841, he wrote a long and intelligible letter to Mrs. Clare, almost the only peculiarity in which is that every word is begun with a capital letter. There is no doubt that at this time he was possessed with the idea that he had two wives—Patty, whom he called his second wife, and his life-long ideal, Mary Joyce. In the letter just referred to he begins "My dear wife Patty," and in a postscript says, "Give my love to the dear boy who wrote to me, and to her who is never forgotten." He wrote verses which he told Dr. Allen were for his wife Mary, and that he intended to take them to her. He made several unsuccessful attempts to escape in the early part of 1841, but in July of that year he contrived to evade both watchers and pursuers, and reached Peterborough after being four days and three nights on the road in a penniless condition, and being so near to dying of starvation that he was compelled to eat grass like the beasts of the field. The day after his return to Northborough he wrote what he called an account of his journey, prefacing the narrative by this remark, "Returned home out of Essex and found no Mary." Mr. Martin gives this extraordinary document in his "Life of Clare." It is a weird, pathetic, and pitiful story—"a tragedy all too deep for tears."

Having finished the journal of his escape he addressed it with a letter to "Mary Clare, Glinton." In this letter he says—"I am not so lonely as I was in Essex, for here I can see Glinton Church, and feeling that my Mary is safe, if not happy I am gratified. Though my home is no home to me, my hopes are not entirely hopeless while even the memory of Mary lives so near to me. God bless you, my dear Mary! Give my love to our dear beautiful family and to your mother, and believe me, as ever I have been and ever shall be, my dearest Mary, your affectionate husband, John Clare." Truly,

"Love's not Time's fool: though rosy lips and cheeks
Within his bending sickle's compass come,
Love alters not with his brief hours and weeks,
But bears it out e'en to the edge of doom."

Clare remained for a short time at Northborough, and was then removed under medical advice to the County Lunatic Asylum at Northampton, of which establishment he continued an inmate until his death in 1864. During

the whole of that time the charge made by the authorities
of the Asylum for his maintenance was paid either by
Earl Fitzwilliam or by his son, the Hon. G. W.
Fitzwilliam. It is to the credit of the managers of the
institution that although the amount paid on his behalf
was that usually charged for patients of the humbler
classes, Clare was always treated in every respect as a
"gentleman patient." He had his favourite window
corner in the common sitting room, commanding a view
of Northampton and the valley of the Nen, and books and
writing materials were provided for him. Unless the
Editor's memory is at fault, he was always addressed
deferentially as " Mr. Clare," both by the officers of the
Asylum and the townspeople; and when Her Majesty
passed through Northampton, in 1844, in her progress to
Burleigh, a seat was specially reserved for the poet near
one of the triumphal arches. There was something
very nearly akin to tenderness in the kindly sympathy
which was shown for him, and his most whimsical
utterances were listened to with gravity, lest he should
feel hurt or annoyed. He was classified in the Asylum
books among the "harmless," and for several years was
allowed to walk in the fields or go into the town at his
own pleasure. His favourite resting-place at Northampton
was a niche under the roof of the spacious portico of All
Saints' Church, and here he would sometimes sit for
hours, musing, watching the children at play, or jotting
down passing thoughts in his pocket note-book. In
course of time it was found expedient not to allow him
to wander beyond the Asylum grounds. He wrote

occasionally to his son Charles, but appears never to have been visited by either relatives or friends. The neglect of his wife and children is inexplicable. It was no doubt while smarting under this treatment that he penned the lines given below, of which an eloquent critic has said that " in their sublime sadness and incoherence they sum up, with marvellous effect, the one great misfortune of the poet's life—his mental isolation—his inability to make his deepest character and thoughts intelligible to others. They read like the wail of a nature cut off from all access to other minds, concentrated at its own centre, and conscious of the impassable gulf which separates it from universal humanity:"—

> I am ! yet what I am who cares, or knows?
> My friends forsake me, like a memory lost.
> I am the self-consumer of my woes,
> They rise and vanish, an oblivious host,
> Shadows of life, whose very soul is lost.
> And yet I am—I live—though I am toss'd.
>
> Into the nothingness of scorn and noise,
> Into the living sea of waking dream,
> Where there is neither sense of life, nor joys,
> But the huge shipwreck of my own esteem
> And all that's dear. Even those I loved the best
> Are strange—nay, they are stranger than the rest.
>
> I long for scenes where man has never trod—
> For scenes where woman never smiled or wept—
> There to abide with my Creator, God,
> And sleep as I in childhood sweetly slept,
> Full of high thoughts, unborn. So let me lie,
> The grass below ; above, the vaulted sky.

"Close up his eyes, & draw the curtain close."

Clare's physical powers slowly declined, and at length he had to be wheeled about the Asylum grounds in a Bath chair. As he felt his end approaching he would frequently say "I have lived too long," or "I want to go home." Until within three days of his death he managed to reach his favourite seat in the window, but was then seized with paralysis, and on the afternoon of the 20th of May, 1864, without a struggle or a sigh his spirit passed away. He was taken home.

In accordance with Clare's own wish, his remains were interred in the churchyard at Helpstone, by the side of those of his father and mother, under the shade of a sycamore tree. The expenses of the funeral were paid by the Hon. G. W. Fitzwilliam. * Two or three years afterwards a coped monument of Ketton stone was erected over Clare's remains. It bears this inscription :—" Sacred to the Memory of John Clare, the Northamptonshire Peasant Poet. Born July 13, 1793. Died May 20, 1864. A Poet is born, not made." In 1869, another memorial was erected in the principal street of Helpstone. The style is Early English : and it bears suitable inscriptions from Clare's Works.

* The oft-repeated statements are incorrect, that the Northampton County Lunatic Asylum is a " pauper asylum," that Clare was " a pauper lunatic," and that Earl Fitzwilliam expressed the wish that he should have " a pauper funeral." The Fitzwilliams have been kind and generous friends of Clare and his family for nearly fifty years, and it is not to be credited that any member of that house ever said anything of the kind. It may be added that Earl Spencer continued his annuity of £10 to Mrs. Clare until her death, Feb. 5th, 1871. In this connection it should also be noted that the Rev. Charles Mossop, of Etton, and Mr. and Mrs. Bellars, of Helpstone, took a lively interest in the welfare of Mrs. Clare and her family, and in May, 1864, Mr. Bellars purchased the poet's cottage at Helpstone, and has set it apart for charitable uses. Lastly, Mr. Joseph Whitaker, of London, in whom is vested the copyright in Clare's poems, paid Mrs. Clare a handsome annuity for the last six or seven years of her life.

In looking back upon such a life as Clare's, so prominent are the human interests which confront us, that those of poetry, as one of the fine arts, are not unlikely to sink for a time completely out of sight. The long and painful strain upon our sympathy to which we are subject as we read the story is such perhaps as the life of no other English poet puts upon us. The spell of the great moral problems by which the lives of so many of our poets seem to have been more or less surrounded makes itself felt in every step of Clare's career. We are tempted to speak in almost fatalistic language of the disastrous gift of the poetic faculty, and to find in that the source of all Clare's woe. The well-known lines—

" We poets in our youth begin in gladness,

But thereof come in the end despondency and
madness "—

ring in our ears, and we remember that these are the words of a poet endowed with a well-balanced mind, and who knew far less than Clare the experience of

" Cold, pain, and labour, and all fleshly ills."

In Clare's case we are tempted to say that the Genius of Poetry laid her fearful hand upon a nature too weak to bear her gifts and at the same time to master the untoward circumstances in which his lot was cast. But too well does poor Clare's history illustrate that interpretation of the myth which pictures Great Pan secretly busy among the reeds and fashioning, with sinister thought, the fatal pipe which shall " make a poet out of a man."

Conclusion.

And yet it may be doubted whether, on the whole, Clare's lot in life, and that of the wife and family who were dependent upon him, was aggravated by the poetic genius which we are thus trying to make the scapegoat for his misfortunes.

It may be that the publicity acquired by the North-amptonshire Peasant Poet simply brings to the surface the average life of the English agricultural labourer in the person of one who was more than usually sensitive to suffering. Unhappily there is too good reason to believe that the privations to which Clare and his household were subject cannot be looked upon as exceptional in the class of society to which both husband and wife belonged, although they naturally acquire a deeper shade from the prospect of competency and comfort which Clare's gifts seemed to promise. In this light, while the miseries of the poet are none the less real and claim none the less of our sympathy, the moral problem of Clare's woes belongs rather to humanity at large than to poets in particular. We are at liberty to hope, then, that the world is all the richer, and that Clare's lot was none the harder, by reason of that dispensation of Providence which has given to English literature such a volume as "The Rural Muse." How many are there who not only fail, as Clare failed, to rise above their circumstances, but who, in addition, leave nothing behind them to enrich posterity! We are indeed the richer for Clare, but with what travail of soul to himself only true poets can know.

Asylum Poems.

ASYLUM POEMS.

'T is Spring, my love, 't is Spring.

'T is Spring, my love, 't is Spring,
And the birds begin to sing :
If 't was Winter, left alone with you,
Your bonny form and face
Would make a Summer place,
And be the finest flower that ever grew.

'T is Spring, my love, 't is Spring,
And the hazel catkins hing,
While the snowdrop has its little blebs of dew ;
But that 's not so white within
As your bosom's hidden skin—
That sweetest of all flowers that ever grew.

The sun arose from bed,
All strewn with roses red,
But the brightest and the loveliest crimson place
Is not so fresh and fair,
Or so sweet beyond compare,
As thy blushing, ever smiling, happy face.

I love Spring's early flowers,
And their bloom in its first hours,
But they never half so bright or lovely seem
As the blithe and happy grace
Of my darling's blushing face,
And the happiness of love's young dream.

Love of Nature.

I love thee, Nature, with a boundless love!
The calm of earth, the storm of roaring woods!
The winds breathe happiness where'er I rove!
There 's life's own music in the swelling floods!
My heart is in the thunder-melting clouds,
The snow-cap't mountain, and the rolling sea!
And hear ye not the voice where darkness shrouds
The heavens? There lives happiness for me!

    *   *   *   *   *

My pulse beats calmer while His lightnings play!
My eye, with earth's delusions waxing dim,
Clears with the brightness of eternal day!
The elements crash round me! It is He!
Calmly I hear His voice and never start.
From Eve's posterity I stand quite free,
Nor feel her curses rankle round my heart.

Love is not here. Hope is, and at His voice—
The rolling thunder and the roaring sea—
My pulses leap, and with the hills rejoice;
Then strife and turmoil are at end for me.
No matter where life's ocean leads me on,
For Nature is my mother, and I rest,
When tempests trouble and the sun is gone,
Like to a weary child upon her breast.

155

The Invitation.

Come hither, my dear one, my choice one, and rare one,
  And let us be walking the meadows so fair,
Where on pilewort and daisies the eye fondly gazes,
  And the wind plays so sweet in thy bonny brown hair.

Come with thy maiden eye, lay silks and satins by;
  Come in thy russet or grey cotton gown;
Come to the meads, dear, where flags, sedge, and reeds
      appear,
  Rustling to soft winds and bowing low down.

Come with thy parted hair, bright eyes, and forehead
      bare;
  Come to the whitethorn that grows in the lane;
To banks of primroses, where sweetness reposes,
  Come, love, and let us be happy again.

Come where the violet flowers, come where the morning
      showers
  Pearl on the primrose and speedwell so blue;
Come to that clearest brook that ever runs round the
      nook
  Where you and I pledged our first love so true.

To the Lark.

Bird of the morn,
When roseate clouds begin
To show the opening dawn
Thou gladly sing'st it in,
And o'er the sweet green fields and happy vales
Thy pleasant song is heard, mixed with the morning
gales.

Bird of the morn,
What time the ruddy sun
Smiles on the pleasant corn
Thy singing is begun,
Heartfelt and cheering over labourers' toil,
Who chop in coppice wild and delve the russet soil.

Bird of the sun,
How dear to man art thou !
When morning has begun
To gild the mountain's brow,
How beautiful it is to see thee soar so blest,
Winnowing thy russet wings above thy twitchy nest.

Bird of the Summer's day,
How oft I stand to hear
Thee sing thy airy lay,
With music wild and clear,
Till thou becom'st a speck upon the sky,
Small as the clods that crumble where I lie.

Thou bird of happiest song,
The Spring and Summer too
Are thine, the months along,
The woods and vales to view.
If climes were evergreen thy song would be
The sunny music of eternal glee.

Graves of Infants.

Infants' gravemounds are steps of angels, where
Earth's brightest gems of innocence repose.
God is their parent, so they need no tear;
He takes them to his bosom from earth's woes,
A bud their lifetime and a flower their close.
Their spirits are the Iris of the skies,
Needing no prayers; a sunset's happy close.
Gone are the bright rays of their soft blue eyes;
Flowers weep in dew-drops o'er them, and the gale
    gently sighs.

Their lives were nothing but a sunny shower,
Melting on flowers as tears melt from the eye.
Each death   *   *   *
Was tolled on flowers as Summer gales went by.
They bowed and trembled, yet they heaved no sigh,
And the sun smiled to show the end was well.
Infants have nought to weep for ere they die;
All prayers are needless, beads they need not tell,
White flowers their mourners are, Nature their passing
    bell.

Bonny Lassie O!

O the evening 's for the fair, bonny lassie O!
To meet the cooler air and join an angel there,
    With the dark dishevelled hair,
        Bonny lassie O!

The bloom 's on the brere, bonny lassie O!
Oak apples on the tree; and wilt thou gang to see
    The shed I've made for thee,
        Bonny lassie O!

'T is agen the running brook, bonny lassie O!
In a grassy nook hard by, with a little patch of sky,
    And a bush to keep us dry,
        Bonny lassie O!

There 's the daisy all the year, bonny lassie O!
There 's the king-cup bright as gold, and the speedwell
    never cold,
    And the arum leaves unrolled,
        Bonny lassie O!

O meet me at the shed, bonny lassie O!
With the woodbine peeping in, and the roses like thy skin
    Blushing, thy praise to win,
        Bonny lassie O!

I will meet thee there at e'en, bonny lassie O!
When the bee sips in the bean, and grey willow branches
lean,
    And the moonbeam looks between,
        Bonny lassie O!

Phœbe of the Scottish Glen.

Agen I'll take my idle pen
.And sing my bonny mountain maid—
Sweet Phœbe of the Scottish glen,
Nor of her censure feel afraid.
I'll charm her ear with beauty's praise,
And please her eye with songs agen—
The ballads of our early days—
To Phœbe of the Scottish glen.

There never was a fairer thing
All Scotland's glens and mountains through.
The siller gowans of the Spring,
Besprent with pearls of mountain dew,
The maiden blush upon the brere,
Far distant from the haunts of men,
Are nothing half so sweet or dear
As Phœbe of the Scottish glen.

How handsome is her naked foot,
Moist with the pearls of Summer dew :
The siller daisy 's nothing to 't,
Nor hawthorn flowers so white to view,
She 's sweeter than the blooming brere,
That blossoms far away from men :
No flower in Scotland 's half so dear
As Phœbe of the Scottish glen.

𝕸𝖆𝖎𝖉 𝖔𝖋 𝖙𝖍𝖊 𝖂𝖎𝖑𝖉𝖊𝖗𝖓𝖊𝖘𝖘.

Maid of the wilderness,
Sweet in thy rural dress,
Fond thy rich lips I press
   Under this tree.

Morning her health bestows,
Sprinkles dews on the rose,
That by the bramble grows:
   Maid happy be.
Womanhood round thee glows,
   Wander with me.

The restharrow blooming,
The sun just a-coming,
Grass and bushes illuming,
   And the spreading oak tree;

Come hither, sweet Nelly,
 * * * *
The morning is loosing
   Its incense for thee.
The pea-leaf has dews on;
   Love wander with me.

143

We'll walk by the river,
And love more than ever ;
There 's nought shall dissever
    My fondness from thee.

Soft ripples the water,
Flags rustle like laughter,
And fish follow after ;
    Leaves drop from the tree.
Nelly, Beauty's own daughter,
    Love, wander with me.

Mary Bateman.

My love she wears a cotton plaid,
    A bonnet of the straw;
Her cheeks are leaves of roses spread,
    Her lips are like the haw.
In truth she is as sweet a maid
    As true love ever saw.

Her curls are ever in my eyes,
    As nets by Cupid flung;
Her voice will oft my sleep surprise,
    More sweet than ballad sung.
O Mary Bateman's curling hair!
    I wake, and there is nothing there.

I wake, and fall asleep again,
The same delights in visions rise;
There's nothing can appear more plain
Than those rose cheeks and those bright eyes.
I wake again, and all alone
Sits Darkness on his ebon throne.

All silent runs the silver Trent,
The cobweb veils are all wet through,
A silver bead 's on every bent,
On every leaf a bleb of dew.
I sighed, the moon it shone so clear :
Was Mary Bateman walking here ?

𝕎hen shall we meet again?

How many times Spring blossoms meek
    Have faded on the land
Since last I kissed that pretty cheek,
    Caressed that happy hand.
Eight time the green 's been painted white
    With daisies in the grass
Since I looked on thy eyes so bright,
    And pressed my bonny lass.

The ground lark sung about the farms,
    The blackbird in the wood,
When fast locked in each other's arms
    By hedgerow thorn we stood.
It was a pleasant Sabbath day,
    The sun shone bright and round,
His light through dark oaks passed, and lay
    Like gold upon the ground.

How beautiful the blackbird sung,
    And answered soft the thrush;
And sweet the pearl-like dew-drops hung
    Upon the white thorn bush.
O happy day, eight years ago!
    We parted without pain:
The blackbird sings, primroses blow;
    When shall we meet again?

The Praise of God.

How cheerful along the gay mead
The daisy and cowslip appear ;
The flocks as they carelessly feed
Rejoice in the Spring of the year.
The myrtles that deck the gay bowers,
The herbage that springs from the sod,
Trees, plants, cooling fruits, and sweet flowers,
All rise to the praise of my God.

Shall man, the great master of all,
The only insensible prove ?
Forbid it, fair gratitude's call ;
Forbid it, devotion and love.
The Lord who such wonders can raise,
And still can destroy with a nod,
My lips shall incessantly praise ;
My soul shall be rapt in my God.

The Lover's Invitation.

Now the wheat is in the ear, and the rose is on the brere,
And blue-caps so divinely blue, with poppies of bright
scarlet hue,
Maiden, at the close o' eve, wilt thou, dear, thy cottage
leave,
And walk with one that loves thee?

When the even's tiny tears bead upon the grassy spears,
And the spider's lace is wet with its pinhead blebs of dew,
Wilt thou lay thy work aside and walk by brooklets dim
descried,
Where I delight to love thee?

While thy footfall lightly press'd tramples by the sky-
lark's nest,
And the cockle's streaky eyes mark the snug place where
it lies,
Mary, put thy work away, and walk at dewy close o' day
With me to kiss and love thee.

There 's something in the time so sweet, when lovers in
the evening meet,
The air so still, the sky so mild, like slumbers of the
cradled child,
The moon looks over fields of love, among the ivy sleeps
the dove:
To see thee is to love thee.

Nature's Darling.

Sweet comes the morning
In Nature's adorning,
And bright shines the dew on the buds of the thorn,
Where Mary Ann rambles
Through the sloe trees and brambles;
She 's sweeter than wild flowers that open at morn;
She 's a rose in the dew;
She 's pure and she 's true;
She 's as gay as the poppy that grows in the corn.

Her eyes they are bright,
Her bosom 's snow white,
And her voice is like songs of the birds in the grove.
She 's handsome and bonny,
And fairer than any,
And her person and actions are Nature's and love.
She has the bloom of all roses,
She 's the breath of sweet posies,
She 's as pure as the brood in the nest of the dove.

Of Earth's fairest daughters,
Voiced like falling waters,
She walks down the meadows, than blossoms more fair.
O her bosom right fair is,
And her rose cheek so rare is,
And parted and lovely her glossy black hair.
Her bosom's soft whiteness!
The sun in its brightness
Has never been seen so bewilderingly fair.

The dewy grass glitters,
The house swallow twitters,
And through the sky floats in its visions of bliss;
The lark soars on high,
.   On cowslips dews lie,
And the last days of Summer are nothing like this.
When Mary Ann rambles
Through hedgerows and brambles,
The soft gales of Spring are the seasons of bliss.

I 'll Dream upon the Days to come.

I 'll lay me down on the green sward,
Mid yellowcups and speedwell blue,
And pay the world no more regard,
But be to Nature leal and true.
Who break the peace of hapless man
 But they who Truth and Nature wrong?
I 'll hear no more of evil's plan,
But live with Nature and her song.

Where Nature's lights and shades are green,
Where Nature's place is strewn with flowers,
Where strife and care are never seen,
There I 'll retire to happy hours,
And stretch my body on the green,
And sleep among the flowers in bloom,
By eyes of malice seldom seen,
And dream upon the days to come.

I 'll lay me by the forest green,
I 'll lay me on the pleasant grass;
My life shall pass away unseen;
I 'll be no more the man I was.
The tawny bee upon the flower,
The butterfly upon the leaf,
Like them I 'll live my happy hour,
A life of sunshine, bright and brief.

In greenwood hedges, close at hand,
Build, brood, and sing the little birds,
The happiest things in the green land,
While sweetly feed the lowing herds,
While softly bleat the roving sheep.
Upon the green grass will I lie,
A Summer's day, to think and sleep.
Or see the clouds sail down the sky.

To Isabel.

Arise, my Isabel, arise!
The sun shoots forth his early ray,
The hue of love is in the skies,
The birds are singing, come away!
O come, my Isabella, come,
With inky tendrils hanging low;
Thy cheeks like roses just in bloom,
That in the healthy Summer glow.

That eye it turns the world away
From wanton sport and recklessness;
That eye beams with a cheerful ray,
And smiles propitiously to bless.
O come, my Isabella, dear!
O come, and fill these longing arms!
Come, let me see thy beauty here,
And bend in worship o'er thy charms.

O come, my Isabella, love!
My dearest Isabella, come!
Thy heart's affection let me prove,
And kiss thy beauty in its bloom.
My Isabella, young and fair,
Thou darling of my home and heart,
Come, love, my bosom's truth to share,
And of its being form a part.

The Shepherd's Daughter.

How sweet is every lengthening day,
    And every change of weather,
When Summer comes, on skies blue grey,
    And brings her hosts together,
Her flocks of birds, her crowds of flowers,
    Her sunny-shining water!
I dearly love the woodbine bowers,
    That hide the Shepherd's Daughter—
In gown of green or brown or blue,
    The Shepherd's Daughter, leal and true.

How bonny is her lily breast!
    How sweet her rosy face!
She 'd give my aching bosom rest,
    Where love would find its place.
While earth is green, and skies are blue,
    And sunshine gilds the water,
While Summer 's sweet and Nature true,
    I 'll love the Shepherd's Daughter—
Her nut brown hair, her clear bright eye,
    My daily thought, my only joy.

She 's such a simple, sweet young thing,
    Dressed in her country costume.
My wits had used to know the Spring,
  .   Till I saw, and loved, and lost 'em.
How quietly the lily lies
    Upon the deepest water !
How sweet to me the Summer skies !
    And so 's the Shepherd's Daughter—
With lily breast and rosy face
    The sweetest maid in any place.

My singing bird, my bonny flower,
    How dearly could I love thee !
To sit with thee one pleasant hour,
    If thou would'st but approve me !
I swear by lilies white and yellow,
    That flower on deepest water,
Would'st thou but make me happy fellow,
    I 'd wed the Shepherd's Daughter !
By all that 's on the earth or water,
I more than love the Shepherd's Daughter.

Lassie, I love thee.

Lassie, I love thee !
The heavens above thee
Look downwards to move thee,
    And prove my love true.
My arms round thy waist, love,
My head on thy breast, love ;
By a true man caressed love,
    Ne'er bid me adieu.

Thy cheek 's full o' blushes,
Like the rose in the bushes,
While my love ardent gushes
    With over delight.
Though clouds may come o'er thee,
Sweet maid, I 'll adore thee,
As I do now before thee :
    I love thee outright.

It stings me to madness
To see thee all gladness,
While I 'm full of sadness
    Thy meaning to guess.
Thy gown is deep blue, love,
In honour of true love :
Ever thinking of you, love,
    My love I 'll confess.

My love ever showing,
Thy heart worth the knowing,
It is like the sun glowing,
    And hid in thy breast.
Thy lover behold me ;
To my bosom I 'll fold thee,
For thou, love, thou 'st just told me,
    So here thou may'st rest.

"Just like the berry browe is my bonny lassie O!
And in the smoky camp lives my bonny lassie O!"

The Gipsy Lass.

The Gipsy Lass.

Just like the berry brown is my bonny lassie O !
And in the smoky camp lives my bonny lassie O !
  Where the scented woodbine weaves
  Round the white-thorn's glossy leaves :
The sweetest maid on earth is my gipsy lassie O !

The brook it runs so clear by my bonny lassie O !
And the blackbird singeth near my bonny lassie O !
  And there the wild briar rose
  Wrinkles the clear stream as it flows
By the smoky camp of my bonny lassie O !

The groundlark singeth high o'er my bonny lassie O !
The nightingale lives nigh my gipsy lassie O !
  They 're with her all the year,
  By the brook that runs so clear,
And there 's none in all the world like my gipsy lassie O !

With a bosom white as snow is my gipsy lassie O !
With a foot like to the roe is my bonny lassie O !
  Like the sweet birds she will sing,
  While echo it will ring :
Sure there 's none in the world like my bonny lassie O !

At the Foot of Clifford Hill.

Who loves the white-thorn tree,
And the river running free ?
There a maiden stood with me
      In Summer weather.
Near a cottage far from town,
While the sun went brightly down
O'er the meadows green and brown,
      We loved together.

How sweet her drapery flowed,
While the moor-cock oddly crowed ;
I took the kiss which love bestowed,
      Under the white-thorn tree.
Soft winds the water curled,
The trees their branches furled ;
Sweetest nook in all the world
      Is where she stood with me.

Calm came the evening air,
The sky was sweet and fair,
In the river shadowed there,
      Close by the hawthorn tree.
Round her neck I clasped my arms,
And kissed her rosy charms ;
O'er the flood the hackle swarms,
      Where the maiden stood with me.

O there 's something falls so dear
On the music of the ear,
Where the river runs so clear,
  And my lover met with me.
At the foot of Clifford Hill
Still I hear the clacking mill,
And the river 's running still
  Under the trysting tree.

To my Wife.—A Valentine.

O once I had a true love,
   As blest as I could be :
Patty was my turtle dove,
   And Patty she loved me.
We walked the fields together,
   By roses and woodbine,
In Summer's sunshine weather,
   And Patty she was mine.

We stopped to gather primroses,
   And violets white and blue,
In pastures and green closes
   All glistening with the dew.
We sat upon green mole-hills,
   Among the daisy flowers,
To hear the small birds' merry trills,
   And share the sunny hours.

The blackbird on her grassy nest
   We would not scare away,
Who nuzzling sat with brooding breast
   On her eggs for half the day.

162

The chaffinch chirruped on the thorn,
    And a pretty nest had she ;
The magpie chattered all the morn
    From her perch upon the tree.

And I would go to Patty's cot,
    And Patty came to me ;
Each knew the other's very thought
    Under the hawthorn tree.
And Patty had a kiss to give,
    And Patty had a smile,
To bid me hope and bid me love,
    At every stopping stile.

We loved one Summer quite away,
    And when another came,
The cowslip close and sunny day,
    It found us much the same.
We both looked on the selfsame thing,
    Till both became as one ;
The birds did in the hedges sing,
    And happy time went on.

The brambles from the hedge advance,
    In love with Patty's eyes :
On flowers, like ladies at a dance,
    Flew scores of butterflies.
I claimed a kiss at every stile,
    And had her kind replies.
The bees did round the woodbine toil,
    Where sweet the small wind sighs.

Then Patty was a slight young thing ;
    Now she 's long past her teens ;
And we 've been married many springs,
    And mixed in many scenes.
And I 'll be true for Patty's sake,
    And she 'll be true for mine ;
And I this little ballad make,
    To be her valentine.

𝔐𝔶 true lobe is a Sailor.

'T was somewhere in the April time,
    Not long before the May,
A-sitting on a bank o' thyme
    I heard a maiden say,
" My true love is a sailor,
    And ere he went away
We spent a year together,
    And here my lover lay.

The gold furze was in blossom,
    So was the daisy too;
The dew-drops on the little flowers
    Were emeralds in hue.
On this same Summer morning,
    Though then the Sabbath day,
He crop 't me Spring pol'ant'uses,
    Beneath the whitethorn may.

He crop't me Spring pol'ant'uses,
    And said if they would keep
They 'd tell me of love's fantasies,
    For dews on them did weep.
And I did weep at parting,
    Which lasted all the week;
And when he turned for starting
    My full heart could not speak.

The same roots grow pol'ant'us' flowers
    Beneath the same haw-tree ;
I crop't them in morn's dewy hours,
    And here love's offerings be.
O come to me my sailor beau
    And ease my aching breast ;
The storms shall cease to rave and blow,
    And here thy life find rest."

The Sailor's Return.

The whitethorn is budding and rushes are green,
The ivy leaves rustle around the ash tree,
On the sweet sunny bank blue violets are seen,
That tremble beneath the wild hum of the bee.
The sunbeams they play on the brook's plashy ripples,
Like millions of suns in each swirl looking on ;
The rush nods and bows till its tasseled head tipples
Right into the wimpled flood, kissing the stones.

'T was down in the cow pasture, just at the gloaming,
I met a young woman sweet tempered and mild,
I said " Pretty maiden, say, where are you roving ?"
" I 'm walking at even," she answered, and smiled.
" Here my sweetheart and I gathered posies at even ;
" It 's eight years ago since they sent him to sea.
" Wild flowers hung with dew are like angels from heaven :
" They look up in my face and keep whispering to me.

" They whisper the tales that were told by my true love ;
" In the evening and morning they glisten with dew ;
" They say (bonny blossoms) ' I ll ne'er get a new love ;
I love her ; she 's kindly.'   I say, " I love him too."
The passing-by stranger 's a stranger no longer ;
He kissed off the teardrop which fell from her e'e ;
With blue-jacket and trousers he is bigger and stronger ;
'T is her own constant Willy returned from the sea.

Birds, why are silent?

Why are ye silent,
    Birds ? ' Where do ye fly ?
Winter 's not violent,
    With such a Spring sky.
The wheatlands are green, snow and frost are away,
Birds, why are ye silent on such a sweet day ?

    By the slated pig-stye
        The redbreast scarce whispers :
Where last Autumn's leaves lie
        The hedge sparrow just lispers.
And why are the chaffinch and bullfinch so still,
While the sulphur primroses bedeck the wood hill ?

    The bright yellow-hammers
        Are strutting about,
All still, and none stammers
        A single note out.
From the hedge starts the blackbird, at brook side to drink:
I thought he 'd have whistled, but he only said "prink."

    The tree-creeper hustles
        Up fir's rusty bark ;
All silent he bustles ;
        We needn't say hark.
There 's no song in the forest, in field, or in wood,
Yet the sun gilds the grass as though come in for good.

How bright the odd daisies
   Peep under the stubbs!
How bright pilewort blazes
   Where ruddled sheep rubs
The old willow trunk by the side of the brook,
Where soon for blue violets the children will look!

By the cot green and mossy
   Feed sparrow and hen:
On the ridge brown and glossy
   They cluck now and then.
The wren cocks his tail o'er his back by the stye,
Where his green bottle nest will be made by and bye.

Here's bunches of chickweed,
   With small starry flowers,
Where red-caps oft pick seed
   In hungry Spring hours.
And blue cap and black cap, in glossy Spring coat,
Are a-peeping in buds without singing a note.

Why silent should birds be
   And sunshine so warm?
Larks hide where the herds be
   By cottage and farm.
If wild flowers were blooming and fully set in the Spring
May-be all the birdies would cheerfully sing.

Meet me to night.

O meet me to-night by the bright starlight,
    Now the pleasant Spring 's begun.
My own dear maid, by the greenwood shade,
    In the crimson set of the sun,
        Meet me to-night.

The sun he goes down with a ruby crown
    To a gold and crimson bed;
And the falling dew, from heaven so blue,
    Hangs pearls on Phœbe's head.
        Love, leave the town.

Come thou with me; 'neath the green-leaf tree
    We 'll crop the bonny sweet brere.
O come, dear maid, 'neath the hazlewood shade,
    For love invites us there.
        Come then with me.

The owl pops, scarce seen, from the ivy green,
    With his spectacles on I ween :
See the moon 's above and the stars twinkle, love;
    Better time was never seen.
        O come, my queen.

The fox he stops, and down he drops
    His head beneath the grass.
The birds are gone; we 're all alone;
    O come, my bonny lass.
        Come, O come !

Young Jenny.

The cockchafer hums down the rut-rifted lane
Where the wild roses hang and the woodbines entwine,
And the shrill squeaking bat makes his circles again
Round the side of the tavern close by the sign.
The sun is gone down like a wearisome queen,
In curtains the richest that ever were seen.

The dew falls on flowers in a mist of small rain,
And, beating the hedges, low fly the barn owls;
The moon with her horns is just peeping again,
And deep in the forest the dog-badger howls;
In best bib and tucker then wanders my Jane
By the side of the woodbines which grow in the lane.

On a sweet eventide I walk by her side;
In green hoods the daisies have shut up their eyes.
Young Jenny is handsome without any pride;
Her eyes (O how bright!) have the hue of the skies.
O 't is pleasant to walk by the side of my Jane
At the close of the day, down the mossy green lane.

We stand by the brook, by the gate, and the stile,
While the even star hangs out his lamp in the sky;
And on her calm face dwells a sweet sunny smile,
While her soul fondly speaks through the light of her eye.
Sweet are the moments while waiting for Jane;
'T is her footsteps I hear coming down the green lane.

Adieu!

"Adieu, my love, adieu!
  Be constant and be true
  As the daisies gemmed with dew,
      Bonny maid."
The cows their thirst were slaking,
Trees the playful winds were shaking;
Sweet songs the birds were making
      In the shade.

The moss upon the tree
  Was as green as green could be,
  The clover on the lea
      Ruddy glowed;
Leaves were silver with the dew,
Where the tall sowthistles grew,
And I bade the maid adieu
      On the road.

Then I took myself to sea,
  While the little chiming bee
  Sung his ballad on the lea,
      Humming sweet;
And the red-winged butterfly
Was sailing through the sky,
Skimming up and bouncing by
      Near my feet.

I left the little birds,
And sweet lowing of the herds,
And couldn't find out words,
      Do you see,
To say to them good bye,
Where the yellow cups do lie ;
So heaving a deep sigh,
      Took to sea.

My bonny Alice and her pitcher.

There 's a bonny place in Scotland,
    Where a little spring is found ;
There Nature shows her honest face
    The whole year round.
Where the whitethorn branches, full of may, .
    Hung near the fountain's rim,
Where comes sweet Alice every day
    And dips her pitcher in ;
A gallon pitcher without ear,
    She fills it with the water clear.

My bonny Alice she is fair ;
    There 's no such other to be found.
Her rosy cheek and dark brown hair —
    The fairest maid on Scotland's ground.
And there the heather's pinhead flowers
    All blossom over bank and brae,
While Alice passes by the bowers
    To fill her pitcher every day ;
The pitcher brown without an ear
    See dips into the fountain clear.

O Alice, bonny, sweet, and fair,
  With roses on her cheeks !
The little birds come drinking there,
  The throstle almost speaks.
He dips his wings and wimples makes
  Upon the fountain clear,
Then vanishes among the brakes
  For ever singing near ;
While Alice, listening, stands to hear,
  And dips her pitcher without ear.

O Alice, bonny Alice, fair,
  Thy pleasant face I love ;
Thy red-rose cheek, thy dark brown hair,
  Thy soft eyes, like a dove.
I see thee by the fountain stand,
  With the sweet smiling face ;
There 's not a maid in all the land
  With such bewitching grace
As Alice, who is drawing near,
  To dip the pitcher without ear.

The maiden I love.

How sweet are Spring wild flowers! They grow past the
    counting.
How sweet are the wood-paths that thread through the
    grove!
But sweeter than all the wild flowers of the mountain
Is the beauty that walks here—the maiden I love.
        Her black hair in tangles
        The rose briar mangles;
        Her lips and soft cheeks,
        Where love ever speaks:
O there 's nothing so sweet as the maiden I love.

It was down in the wild flowers, among brakes and
    brambles,
I met the sweet maiden so dear to my eye,
In one of my Sunday morn midsummer rambles,
Among the sweet wild blossoms blooming close by.
        Her hair it was coal black,
        Hung loose down her back;
        In her hand she held posies
        Of blooming primroses,
The maiden who passed on the morning of love.

176

Coal black was her silk hair that shaded white shoulders;
Ruby red were her ripe lips, her cheeks of soft hue;
Her sweet smiles, enchanting the eyes of beholders,
Thrilled my heart as she rambled the wild blossoms
    through.
        Like the pearl, her bright eye;
        In trembling delight I
        Kissed her cheek, like a rose
        In its gentlest repose.
O there 's nothing so sweet as the maiden I love!

To Jenny Lind.

I cannot touch the harp again,
    And sing another idle lay,
To cool a maddening, burning brain,
    And drive the midnight fiend away.
Music, own sister to the soul,
    Bids roses bloom on cheeks all pale;
And sweet her joys and sorrows roll
    When sings the Swedish Nightingale.

*   *   *   *   *   *

I cannot touch the harp again;
    No chords will vibrate on the string.
Like broken flowers upon the plain,
    My heart e'en withers while I sing.
Æolian harps have witching tones,
    On morning or the evening gale;
No melody their music owns
    As sings the Swedish nightingale.

Little Trotty Wagtail.

Little trotty wagtail he went in the rain,
And twittering, tottering sideways he ne'er got straight
    again.
He stooped to get a worm, and looked up to get a fly,
And then he flew away ere his feathers they were dry.

Little trotty wagtail he waddled in the mud,
And left his little footmarks, trample were he would.
He waddled in the water-pudge, and waggle went his
    tail,
And chirrupt up his wings to dry upon the garden rail.

Little trotty wagtail, you nimble all about,
And in the dimpling water-pudge you waddle in and
    out ;
Your home is nigh at hand, and in the warm pig-stye,
So, little Master Wagtail, I 'll bid you a good bye.

The Forest Maid.

O once I loved a pretty girl, and dearly love her still;
I courted her in happiness for two short years or more.
And when I think of Mary it turns my bosom chill,
For my little of life's happiness is faded and is o'er.
O fair was Mary Littlechild, and happy as the bee,
And sweet was bonny Mary as the song of forest bird;
And the smile upon her red lips was very dear to me,
And her tale of love the sweetest that my ear has ever
        heard.

O the flower of all the forest was Mary Littlechild;
There 's few could be so dear to me and none could be so
        fair.
While many love the garden flowers I still esteem the
        wild,
And Mary of the forest is the fairest blossom there.
She 's fairer than the may flowers that bloom among the
        thorn,
She 's dearer to my eye than the rose upon the brere;
Her eye is brighter far than the bonny pearls of morn,
And the name of Mary Littlechild is to me ever dear.

O once I loved a pretty girl.   The linnet in its mirth
Was never half so blest as I with Mary Littlechild—
The rose of the creation, and the pink of all the earth,
The flower of all the forest, and the best for being wild.
O sweet are dews of morning, ere the Autumn blows so
     chill,
And sweet are forest flowers in the hawthorn's mossy
     shade,
But nothing is so fair, and nothing ever will
Bloom like the rosy cheek of my bonny Forest Maid.

Bonny Mary O!

The morning opens fine, bonny Mary O!
The robin sings his song by the dairy O!
Where the little Jenny wrens cock their tails among the
　　hens,
　　Singing morning's happy songs with Mary O!

The swallow 's on the wing, bonny Mary O!
Where the rushes fringe the spring, bonny Mary O!
Where the cowslips do unfold, shaking tassels all of gold,
　　Which make the milk so sweet, bonny Mary O!

There 's the yellowhammer's nest, bonny Mary O!
Where she hides her golden breast, bonny Mary O!
On her mystic eggs she dwells, with strange writing on
　　their shells,
　　Hid in the mossy grass, bonny Mary O!

There the spotted cow gets food, bonny Mary O!
And chews her peaceful cud, bonny Mary O!
In the mole-hills and the bushes, and the clear brook
　　fringed with rushes,
　　To fill the evening pail, bonny Mary O!

*　　　*　　　*　　　*　　　*

Where the gnat swarms fall and rise under evenings'
    mellow skies,
  And on flags sleep dragon flies, bonny Mary O!

  And I will meet thee there, bonny Mary O!
  When a-milking you repair, bonny Mary O!
And I 'll kiss thee on the grass, my buxom, bonny lass,
  And be thine own for aye, bonny Mary O!

Love's Emblem.

Go rose, my Chloe's bosom grace :
    How happy should I prove,
Could I supply that envied place
    With never-fading love.

Accept, dear maid, now Summer glows,
    This pure, unsullied gem,
Love's emblem in a full-blown rose,
    Just broken from the stem.

Accept it as a favourite flower
    For thy soft breast to wear ;
'T will blossom there its transient hour,
    A favourite of the fair.

Upon thy cheek its blossom glows,
    As from a mirror clear,
Making thyself a living rose,
    In blossom all the year.

It is a sweet and favourite flower
    To grace a maiden's brow,
Emblem of love without its power—
    A sweeter rose art thou.

The rose, like hues of insect wing,
 May perish in an hour;
'T is but at best a fading thing,
 But thou 'rt a living flower.

The roses steeped in morning dews
 Would every eye enthrall,
But woman, she alone subdues;
 Her beauty conquers all.

The Morning Walk.

The linnet sat upon its nest,
By gales of morning softly prest,
His green wing and his greener breast
    Were damp with dews of morning :
The dog-rose near the oaktree grew,
Blush'd swelling 'neath a veil of dew,
A pink's nest to its prickles grew,
    Right early in the morning.

The sunshine glittered gold, the while
A country maiden clomb the stile ;
Her straw hat couldn't hide the smile
    That blushed like early morning.
The lark, with feathers all wet through,
Looked up above the glassy dew,
And to the neighbouring corn-field flew,
    Fanning the gales of morning.

In every bush was heard a song,
On each grass blade, the whole way long,
A silver shining drop there hung,
    The milky dew of morning.
Where stepping-stones stride o'er the brook
The rosy maid I overtook.
How ruddy was her healthy look,
    So early in the morning !

I took her by the well-turned arm,
And led her over field and farm,
And kissed her tender cheek so warm,
 A rose in early morning.
The spiders' lacework shone like glass,
Tied up to flowers and cat-tail grass ;
The dew-drops bounced before the lass,
 Sprinkling the early morning.

Her dark curls fanned among the gales,
The skylark whistled o'er the vales,
I told her love's delightful tales
 Among the dews of morning.
She crop't a flower, shook off the dew,
And on her breast the wild rose grew ;
She blushed as fair, as lovely, too—
 The living rose of morning.

To Miss C——.

Thy glance is the brightest,
Thy voice is the sweetest,
Thy step is the lightest,
Thy shape the completest :
Thy waist I could span, dear,
Thy neck 's like a swan's, dear,
And roses the sweetest
On thy cheeks do appear.

The music of Spring
Is the voice of my charmer.
When the nightingales sing
She 's as sweet ; who would harm her ?
Where the snowdrop or lily lies
They show her face, but her eyes
Are the dark clouds, yet warmer,
From which the quick lightning flies
O'er the face of my charmer.

Her faith is the snowdrop,
So pure on its stem ;
And love in her bosom
She wears as a gem ;
She is young as Spring flowers,
And sweet as May showers,
Swelling the clover buds, and bending the stem,
She 's the sweetest of blossoms, she love's favourite
gem.

I pluck Summer Blossoms.

I pluck Summer blossoms,
And think of rich bosoms—
The bosoms I 've leaned on, and worshipped, and won.
The rich valley lilies,
The wood daffodillies,
Have been found in our rambles when Summer begun.

Where I plucked thee the bluebell,
'T was where the night dew fell,
And rested till morn in the cups of the flowers;
I shook the sweet posies,
Bluebells and brere roses,
As we sat in cool shade in Summer's warm hours.

Bedlam-cowslips and cuckoos,
With freck'd lip and hooked nose,
Growing safe near the hazel of thicket and woods,
And water blobs, ladies' smocks,
Blooming where haycocks
May be found, in the meadows, low places, and floods.

And cowslips a fair band
For May ball or garland,
That bloom in the meadows as seen by the eye ;
And pink ragged robin,
Where the fish they are bobbing
Their heads above water to catch at the fly.

Wild flowers and wild roses !
'T is love makes the posies
To paint Summer ballads of meadow and glen.
Floods can't drown it nor turn it,
Even flames cannot burn it ;
Let it bloom till we walk the green meadows again.

The March Nosegay.

The bonny March morning is beaming
    In mingled crimson and grey,
White clouds are streaking and creaming
    The sky till the noon of the day ;
The fir deal looks darker and greener,
    And grass hills below look the same ;
The air all about is serener,
    The birds less familiar and tame.

Here 's two or three flowers for my fair one,
    Wood primroses and celandine too ;
I oft look about for a rare one
    To put in a posy for you.
The birds look so clean and so neat,
    Though there 's scarcely a leaf on the grove ;
The sun shines about me so sweet,
    I cannot help thinking of love.

So where the blue violets are peeping,
    By the warm sunny sides of the woods,
And the primrose, 'neath early morn weeping,
    Amid a large cluster of buds,
(The morning it was such a rare one,
    So dewy, so sunny, and fair,)
I sought the wild flowers for my fair one,
    To wreath in her glossy black hair.

Left alone.

Left in the world alone,
  Where nothing seems my own,
And everything is weariness to me,
  'T is a life without an end,
  'T is a world without a friend,
And everything is sorrowful I see.

  There 's the crow upon the stack,
  And other birds all black,
While bleak November 's frowning wearily ;
  And the black cloud 's dropping rain,
  Till the floods hide half the plain,
And everything is dreariness to me.

  The sun shines wan and pale,
  Chill blows the northern gale,
And odd leaves shake and quiver on the tree,
  While I am left alone,
  Chilled as a mossy stone,
And all the world is frowning over me.

To Mary.

Mary, I love to sing
About the flowers of Spring,
      For they resemble thee.
In the earliest of the year
Thy beauties will appear,
      And youthful modesty.

Here 's the daisy's silver rim,
With gold eye never dim,
      Spring's earliest flower so fair.
Here the pilewort's golden rays
Set the cow green in a blaze,
      Like the sunshine in thy hair.

Here 's forget-me-not so blue ;
Is there any flower so true ?
      Can it speak my happy lot ?
When we courted in disguise
This flower I used to prize,
      For it said " Forget-me-not."

Speedwell !   And when we meet
In the meadow paths so sweet,
      Where the flowers I gave to thee
All grew beneath the sun,
May thy gentle heart be won,
      And I be blest with thee.

The Nightingale.

This is the month the nightingale, clod brown,
Is heard among the woodland shady boughs :
This is the time when in the vale, grass-grown,
The maiden hears at eve her lover's vows,
What time the blue mist round the patient cows
Dim rises from the grass and half conceals
Their dappled hides.   I hear the nightingale,
That from the little blackthorn spinney steals
To the old hazel hedge that skirts the vale,
And still unseen sings sweet.   The ploughman feels
The thrilling music as he goes along,
And imitates and listens ; while the fields
Lose all their paths in dusk to lead him wrong,
Still sings the nightingale her soft melodious song.

The Dying Child.

He could not die when trees were green,
   For he loved the time too well.
His little hands, when flowers were seen,
   Were held for the bluebell,
      As he was carried o'er the green.

His eye glanced at the white-nosed bee ;
   He knew those children of the Spring :
When he was well and on the lea
   He held one in his hands to sing,
      Which filled his heart with glee.

Infants, the children of the Spring !
   How can an infant die
When butterflies are on the wing,
   Green grass, and such a sky ?
      How can they die at Spring ?

He held his hands for daisies white,
   And then for violets blue,
And took them all to bed at night
   That in the green fields grew,
      As childhood's sweet delight.

And then he shut his little eyes,
    And flowers would notice not;
Bird's nests and eggs caused no surprise,
    He now no blossoms got :
        They met with plaintive sighs.

When Winter came and blasts did sigh,
    And bare were plain and tree,
As he for ease in bed did lie
    His soul seemed with the free,
        He died so quietly.

Mary.

The skylark mounts up with the morn,
The valleys are green with the Spring,
The linnets sit in the whitethorn,
To build mossy dwellings and sing;
I see the thornbush getting green,
I see the woods dance in the Spring, ·
But Mary can never be seen,
Though the all-cheering Spring doth begin.

I see the grey bark of the oak
Look bright through the underwood now;
To the plough plodding horses they yoke,
But Mary is not with her cow.
The birds almost whistle her name:
Say, where can my Mary be gone?
The Spring brightly shines, and 't is shame
That she should be absent alone.

The cowslips are out on the grass,
Increasing like crowds at a fair;
The river runs smoothly as glass,
And the barges float heavily there;
The milkmaid she sings to her cow,
But Mary is not to be seen;
Can Nature such absence allow
At milking on pasture and green?

When Sabbath-day comes to the green,
The maidens are there in their best,
But Mary is not to be seen,
Though I walk till the sun 's in the west.
I fancy still each wood and plain,
Where I and my Mary have strayed,
When I was a young country swain,
And she was the happiest maid.

But woods they are all lonely now,
And the wild flowers blow all unseen;
The birds sing alone on the bough,
Where Mary and I once have been.
But for months she now keeps away,
And I am a sad lonely hind;
Trees tell me so day after day,
As slowly they wave in the wind.

Birds tell me, while swaying the bough,
That I am all threadbare and old;
The very sun looks on me now
As one dead, forgotten, and cold.
Once I 'd a place where I could rest, ·
And love, for then I was free;
That place was my Mary's dear breast
And hope was still left unto me.

The Spring comes brighter day by day,
 And brighter flowers appear,
And though she long has kept away
 Her name is ever dear.
Then leave me still the meadow flowers,
 Where daffies blaze and shine;
Give but the Spring's young hawthorn bower,
 For then sweet Mary 's mine.

Clock=a=clay.

In the cowslip pips I lie,
Hidden from the buzzing fly,
While green grass beneath me lies,
Pearled with dew like fishes' eyes,
Here I lie, a clock-a-clay.
Waiting for the time o' day.

While the forest quakes surprise,
And the wild wind sobs and sighs,
My home rocks as like to fall,
On its pillar green and tall;
When the pattering rain drives by
Clock-a-clay keeps warm and dry.

Day by day and night by night,
All the week I hide from sight;
In the cowslip pips I lie,
In the rain still warm and dry;
Day and night, and night and day,
Red, black-spotted clock-a-clay.

My home shakes in wind and showers,
Pale green pillar topped with flowers,
Bending at the wild wind's breath,
Till I touch the grass beneath;
Here I live, lone clock-a-clay,
Watching for the time of day.

Spring.

Come, gentle Spring, and show thy varied greens
In woods, and fields, and meadows, by clear brooks.
Come, gentle Spring, and bring thy sweetest scenes,
Where peace, with solitude, the loveliest looks;
    Where the blue unclouded sky
    Spreads the sweetest canopy,
And Study wiser grows without her books.

Come hither, gentle May, and with thee bring
Flowers of all colours, and the wild briar rose;
Come in wind-floating drapery, and bring
Fragrance and bloom, that Nature's love bestows—
    Meadow pinks and columbines,
    Kecksies white and eglantines,
And music of the bee that seeks the rose.

Come, gentle Spring, and bring thy choicest looks,
Thy bosom graced with flowers, thy face with smiles;
Come, gentle Spring, and trace thy wandering brooks,
Through meadow gates, o'er footpath crooked stiles;
    Come in thy proud and best array,
    April dews and flowers of May,
And singing birds that come where heaven smiles.

Evening.

In the meadow's silk grasses we see the black snail,
Creeping out at the close of the eve, sipping dew,
While even's one star glitters over the vale,
Like a lamp hung outside of that temple of blue.
I walk with my true love adown the green vale,
The light feathered grasses keep tapping her shoe ;
In the whitethorn the nightingale sings her sweet tale,
And the blades of the grasses are sprinkled with dew.

If she stumbles I catch her and cling to her neck,
As the meadow-sweet kisses the blush of the rose :
Her whisper none hears, and the kisses I take
The mild voice of even will never disclose.
Her hair hung in ringlets adown her sweet cheek,
That blushed like the rose in the hedge hung with dew ;
Her whisper was fragrance, her face was so meek—
The dove was the type on't that from the bush flew.

The Swallow.

Swift goes the sooty swallow o'er the heath,
Swifter than skims the cloud-rack of the skies;
As swiftly flies its shadow underneath,
And on his wing the twittering sunbeam lies,
As bright as water glitters in the eyes
Of those it passes; 't is a pretty thing,
The ornament of meadows and clear skies:
With dingy breast and narrow pointed wing,
Its daily twittering is a song to Spring.

Jockey and Jenny.

" Will Jockey come to-day, mither ?
       Will Jockey come to-day ?
He 's taen sic likings to my brither
       He 's sure to come the day."
" Haud yer tongue, lass, mind your rockie ;
But th' other day ye wore a pockie.
What can ye mean to think o' Jockey ?
Ye 've bin content the season long,
Ye 'd best keep to your harmless song."

" Ye 'll soon see falling tears, mither,
       If love 's a sin in youth ;
He leuks to me, and talks wi' brither,
       But I know the secret truth.
He 's courted me the year, mither ;
Judge not the matter queer, mither ;
Ye 're a' the while as dear, mither,
       As ye 've been the Summer long.
       I cannot sing my song.

I 'll hear nae farder preaching, mither ;
    I'se bin a child ower lang ;
He led me frae the teaching, mither,
    And wherefore did he wrang ?
I ken he often tauks wi' brither ;
I neither look at ane or 'tither ;
You ken as well as I, mither,
      There 's nae love in my song,
      Though I 've sang the Summer long."

" Nae, dinna be sae saucy, lassie,
    I may be kenned ye ill.
If love has taen the hold, lassie,
    There 's nae cure i' the pill."
" Nae, I dinna want a pill, mither ;
He leuks at me and tauks to ither ;
And twice we 've bin at kirk thegither.
I 'm 's well now as a' Summer long,
But somehow canna sing a song.

He comes and talks to brither, mither,
    But leuks his thoughts at me ;
He always says gude neet to brither,
    And looks gude neet to me."
" Lassie, ye seldom vexed yer mither ;
Ye 're ower too fair a flower to wither ;
So be ye are to come thegither,
I 'll be nae damp to yer new claes ;
Cheer up and sing o'er ' Loggan braes.' "

Jockey comes o' Sabbath days,
His face is not a face o'er brassy ;
Her mither sits to praise the claes ;
Holds him her box ; to win the lassie
He taks a pinch, and greets wi' granny,
And helps his chair up nearer Jenny,
And vows he loves her muir than any.
She thinks her mither seldom wrong,
And " Loggan braes " is her daily song.

The face I love so dearly.

Sweet is the violet, th' scented pea,
Haunted by red-legged, sable bee,
But sweeter far than all to me
    Is she I love so dearly;
Than perfumed pea and sable bee,
    The face I love so dearly.

Sweeter than hedgerow violets blue,
Than apple blossoms' streaky hue,
Or black-eyed bean-flower blebbed with dew
    Is she I love so dearly ;
Than apple flowers or violets blue
    Is she I love so dearly.

Than woodbine upon branches thin,
The clover flower, all sweets within,
Which pensive bees do gather in,
    Three times as sweet, or nearly,
Is the cheek, the eye, the lip, the chin
    Of her I love so dearly.

The Beanfield.

A beanfield full in blossom smells as sweet
As Araby, or groves of orange flowers ;
Black-eyed and white, and feathered to one's feet,
How sweet they smell in morning's dewy hours !
When seething night is left upon the flowers,
And when morn's sun shines brightly o'er the field,
The bean bloom glitters in the gems of showers,
And sweet the fragrance which the union yields
To battered footpaths crossing o'er the fields.

Where she told her love.

I saw her crop a rose
Right early in the day,
And I went to kiss the place
Where she broke the rose away ;
And I saw the patten rings
Where she o'er the stile had gone,
And I love all other things
Her bright eyes look upon.
If she looks upon the hedge or up the leafing tree,
That whitethorn or the brown oak are made dearer
    things to me.

I have a pleasant hill
Which I sit upon for hours,
Where she crop't some sprigs of thyme
And other little flowers ;
And she muttered as she did it
As does beauty in a dream,
And I loved her when she hid it
On her breast, so like to cream,
Near the brown mole on her neck that to me a
    diamond shone ;
Then my eye was like to fire, and my heart was
    like to stone.

There is a small green place
Where cowslips early curled,
Which on Sabbath day I traced,
The dearest in the world.
A little oak spreads o'er it,
And throws a shadow round,
A green sward close before it,
The greenest ever found :
There is not a woodland nigh nor is there a green
grove,
Yet stood the fair maid nigh me and told me all
her love.

Milking o' the Rye.

Young Jenny wakens at the dawn,
Fresh as carnations newly blown,
And o'er the pasture every morn
   Goes milking o' the kye.
She sings her songs of happy glee,
While round her swirls the humble bee;
The butterfly, from tree to tree,
   Goes gaily flirting by.

Young Jenny was a bonny thing
As ever wakened in the Spring,
And blythe she to herself could sing
   At milking o' the kye.
She loved to hear the old crows croak
Upon the ash tree and the oak,
And noisy pies that almost spoke
   At milking o' the kye.

She crop't the wild thyme every night,
Scenting so sweet the dewy light,
And hid it in her breast so white
   At milking o' the kye.
I met and clasped her in my arms,
The finest flower on twenty farms;
Her snow-white breast my fancy warms
   At milking o' the kye.

A Lover's Vows.

Scenes of love and days of pleasure,
    I must leave them all, lassie.
Scenes of love and hours of leisure,
    All are gone for aye, lassie.
No more thy velvet-bordered dress
My fond and longing een shall bless,
Thou lily in the wilderness;
    And who shall love thee then, lassie?
Long I've watched thy look so tender,
Often clasped thy waist so slender:
Heaven, in thine own love defend her,
    God protect my own lassie.

By all the faith I 've shown afore thee,
    I 'll swear by more than that, lassie:
By heaven and earth I 'll still adore thee,
    Though we should part for aye, lassie!
By thy infant years so loving,
By thy woman's love so moving,
That white breast thy goodness proving,
    I 'm thine for aye, through all, lassie!
By the sun that shines for ever,
By love's light and its own Giver,
Who loveth truth and leaveth never,
    I 'm thine for aye, through all, lassie!

𝕿𝖍𝖊 𝕱𝖆𝖑𝖑 𝖔𝖋 𝖙𝖍𝖊 𝖄𝖊𝖆𝖗.

The Autumn 's come again,
And the clouds descend in rain,
And the leaves are fast falling in the wood ;
The Summer's voice is still,
Save the clacking of the mill
And the lowly-muttered thunder of the flood.

There 's nothing in the mead
But the river's muddy speed,
And the willow leaves all littered by its side.
Sweet voices are all still
In the vale and on the hill,
And the Summer's blooms are withered in their pride.

Fled is the cuckoo's note
To countries far remote,
And the nightingale is vanished from the woods ;
If you search the lordship round
There is not a blossom found,
And where the hay-cock scented is the flood.

213

My true love 's fled away
Since we walked 'mid cocks of hay,
On the Sabbath in the Summer of the year;
And she 's nowhere to be seen
On the meadow or the green,
But she 's coming when the happy Spring is near.

When the birds begin to sing,
And the flowers begin to spring,
And the cowslips in the meadows reappear,
When the woodland oaks are seen
In their monarchy of green,
Then Mary and love's pleasures will be here.

Autumn.

I love the fitful gust that shakes
    The casement all the day,
And from the glossy elm tree takes
    The faded leaves away,
Twirling them by the window pane
With thousand others down the lane.

I love to see the shaking twig
    Dance till the shut of eve,
The sparrow on the cottage rig,
    Whose chirp would make believe
That Spring was just now flirting by,
In Summer's lap with flowers to lie.

I love to see the cottage smoke
    Curl upwards through the trees,
The pigeons nestled round the cote
    On November days like these;
The cock upon the dunghill crowing,
The mill sails on the heath a-going.

The feather from the raven's breast
    Falls on the stubble lea,
The acorns near the old crow's nest
    Drop pattering down the tree;
The grunting pigs, that wait for all,
Scramble and hurry where they fall.

Early Love.

The Spring of life is o'er with me,
    And love and all gone by;
Like broken bough upon yon tree,
    I 'm left to fade and die.
Stern ruin seized my home and me,
    And desolate 's my cot:
Ruins of halls, the blasted tree,
    Are emblems of my lot.

I lived and loved, I woo'd and won,
    Her love was all to me,
But blight fell o'er that youthful one,
    And like a blasted tree
I withered, till I all forgot
    But Mary's smile on me;
She never lived where love was not,
    And I from bonds was free.

The Spring it clothed the fields with pride,
    When first we met together;
And then unknown to all beside
    We loved in sunny weather;
We met where oaks grew overhead,
    And whitethorns hung with may;
Wild thyme beneath her feet was spread,
    And cows in quiet lay.

I thought her face was sweeter far
    Than aught I 'd seen before—
As simple as the cowslips are
    Upon the rushy moor :
She seemed the muse of that sweet spot,
    The lady of the plain,
And all was dull where she was not,
    Till we met there again.

Evening.

'T is evening : the black snail has got on his track,
    And gone to its nest is the wren,
And the packman snail, too, with his home on his back,
    Clings to the bowed bents like a wen.

The shepherd has made a rude mark with his foot
    Where his shadow reached when he first came,
And it just touched the tree where his secret love cut
    Two letters that stand for love's name.

The evening comes in with the wishes of love,
    And the shepherd he looks on the flowers,
And thinks who would praise the soft song of the dove,
    And meet joy in these dew-falling hours.

For Nature is love, and finds haunts for true love,
    Where nothing can hear or intrude ;
It hides from the eagle and joins with the dove,
    In beautiful green solitude.

A Valentine.

Here 's a valentine nosegay for Mary,
    Some of Spring's earliest flowers ;
The ivy is green by the dairy,
    And so are these laurels of ours.
Though the snow fell so deep and the winter was dreary,
The laurels are green and the sparrows are cheery.

The snowdrops in bunches grow under the rose,
And aconites under the lilac, like fairies ;
The best in the bunches for Mary I chose,
Their looks are as sweet and as simple as Mary's.
The one will make Spring in my verses so bare,
The other set off as a braid thy dark hair.

Pale primroses, too, at the old parlour end,
Have bloomed all the winter 'midst snows cold and dreary,
Where the lavender-cotton kept off the cold wind,
Now to shine in my valentine nosegay for Mary ;
And appear in my verses all Summer, and be
A memento of fondness and friendship for thee.

Here 's the crocus half opened, that spreads into gold,
Like branches of sunbeams left there by a fairy :
I place them as such in these verses so cold,
But they 'll bloom twice as bright in the presence of Mary.
These garden flowers crop't, I will go to the field,
And see what the valley and pasture land yield.

Here peeps the pale primrose from the skirts of the wild
    wood,
And violet blue 'neath the thorn on the green ;
The wild flowers we plucked in the days of our childhood,
On the very same spot, as no changes have been—
In the very same place where the sun kissed the leaves,
And the woodbine its branches of thorns interweaves.

And here in the pasture, all swarming with rushes,
Is a cowslip as blooming and forward as Spring ;
And the pilewort like sunshine grows under the bushes,
While the chaffinch there sitting is trying to sing ;
And the daisies are coming, called " stars of the earth,"
To bring to the schoolboy his Springtime of mirth.

Here, then, is the nosegay : how simple it shines !
It speaks without words to the ear and the eye ;
The flowers of the Spring are the best valentines ;
They are young, fair, and simple, and pleasingly shy.
That you may remain so and your love never vary,
I send you these flowers as a valentine, Mary.

To Liberty.

O spirit of the wind and sky,
Where doth thy harp neglected lie ?
Is there no heart thy bard to be,
To wake that soul of melody ?
Is liberty herself a slave ?
No!   God forbid it !   On, ye brave !

I 've loved thee as the common air,
And paid thee worship everywhere :
In every soil beneath the sun
Thy simple song my heart has won.
And art thou silent ?   Still a slave ?
And thy sons living ?   On, ye brave !

Gather on mountain and on plain !
Make gossamer the iron chain !
Make prison walls as paper screen,
That tyrant maskers may be seen !
Let earth as well as heaven be free !
So, on, ye brave, for liberty !

I 've loved thy being from a boy :
The Highland hills were once my joy :
Then morning mists did round them lie,
Like sunshine in the happiest sky.
The hills and valley seemed my own,
When Scottish land was freedom's throne

And Scottish land is freedom's still :
Her beacon fires, on every hill,
Have told, in characters of flame,
Her ancient birthright to her fame.
A thousand hills will speak again,
In fire, that language ever plain

To sychophants and fawning knaves,
That Scotland ne'er was made for slaves !
Each fruitful vale, each mountain throne,
Is ruled by Nature's laws alone ;
And nought but falsehood's poisoned breath
Will urge the claymore from its sheath.

O spirit of the wind and sky,
Where doth thy harp neglected lie ?
Is there no harp thy bard to be,
To wake that soul of melody ?
Is liberty herself a slave ?
No ! God forbid it ! On, ye brave !

Approach of Winter.

The Autumn day now fades away,
　　The fields are wet and dreary ;
The rude storm takes the flowers of May,
　　And Nature seemeth weary ;
The partridge coveys, shunning fate,
　　Hide in the bleaching stubble,
And many a bird, without its mate,
　　Mourns o'er its lonely trouble.

On hawthorns shine the crimson haw,
　　Where Spring brought may-day blossoms :
Decay is Nature's cheerless law—
　　Life's Winter in our bosoms.
The fields are brown and naked all,
　　The hedges still are green,
But storms shall come at Autumn's fall,
　　And not a leaf be seen.

Yet happy love, that warms the heart
　　Through darkest storms severe,
Keeps many a tender flower to start
　　When Spring shall re-appear.
Affection's hope shall roses meet,
　　Like those of Summer bloom,
And joys and flowers shall be as sweet
　　In seasons yet to come.

Mary Dove.

Sweet Summer, breathe your softest gales
    To charm my lover's ear :
Ye zephyrs, tell your choicest tales
    Where'er she shall appear ;
And gently wave the meadow grass
    Where soft she sets her feet,
For my love is a country lass,
    And bonny as she 's sweet.

The hedges only seem to mourn,
    The willow boughs to sigh,
Though sunshine o'er the meads sojourn,
    To cheer me where I lie :
The blackbird in the hedgerow thorn
    Sings loud his Summer lay ;
He seems to sing, both eve and morn,
    " She wanders here to-day."

The skylark in the summer cloud
    One cheering anthem sings,
And Mary often wanders out
    To watch his trembling wings.

* * * * * * *

I 'll wander down the river way,
    And wild flower posies make,
For Nature whispers all the day
    She can't her promise break.
The meads already wear a smile,
    The river runs more bright,
For down the path and o'er the stile
    The maiden comes in sight.

The scene begins to look divine;
    We 'll by the river walk.
Her arm already seems in mine,
    And fancy hears her talk.
A vision, this, of early love:
    The meadow, river, rill,
Scenes where I walked with Mary Dove,
    Are in my memory still.

Spring's Nosegay.

The prim daisy's golden eye
On the fallow land doth lie,
Though the Spring is just begun :
    Pewits watch it all the day,
    And the skylark's nest of hay
Is there by its dried leaves in the sun.

There the pilewort, all in gold,
'Neath the ridge of finest mould,
Blooms to cheer the ploughman's eye :
    There the mouse his hole hath made,
    And 'neath the golden shade
Hides secure when the hawk is prowling by.

Here 's the speedwell's sapphire blue :
Was there anything more true
To the vernal season still ?
    Here it decks the bank alone,
    Where the milkmaid throws a stone
At noon, to cross the rapid, flooded rill.

Here the cowslip, chill with cold,
On the rushy bed behold,
It looks for sunshine all the day.
Here the honey bee will come,
For he has no sweets at home ;
Then quake his weary wing and fly away.

And here are nameless flowers,
Culled in cold and rawky hours
For my Mary's happy home.
They grew in murky blea,
Rush fields and naked lea,
But suns will shine and pleasing Spring will come.

The Lost One.

I seek her in the shady grove,
    And by the silent stream ;
I seek her where my fancies rove,
    In many a happy dream ;
I seek her where I find her not,
    In Spring and Summer weather :
My thoughts paint many a happy spot,
    But we ne'er meet together.

The trees and bushes speak my choice,
    And in the Summer shower
I often hear her pleasant voice,
    In many a silent hour :
I see her in the Summer brook,
    In blossoms sweet and fair ;
In every pleasant place I look
    My fancy paints her there.

The wind blows through the forest trees,
    And cheers the pleasant day ;
There her sweet voice is sure to be
    To lull my cares away.
The very hedges find a voice,
    So does the gurgling rill ;
But still the object of my choice
    Is lost and absent still.

228

The Tell=tale Flowers.

And has the Spring's all glorious eye
    No lesson to the mind?
The birds that cleave the golden sky—
    Things to the earth resigned—
Wild flowers that dance to every wind—
Do they no memory leave behind?

Aye, flowers! The very name of flowers,
    That bloom in wood and glen,
Brings Spring to me in Winter's hours,
    And childhood's dreams again.
The primrose on the woodland lea
Was more than gold and lands to me.

The violets by the woodland side
    Are thick as they could thrive;
I 've talked to them with childish pride
    As things that were alive:
I find them now in my distress—
They seem as sweet, yet valueless.

The cowslips on the meadow lea,
    How have I run for them!
I looked with wild and childish glee
    Upon each golden gem:
And when they bowed their heads so shy
I laughed, and thought they danced for joy.

And when a man, in early years,
      How sweet they used to come,
And give me tales of smiles and tears,
      And thoughts more dear than home:
Secrets which words would then reprove—
They told the names of early love.

The primrose turned a babbling flower
      Within its sweet recess :
I blushed to see its secret bower,
      And turned her name to bless.
The violets said the eyes were blue :
I loved, and did they tell me true ?

The cowslips, blooming everywhere,
      My heart's own thoughts could steal :
I nip't them that they should not hear :
      They smiled, and would reveal ;
And o'er each meadow, right or wrong,
They sing the name I 've worshipped long.

The brook that mirrored clear the sky—
      Full well I know the spot ;
The mouse-ear looked with bright blue eye,
      And said " Forget-me-not."
And from the brook I turned away,
But heard it many an after day.

The king-cup on its slender stalk,
    Within the pasture dell,
Would picture there a pleasant walk
    With one I loved so well.
It said " How sweet at eventide
'T would be, with true love at thy side."

And on the pasture's woody knoll
    I saw the wild bluebell,
On Sundays where I used to stroll
    With her I loved so well :
She culled the flowers the year before ;
These bowed, and told the story o'er.

And every flower that had a name
    Would tell me who was fair ;
But those without, as strangers, came
    And blossomed silent there :
I stood to hear, but all alone :
They bloomed and kept their thoughts unknown.

But seasons now have nought to say,
    The flowers no news to bring :
Alone I live from day to day—
    Flowers deck the bier of Spring ;
And birds upon the bush or tree
All sing a different tale to me.

The Skylark.

Although I 'm in prison
    Thy song is uprisen,
Thou 'rt singing away to the feathery cloud,
    In the blueness of morn,
    Over fields of green corn,
With a song sweet and trilling, and rural and loud.

    When the day is serenest,
    When the corn is the greenest,
Thy bosom mounts up and floats in the light,
    And sings in the sun,
    Like a vision begun
Of pleasure, of love, and of lonely delight.

    The daisies they whiten
    Plains the sunbeams now brighten,
And warm thy snug nest where thy russet eggs lie,
    From whence thou 'rt now springing,
    And the air is now ringing,
To show that the minstrel of Spring is on high.

The cornflower is blooming,
The cowslip is coming,
And many new buds on the silken grass lie :
On the earth's shelt'ring breast
Thou hast left thy brown nest,
And art towering above it, a speck in the sky.

Thou 'rt the herald of sunshine,
And the soft dewy moonshine
Gilds sweetly the sleep of thy brown speckled breast :
Thou 'rt the bard of the Spring,
On thy brown russet wing,
And of each grassy close thou 'rt the poet and guest.

There 's the violet confiding,
In the mossy wood riding,
And primrose beneath the old thorn in the glen,
And the daisies that bed
In the sheltered homestead—
Old friends with old faces, I see them again.

And thou, feathered poet,
I see thee, and know it—
Thou 'rt one of the minstrels that cheered me last
Spring :
With Nature thou 'rt blest,
And green grass round thy nest
Will keep thee still happy to mount up and sing.

Poets love Nature.—A Fragment.

Poets love Nature, and themselves are love,
Though scorn of fools, and mock of idle pride.
The vile in nature worthless deeds approve,
They court the vile and spurn all good beside.
Poets love Nature ; like the calm of Heaven,
Like Heaven's own love, her gifts spread far and wide :
In all her works there are no signs of leaven
     *   *   *   *   *   *
Her flowers   *   *   *   *
They are her very Scriptures upon earth,
And teach us simple mirth where'er we go.
Even in prison they can solace me,
For where they bloom God is, and I am free.

"O for the pasture, field and en,
When shall I see such res' again."

Home Yearnings.

Home Yearnings.

O for that sweet, untroubled rest
        That poets oft have sung!—
The babe upon its mother's breast,
        The bird upon its young,
The heart asleep without a pain—
When shall I know that sleep again?

When shall I be as I have been
        Upon my mother's breast—
Sweet Nature's garb of verdant green
        To woo to perfect rest—
Love in the meadow, field, and glen,
And in my native wilds again?

The sheep within the fallow field,
        The herd upon the green,
The larks that in the thistle shield,
        And pipe from morn to e'en—
O for the pasture, fields, and fen!
When shall I see such rest again?

I love the weeds along the fen,
        More sweet than garden flowers,
For freedom haunts the humble glen
        That blest my happiest hours.
Here prison injures health and me:
I love sweet freedom and the free.

The crows upon the swelling hills,
  The cows upon the lea,
Sheep feeding by the pasture rills,
  Are ever dear to me,
Because sweet freedom is their mate,
While I am lone and desolate.

I loved the winds when I was young,
  When life was dear to me;
I loved the song which Nature sung,
  Endearing liberty;
I loved the wood, the vale, the stream,
For there my boyhood used to dream.

There even toil itself was play;
  'T was pleasure e'en to weep;
'T was joy to think of dreams by day,
  The beautiful of sleep.
When shall I see the wood and plain,
And dream those happy dreams again?

𝔐𝔶 𝔖𝔠𝔥𝔬𝔬𝔩𝔟𝔬𝔶 𝔇𝔞𝔶𝔰.

The Spring is come forth, but no Spring is for me
Like the Spring of my boyhood on woodland and lea,
When flowers brought me heaven and knew me again,
In the joy of their blooming o'er mountain and plain.
My thoughts are confined and imprisoned : O when
Will freedom find me my own valleys again?

The wind breathes so sweet, and the day is so calm;
In the woods and the thicket the flowers look so warm;
And the grass is so green, so delicious and sweet;
O when shall my manhood my youth's valleys meet—
The scenes where my children are laughing at play—
The scenes that from memory are fading away?

The primrose looks happy in every field;
In strange woods the violets their odours will yield,
And flowers in the sunshine, all brightly arrayed,
Will bloom just as fresh and as sweet in the shade,
But the wild flowers that bring me most joy and content
Are the blossoms that glow where my childhood was spent.

The trees are all naked, the bushes are bare,
And the fields are as brown as if Winter was there ;
But the violets are there by the dykes and the dell,
Where I played "hen and chickens" and heard the
    church bell,
Which called me to prayer-book and sermons in vain :
O when shall I see my own valleys again ?

The churches look bright as sun at noon-day ;
There the meadows look green ere the winter 's away ;
There the pooty still lies for the schoolboy to find,
And a thought often brings these sweet places to mind ;
Where trees waved and wind moaned ; no music so well :
There nought sounded harsh but the school-calling bell.

There are spots where I played, there are spots where I
    loved,
There are scenes where the tales of my choice where ap-
    proved,
As green as at first, and their memory will be
The dearest of life's recollections to me.
The objects seen there, in the care of my heart,
Are as fair as at first, and will never depart.

Though no names are mentioned to sanction my themes,
Their hearts beat with mine, and make real my dreams ;
Their memories with mine their diurnal course run,
True as night to the stars and as day to the sun ;
And as they are now so their memories will be,
While sense, truth, and reason remain here with me.

Love lives beyond the Tomb.

Love lives beyond the tomb,
And earth, which fades like dew !
I love the fond,
The faithful, and the true.

Love lives in sleep :
'T is happiness of healthy dreams :
Eve's dews may weep,
But love delightful seems.

'T is seen in flowers,
And in the morning's pearly dew ;
In earth's green hours,
And in the heaven's eternal blue.

'T is heard in Spring,
When light and sunbeams, warm and kind,
On angel's wing
Bring love and music to the mind.

239

And where 's the voice,
So young, so beautiful, and sweet
As Nature's choice,
Where Spring and lovers meet ?

Love lives beyond the tomb,
And earth, which fades like dew !
I love the fond,
The faithful, and the true.

My early Home.

Here sparrows build upon the trees,
 And stockdove hides her nest;
The leaves are winnowed by the breeze
 Into a calmer rest;
The black-cap's song was very sweet,
 That used the rose to kiss;
It made the Paradise complete:
 My early home was this.

The red-breast from the sweetbriar bush
 Drop't down to pick the worm;
On the horse-chestnut sang the thrush,
 O'er the house where I was born;
The moonlight, like a shower of pearls,
 Fell o'er this " bower of bliss,"
And on the bench sat boys and girls:
 My early home was this.

The old house stooped just like a cave,
 Thatched o'er with mosses green;
Winter around the walls would rave,
 But all was calm within;
The trees are here all green agen,
 Here bees the flowers still kiss,
But flowers and trees seemed sweeter then:
 My early home was this.

Mary Appleby.

I look upon the hedgerow flower,
I gaze upon the hedgerow tree,
I walk alone the silent hour,
And think of Mary Appleby.
I see her in the brimming streams,
I see her in the gloaming hour,
I hear her in my Summer dreams
Of singing bird and blooming flower.

For Mary is the dearest bird,
And Mary is the sweetest flower,
That in Spring bush was ever heard—
That ever bloomed on bank or bower.
O bonny Mary Appleby !
The sun did never sweeter shine
Than when in youth I courted thee,
And, dreaming, fancied you'd be mine.

The lark above the meadow sings,
Wood pigeons coo in ivied trees,
The butterflies, on painted wings,
Dance daily with the meadow bees.
All Nature is in happy mood,
The sueing breeze is blowing free,
And o'er the fields, and by the wood,
I think of Mary Appleby.

O bonny Mary Appleby ;
My once dear Mary Appleby !
A crown of gold thy own should be,
My handsome Mary Appleby !
Thy face is like the Summer rose,
Its maiden bloom is all divine,
And more than all the world bestows
I 'd give had Mary e'er been mine.

Among the Green Bushes.

Among the green bushes the songs of the thrushes
Are answering each other in music and glee,
While the magpies and rooks, in woods, hedges, near
    brooks,
Mount their Spring dwellings on every high tree.
There meet me at eve, love, we 'll on grassy banks lean
    love,
And crop a white branch from the scented may tree,
Where the silver brook wimples and the rosy cheek
    dimples,
Sweet will the time of that courting hour be.

We 'll notice wild flowers, love, that grow by thorn
    bowers, love,
Though sinful to crop them now beaded with dew ;
The violet is thine, love, the primrose is mine, love,
To Spring and each other so blooming and true.
With dewdrops all beaded, the feather grass seeded,
The cloud mountains turn to dark woods in the sky ;
The daisy bud closes, while sleep the hedge roses ;
There 's nothing seems wakeful but you love and I.

Larks sleep in the rushes, linnets perch on the bushes,
While mag 's on her nest with her tail peeping out ;
The moon it reveals her, yet she thinks night conceals her,
Though birdnesting boys are not roving about.
The night winds won't wrong her, nor aught that belong
      her,
For night is the nurse of all Nature in sleep ;
The moon, love, is keeping a watch o'er the sleeping,
And dews for real pleasure do nothing but weep.

Among the green bushes we 'll sit with the thrushes,
And blackbirds and linnets, an hour or two long,
That are up at the dawning, by times in the morning,
To cheer thee when milking with music and song.
Then come at the eve, love, and where the banks lean,
      love,
By the brook that flows on in its dribbles of song ;
While the moon looks so pale, love, and the trees look so
      hale, love,
I will tell thee a tale, love, an hour or two long.

To Jane.

The lark 's in the sky, love,
    The flowers on the lea,
The whitethorn 's in bloom, love,
    To please thee and me;
'Neath its shade we can rest, love,
    And sit on the hill,
And as last we met, love,
    Enjoy the Spring still.

The Spring is for lovers,
    The Spring is for joy :
O'er the moor, where the plovers
    Whirr, startled, and cry,
We'll seek the white hawthorn, love,
    And sit on the hill;
In the sweet sunny morn, love,
    We'll be lovers still;

Where the partridge is craking
    From morning to e'en,
In the wheat lands awaking,
    The sprouts young and green,
Where the brook dribbles past, love,
    Down the willowy glen,
And as we met last, love,
    Be lovers again.

The lark 's in the grass, love,
　　A-building her nest ;
And the brook 's running fast, love,
　　'Neath the carrion-crow's nest :
There the wild woodbines twine, love ;
　　And, till the day 's gone,
Sun 's set, and stars shine, love,
　　I 'll call thee my own.

The Old Year.

The Old Year 's gone away
To nothingness and night:
We cannot find him all the day,
Nor hear him in the night:
He left no footstep, mark, or place,
In either shade or sun :
The last year he 'd a neighbour's face,
In this he 's known by none.

All nothing everywhere :
Mists we on mornings see
Have more of substance when they 're here
And more of form than he.
He was a friend by every fire,
In every cot and hall—
A guest to every heart's desire,
And now he 's nought at all.

Old papers thrown away,
Old garments cast aside,
The talk of yesterday,
Are things identified ;
But time once torn away
No voices can recall :
The eve of New Year's Day
Left the Old Year lost to all.

Miscellaneous Poems.

MISCELLANEOUS POEMS.

Maping; or, Love and Flowers.

Upon a day, a merry day,
    When summer in her best,
Like Sunday belles, prepares for play,
    And joins each merry guest,
A maid, as wild as is a bird
    That never knew a cage,
Went out her parents' kine to herd,
    And Jocky, as her page,

Must needs go join her merry toils ;
    A silly shepherd he,
And little thought the aching broils
    That in his heart would be ;
For he as yet knew nought of love,
    And nought of love knew she ;
Yet without learning love can move
    The wildest to agree.

The wind, enamoured of the maid,
    Around her drapery swims,
And moulds in luscious masquerade
    Her lovely shape and limbs.
Smith's " Venus stealing Cupid's bow "
    In marble hides as fine ;
But hers were life and soul, whose glow
    Makes meaner things divine.

In sooth she was a lovely toy—
    A worship-moving thing
As ever brought the season joy,
    Or beautified the Spring ;
So sweet a thing no heart might hurt,
    Gay as a butterfly ;
Tho' Cupid chased 't was half in sport—
    He meant not to destroy.

When speaking, words with breathing grace
    Her sweet lips seeming wooed,
Pausing to leave so sweet a place
    Ere they could part for good—
Those lips that pouted from her face,
    As the wild rose bursts the bud
Which June, so eager to embrace,
    Tempts from beneath its hood.

Her eyes, like suns, did seem to light
    The beauties of her face,
Suffusing all her forehead white
    And cheeks of rosy grace.

Her bosom swelled to pillows large,
    Till her so taper waist
Scarce able seemed to bear the charge
    Of each lawn-bursting breast.

A very flower! how she did shine,
    Her beauty all displaying!
In truth this modern Proserpine
    Might set the angels maying,
As, like a fairy mid the flowers,
    She flew to this, now that;
And some she braided in her hair—
    Some wreathed within her hat.

Then off she skipt, in bowers to hide,
    By Cupid led, I ween,
Putting her bosom's lawn aside,
    To place some thyme atween.
The shepherd saw her skin so white—
    Two twin suns newly risen:
Tho' love had chained him there till night,
    Who would have shunned the prison?

Then off again she skipt, and flew
    With foot so light and little
That Cinderella's fancy shoe
    Had fit her to a tittle.
The shepherd's heart, like playing coal,
    Beat as 't would leave the socket:
He sighed, but thought it, silly fool,
    The watch within his pocket.

And then he tried a song to sing,
  But sighs arose and drop't it;
He thought the winds, poor silly thing,
  Blew in his face and stopt it.
And then he tried to sing again,
  But sighs again did flutter
Around his heart, and " What a pain !"
  . Was all that he could utter.

" Fair flower," said he. " Who's that ?" quoth she,
  And tied her flowers together ;
Then sought for more : " Ah ; woe is me !"
  He said, or sighed it, rather :
Then grasped her arm that, soft and white,
  Like to a pillow dinted,
And flushing red as at a bite,
  His fingers there were printed ;
And " Ah !" he sighed, to mark the sight
  That rudeness unmeant hinted.

And, Daphne-like, she blushed and flew,
  Though but to vex his pain ;
And soon, to see if he'd pursue,
  She turned to smile again ;
And, like a bird with injured wing,
  That flutters but not flies,
She waited for the sheepish thing
  To catch her by surprise.

But bold in love grow silly sheep,
    And so right bold grew he ;
He ran ; she fled ; and at bo-peep
    She met him round a tree.
A thorn, enamoured like the swain,
    Caught at her lily arm,
And then good faith, to ease her pain,
    Love had a double charm.

She sighed ; he wished it well, I wis ;
    The place was sadly swollen ;
And then he took a willing kiss,
    And made believe 't was stolen ;
Then made another make-believe,
    . Till thefts grew past concealing,
For when love once begins to thieve
    There grows no end to stealing.

They played and toyed till down the skies
    The sun had taken flight,
And still a sun was in her eyes
    To keep away the night ;
And there he talked of love so well,
    Or else he talked so ill,
That soon the priest was sought to tell
    The story better still.

Two Sonnets to Mary.

I.

I met thee like the morning, though more fair,
And hopes 'gan travel for a glorious day;
And though night met them ere they were aware,
Leading the joyous pilgrims all astray,
Yet know I not, though they did miss their way,
That joyed so much to meet thee, if they are
To blame or bless the fate that bade such be.
Thou seem'dst an angel when I met thee first,
Nor has aught made thee otherwise to me:
Possession has not cloyed my love, nor curst
Fancy's wild visions with reality.
Thou art an angel still; and Hope, awoke
From the fond spell that early raptures nurst,
Still feels a joy to think that spell ne'er broke.

II.

The flower that 's gathered beauty soon forsakes :
The bliss grows feeble as we gain the prize ;
Love dreams of joy, and in possession wakes,
Scarce time enough to hail it ere it dies :
Life intermingles, with its cares and sighs,
And rapture's dreams are ended.   Heavenly flower !
It is not so with thee !   Still fancy's power
Throws rainbow halos round thee, and thine eyes,
That once did steal their sapphire blue from even,
Are beaming on ; thy cheeks' bewitching dye,
Where partial roses all their blooms had given,
Still in fond memory with the rose can vie ;
And thy sweet bosom, which to view was heaven,
No lily yet a fairer hue supplies.

The Vanities of Life.

[The reader has been made acquainted with the circumstances
under which this poem was written. It was included by
Mr. J. H. Dixon in his " Ballads and Songs of the
Peasantry of England" (edited by Robert Bell), with the
following prefatory note ;—" The poem was, probably, as
Clare supposes, written about the commencement of the
18th century, and the unknown author appears to have
been deeply imbued with the spirit of the popular
devotional writers of the preceding century, as Herbert,
Quarles, &c., but seems to have modelled his smoother and
more elegant versification after that of the poetic school of
his own times." Montgomery's criticism on publishing it
in the " Sheffield Iris" was as follows :—" Long as the
poem appears to the eye, it will abundantly repay the
trouble of perusal, being full of condensed and admirable
thought, as well as diversified with exuberant imagery, and
embellished with peculiar felicity of language. The moral
points in the closing couplets of the stanzas are often
powerfully enforced."]

" Vanity of vanities, all is vanity."—*Solomon.*

What are life's joys and gains ?
What pleasures crowd its ways,
That man should take such pains
To seek them all his days ?

Sift this untoward strife
On which the mind is bent :
See if this chaff of life
Is worth the trouble spent.

Is pomp thy heart's desire ?
Is power thy climbing aim ?
Is love thy folly's fire ?
Is wealth thy restless game ?
Pomp, power, love, wealth, and all
Time's touchstone shall destroy,
And, like base coin, prove all
Vain substitutes for joy.

Dost think that pride exalts
Thyself in other's eyes,
And hides thy folly's faults,
Which reason will despise ?
Dost strut, and turn, and stride,
Like a walking weathercock ?
The shadow by thy side
Will be thy ape, and mock.

Dost think that power's disguise
Can make thee mighty seem ?
It may in folly's eyes,
But not in worth's esteem,
When all that thou canst ask,
And all that she can give,
Is but a paltry mask
Which tyrants wear and live.

Go, let thy fancies range
And ramble where they may ;
View power in every change,
And what is the display ?
—The county magistrate,
The lowest shade in power,
To rulers of the state,
The meteors of an hour :—

View all, and mark the end
Of every proud extreme,
Where flattery turns a friend,
And counterfeits esteem ;
Where worth is aped in show,
That doth her name purloin,
Like toys of golden glow
Oft sold for copper coin.

Ambition's haughty nod
With fancies may deceive,
Nay, tell thee thou'rt a god,
And wilt thou such believe ?
Go, bid the seas be dry ;
Go, hold earth like a ball,
Or throw her fancies by,
For God can do it all.

Dost thou possess the dower
Of laws to spare or kill ?
Call it not heavenly power
When but a tyrant's will.

Think what thy God would do,
And know thyself a fool,
Nor, tyrant-like, pursue
Where He alone can rule.

Dost think, when wealth is won,
Thy heart has its desire?
Hold ice up to the sun,
And wax before the fire;
Nor triumph o'er the reign
Which they so soon resign:
Of this world weigh the gain,
Insurance safe is thine.

Dost think life's peace secure
In houses and in land?
Go, read the fairy lure,
And twist a cord in sand;
Lodge stones upon the sky,
Hold water in a sieve,
Nor give such tales the lie,
And still thine own believe.

Whoso with riches deals,
And thinks peace bought and sold,
Will find them slipping eels,
That slide the firmest hold:
Though sweet as sleep with health
Thy lulling luck may be,
Pride may o'erstride thy wealth,
And check prosperity.

Dost think that beauty's power
Life sweetest pleasure gives ?
Go, pluck the summer flower,
And see how long it lives :
Behold, the rays glide on
Along the summer plain
Ere thou canst say they're gone :—
Know such is beauty's reign.

Look on the brightest eye,
Nor teach it to be proud ;
View next the clearest sky,
And thou shalt find a cloud ;
Nor call each face ye meet
An angel's, 'cause it 's fair,
But look beneath your feet,
And think of what ye are.

Who thinks that love doth live
In beauty's tempting show,
Shall find his hopes ungive,
And melt in reason's thaw.
Who thinks that pleasure lies
In every fairy bower,
Shall oft, to his surprise,
Find poison in the flower.

Dost lawless pleasures grasp ?
Judge not they 'll bring thee joy :
Their flowers but hide the asp,
Whose poison will destroy.

Who trusts a harlot's smile,
And by her wiles is led,
Plays, with a sword the while
Hung dropping o'er his head.

Dost doubt my warning song?
Then doubt the sun gives light,
Doubt truth to teach thee wrong,
Think wrong alone is right;
And live as lives the knave,
Intrigue's deceiving guest;
Be tyrant, or be slave,
As suits thy ends the best.

Or pause amid thy toils
For visions won and lost,
And count the fancied spoils,
If e'er they quit the cost:
And if they still possess
Thy mind, as worthy things,
Pick straws with Bedlam Bess,
And call them diamond rings.

Thy folly 's past advice,
Thy heart 's already won,
Thy fall 's above all price,
So go, and be undone;
For all who thus prefer
The seeming great for small
Shall make wine vinegar,
And sweetest honey gall.

Would'st heed the truths I sing,
To profit wherewithal,
Clip folly's wanton wing,
And keep her within call.
I've little else to give,
But thou canst easy try ;
The lesson how to live
Is but to learn to die.

March.

[From HONE'S " *Year Book.*"]

The insect world, now sunbeams higher climb,
Oft dream of Spring, and wake before their time :
Bees stroke their little legs across their wings,
And venture short flights where the snow-drop hings
Its silver bell, and winter aconite
Its buttercup-like flowers that shut at night,
With green leaf furling round its cup of gold,
Like tender maiden muffled from the cold :
They sip and find their honey-dreams are vain,
Then feebly hasten to their hives again.
The butterflies, by eager hopes undone,
Glad as a child come out to greet the sun,
Beneath the shadows of a sunny shower
Are lost, nor see to-morrow's April flower.

The Old Man's Lament.

Youth has no fear of ill, by no cloudy days annoyed,
But the old man's all hath fled, and his hopes have met
  their doom :
The bud hath burst to flower, and the flower been long
  destroyed,
The root also is withered ; I no more can look for bloom.
So I have said my say, and I have had my day,
And sorrow, like a young storm, creeps dark upon my
  brow ;
Hopes, like to summer clouds, have all blown far away,
And the world's sunny side is turned over with me now,
And I am left a lame bird upon a withered bough.

I look upon the past : 't is as black as winter days,
But the worst is not yet over ; there are blacker days to
  come.
O, I would I had but known of the wide world's many
  ways,
But youth is ever blind, so I e'en must meet my doom.
Joy once gave brightest forecasts of prospects that are past,
But now, like a looking glass that 's turned to the wall,
Life is nothing but a blank, and the sunny shining past
Is overcast in glooms that my every hope enthrall,
While troubles daily thicken in the wind ere they fall.

Life smiled upon me once, as the sun upon the rose;
My heart, so free and open, guessed in every face a friend:
Though the sweetest flower must fade, and the sweetest
season close,
Yet I never gave it thought that my happiness would end,
Till the warmest-seeming friends grew the coldest at the
close,
As the sun from lonely night hides its haughty shining
face,
Yet I could not think them gone, for they turned not open
foes,
While memory fondly mused, former favours to retrace,
So I turned, but only found that my shadow kept its
place.

And this is nought but common life, which everybody
finds
As well as I, or more 's the luck of those that better
speed.
I'll mete my lot to bear with the lot of kindred minds,
And grudge not those who say they for sorrow have no
need.
Why should I, when I know that it will not aid a nay?
For Summer is the season; even then the little fly
Finds friends enow, indeed, both for leisure and for play;
But on the winter window it must crawl alone to die:
Such is life, and such am I—a wounded, stricken fly.

Spring Flowers.

Bowing adorers of the gale,
Ye cowslips delicately pale,
     Upraise your loaded stems;
Unfold your cups in splendour; speak!
Who decked you with that ruddy streak
     And gilt your golden gems?

Violets, sweet tenants of the shade,
In purple's richest pride arrayed,
     Your errand here fulfil;
Go, bid the artist's simple stain
Your lustre imitate—in vain—
     And watch your Maker's skill.

Daisies, ye flowers of lowly birth,
Embroiders of the carpet earth,
     That stud the velvet sod,
Open to Spring's refreshing air,
In sweetest smiling bloom declare
     Your Maker and your God.

ℜoem on ℜeath.

[This poem, like that entitled "The Vanities of Life," is an imitation. In his Diary, Clare says—"Wednesday, July 27, 1825. Received the 28th No. [June the 28th] of the 'Every-Day Book,' in which is inserted a poem of mine which I sent under the assumed name of James Gilderoy, from Sunfleet, as being the production of Andrew Marvell, and printed in the 'Miscellanies' of the Spalding Antiquaries [the members of the Spalding Club]. I shall venture again under another name after a while." Hone accepted the contribution without detecting the disguise, but Clare's next venture of the same description, "A Farewell and Defiance to Love," which he says in his Diary, August 2nd, he fathered on Sir John Harrington," was unsuccessful.]

Why should man's high aspiring mind
Burn in him with so proud a breath,
When all his haughty views can find
    In this world yields to Death ?
The fair, the brave, the vain, the wise,
The rich, the poor, and great, and small,
Are each but worm's anatomies
    To strew his quiet hall.

Power may make many earthly gods,
Where gold and bribery's guilt prevails,
But Death's unwelcome, honest odds
    Kick o'er the unequal scales.
The flatter'd great may clamours raise
Of power, and their own weakness hide,
But Death shall find unlooked-for ways
    To end the farce of pride.

An arrow hurtel'd e'er so high,
With e'en a giant's sinewy strength,
In Time's untraced eternity
    Goes but a pigmy length ;
Nay, whirring from the tortured string,
With all its pomp of hurried flight,
'T is by the skylark's little wing
    Outmeasured in its height.

Just so man's boasted strength and power
Shall fade before Death's lightest stroke,
Laid lower than the meanest flower,
    Whose pride o'er-top't the oak ;
And he who, like a blighting blast,
Dispeopled worlds with war's alarms
Shall be himself destroyed at last
    By poor despised worms.

Tyrants in vain their powers secure,
And awe slaves' murmurs with a frown,
For unawed Death at last is sure
    To sap the Babels down.

A stone thrown upward to the skye
Will quickly meet the ground agen ;
So men-gods of earth's vanity
    Shall drop at last to men ;

And Power and Pomp their all resign,
Blood-purchased thrones and banquet halls.
Fate waits to sack Ambition's shrine
    As bare as prison walls,
Where the poor suffering wretch bows down
To laws a lawless power hath passed ;
And pride, and power, and king, and clown
    Shall be Death's slaves at last.

Time, the prime minister of Death !
There 's nought can bribe his honest will.
He stops the richest tyrant's breath
    And lays his mischief still.
Each wicked scheme for power all stops,
With grandeurs false and mock display,
As eve's shades from high mountain tops
    Fade with the rest away.

Death levels all things in his march ;
Nought can resist his mighty strength ;
The palace proud, triumphal arch,
    Shall mete its shadow's length.
The rich, the poor, one common bed
Shall find in the unhonoured grave,
Where weeds shall grow alike o'er head
    Of tyrant and of slave.

The Wanton Chloe.—A Pastoral.

Young Chloe looks sweet as the rose,
And her love might be reckoned no less,
But her bosom so freely bestows
That all may a portion possess.
Her smiles would be cheering to see,
But so freely they 're lavished abroad
That each silly swain, like to me,
Can boast what the wanton bestowed.

Her looks and her kisses so free
Are for all, like the rain and the sky ;
As the blossom love is to the bee,
Each swain is as welcome as I.
And though I my folly can see,
Yet still must I love and adore,
Though I know the love whispered to me
Has been told to so many before.

'T is sad that a bosom so fair,
And soft lips so seemingly sweet,
Should study false ways, to ensnare,
And breathe in their kisses deceit.
But beauty 's no guide to the best :
The rose, that out-blushes the morn,
While it tempts the glad eye to its breast,
Will pierce the fond hand with a thorn.

Yet still must I love, silly swain!
And put up with all her deceit,
And try to be jealous, in vain,
For I cannot help thinking her sweet.
I see other swains in her bower,
And I sigh, and excuse what I see,
While I say to myself, " Is the flower
Any worse when it 's kissed by the bee?"

The Old Shepherd.

'T is pleasant to bear recollections in mind
 Of joys that time hurries away—
To look back on smiles that have passed like the wind,
 And compare them with frowns of to-day.
'T was the constant delight of Old Robin, forsooth,
 On the past with clear vision to dwell—
To recount the fond loves and raptures of youth,
 And tales of lost pleasures to tell.

" 'T is now many years," like a child, he would say,
 " Since I joined in the sports of the green—
Since I tied up the flowers for the garland of May,
 And danced with the holiday queen.
My memory looks backward in sorrowful pride,
 And I think, till my eyes dim with tears,
Of the past, where my happiness withered and died,
 And the present dull, desolate years.

I love to be counting, while sitting alone,
 With many a heart-aching sigh,
How many a season has rapidly flown,
 And springs, with their summers, gone by,
Since Susan the pride of the village was deemed,
 To whom youth's affections I gave ;
Whom I led to the church, and beloved and esteemed,
 And followed in grief to the grave.

Life's changes for many hours musings supply ;
    Both the past and the present appear ;
I mark how the years that remain hurry by,
    And feel that my last must be near.
The youths that with me to man's summer did bloom
    Have dwindled away to old men,
And maidens, like flowers of the Spring, have made room
    For many new blossoms since then.

I have lived to see all but life's sorrows pass by,
    Leaving changes, and pains, and decay,
Where nought is the same but the wide-spreading sky,
    And the sun that awakens the day.
The green, where I tended my sheep when a boy,
    Has yielded its pride to the plough ;
And the shades where my infancy revelled in joy
    The axe has left desolate now.

Yet a bush lingers still, that will urge me to stop—
    (What heart can such fancies withstand ?)
Where Susan once saw a bird's nest on the top,
    And I reached her the eggs with my hand :
And so long since the day I remember so well,
    It has stretched to a sizable tree,
And the birds yearly come in its branches to dwell,
    As far from a giant as me.

On a favourite spot, by the side of a brook,
    When Susan was just in her pride,
A ripe bunch of nuts from her apron she took,
    To plant as she sat by my side.

They have grown up with years, and on many a bough
    Cluster nuts like their parents agen,
Where shepherds no doubt have oft sought them ere now,
    To please other Susans since then.

The joys that I knew when my youth was in prime,
    Like a dream that 's half ended, are o'er;
And the faces I knew in that changeable time
    Are met with the living no more.
I have lived to see friends that I loved pass away
    With the pleasures their company gave:
I have lived to see love, with my Susan, decay,
    And the grass growing green on her grave. "

"Though pride look disdainfully on thee,
  Scorning scenes so mean as thine;
Although fortune frown upon thee,
  Lovely blossom, ne'er repine."

To a Rosebud in Humble Life.

To a Rosebud in Humble Life.

Sweet, uncultivated blossom,
    Reared in Spring's refreshing dews,
Dear to every gazer's bosom,
    Fair to every eye that views ; —
Opening bud, whose youth can charm us,
    Thine be many a happy hour :
Spreading rose, whose beauties warm us—
    Flourish long, my lovely flower.

Though pride look disdainful on thee,
    Scorning scenes so mean as thine,
Although fortune frown upon thee,
    Lovely blossom, ne'er repine :
Health unbought is ever with thee,
    Which their wealth can never gain ;
Innocence doth garments give thee,
    Such as fashion apes in vain.

When fit time and reason grant thee
    Leave to quit the parent tree,
May some happy hand transplant thee
    To a station suiting thee.
On some lover's faithful bosom
    May'st thou then thy sweets resign ;
And may each unfolding blossom
    Open charms as sweet as thine.

Till that time may joys unceasing
  Thy bard's every wish fulfil.
When that 's come may joys increasing
  Make thee blest and happier still.
Flourish fair, thou flower of Jessies,
  Pride of each admiring swain—
Envy of despairing lasses—
  Queen of Walkherd's lovely plain.

The Triumphs of Time.

[From "*The Champion.*"]

Emblazoned Vapour!   Half-eternal Shade!
That gathers strength from ruin and decay ;—
Emperor of empires! (for the world hath made
No substance that dare take thy shade away ;)
Thy banners nought but victories display :
In undisturbed success thou 'rt grown sublime :
Kings are thy subjects, and their sceptres lay
Round thy proud footstool : tyranny and crime
Thy serving vassals are.   Then hail, victorious Time!

The elements that wreck the marble dome
Proud with the polish of the artisan—
Bolts that crash shivering through the humble home,
Traced with the insignificance of man—
Are architects of thine, and proudly plan
Rich monuments to show thy growing prime :
Earthquakes that rend the rocks with dreadful span,
Lightnings that write in characters sublime,
Inscribe their labours all unto the praise of Time.

Thy palaces are kingdoms lost to power;
The ruins of ten thousand thrones thy throne;
Thy crown and sceptre the dismantled tower,
A place of kings, yet left to be unknown,
Now with triumphing ivy overgrown—
Ivy oft plucked on Victory's brow to shine—
That fades in crowns of kings, preferring stone;
It only prospers where they most decline,
To flourish o'er their fate, and live alone in thine.

Thy dwellings are in ruins made sublime.
Impartial Monitor, no dream of fear,
No dread of treason for a royal crime,
Deters thee from thy purpose : everywhere
Thy power is shown : thou art arch-emperor here :
Thou soil'st the very crowns with stains and rust;
On royal robes thy havoc doth appear;
The little moth, to thy proud summons just,
Dares scarlet pomp to scorn, and eats it into dust.

Old shadows of magnificence, where now—
Where now and what your grandeur ?   Come and see
Busts broken and thrown down, with wreathless brow,
Walls stained with colours, not of paint, but thee,
Moss, lichens, ferns, and lonely elder tree;
That upon ruins gladly climb to bloom,
And add a beauty where 't is vain to be,
Like to the soft moonlight in a prison's gloom,
Or lovely maid in youth death-smitten for the tomb.

Pride may build palaces and splendid halls ;
Power may display its victories and be brave ;
The eye finds weakest spots in strongest walls,
And meets no strength that can out-wear the grave.
Nature, thy handmaid and imperial slave,
The pomp of splendour's finery never heeds :
Kings reign and die : pride may no respite crave ;
Nature in barrenness ne'er mourns thy deeds :
Graves, poor and rich alike, she overruns with weeds.

In thy proud eye, imperial Arbiter,
An insect small to prize appeareth man ;
His pomp and honours have o'er thee no spell,
To win thy purpose from the little span
Allotted unto life in Nature's plan ;
Trifles to him thy favour can engage ;
High he looks up, and soon his race is run,
While the small daisy upon Nature's page,
On which he sets his foot, gains endless heritage.

Look at the farces played in every age
By puny empires, vaunting vain display,
And blush to read the historian's fulsome page,
Where kings are worshipped like to gods in clay.
Their pride the earth disdained and swept away,
By thee, a shadow, worsted of their all—
Legions of soldiers, battle's dread array—
Kings' speeches—golden bribes—nought saved their
    fall ;
All 'neath thy feet are laid, thy robe their funeral pall.

How feeble and how vain, compared to thine,
The glittering pageantry of earthly kings,
Though in their little light they would outshine
Thy splendid sun : yet soon thy vengeance flings
Its gloom around their crowns, poor puny things.
What then remains of all that great hath been ?
A tattered state, that as a mockery clings
To greatness, and concludes the idle scene—
In life how mighty thought, and found in death how mean.

Thus Athens lingers on, a nest of slaves,
And Babylon 's an almost doubted name :
Thou with thy finger writ'st upon their graves,
On one obscurity, the other shame.
The richest greatness or the proudest fame
Thy sport concludeth as a farce at last :
They were and would be, but are not the same :
Tyrants, that made all subject where they passed,
Become a common jest for laughter at the last.

Here where I stand* thy voice breathes from the ground
A buried tale of sixteen hundred years,
And many a Roman fragment, littered round,
In each new-rooted mole-hill reappears.
Ah ! what is fame, that honour so reveres ?
And what is Victory's laurel-crowned event
When thy unmasked intolerance interferes ?
A Cæsar's deeds are left to banishment,
Indebted e'en to moles to show us where he went.

* A Roman encampment near Helpstone.

A mighty poet thou, and every line
Thy grand conception traces is sublime :
No language doth thy god-like works confine ;
Thy voice is earth's grand polyglot, O Time !
Known of all tongues, and read in every clime,
Changes of language make no change in thee :
Thy works have worsted centuries of their prime,
Yet new editions every day we see—
Ruin thy moral theme, its end eternity.

A satirist, too, thy pen is deadly keen ;
Thou turnest things that once did wonder claim
To jests ridiculous and memories mean ;—
The Egyptian pyramids, without a name,
Stand monuments to chaos, not to fame—
Stone jests of kings which thou in sport did'st save,
As towering satires of pride's living shame—
Beacons to prove thy overbearing wave
Will make all fame at last become its owner's grave.

Mighty survivors !   Thou shalt see the hour
When all the grandeur that the earth contains—
Its pomp, its splendour, and its hollow power—
Shall waste like water from its weakened veins,
And not a shadow or a myth remain—
When names and fames of which the earth is full,
And books, with all their knowledge urged in vain—
When dead and living shall be void and null,
And Nature's pillow be at last a human skull.

E'en temples raised to worship and to prayer,
Sacred from ruin in all eyes but thine,
Are laid as level, and are left as bare,
As spots with no pretensions to resign ;
Nor lives one relic that was deemed divine.
By thee, great sacrilegious Shade, all, all
Are swept away, and common weeds enshrine
That place of tombs and memories prodigal—
Itself a tomb at last, the record of its fall.

All then shall mingle fellowship with one,
And earth be strewn with wrecks of human things,
When tombs are broken up and memory 's gone
Of proud aspiring mortals, crowned as kings,
Mere insects, sporting upon waxen wings
That melt at thy all-mastering energy ;
And, when there 's nought to govern, thy fame springs
To new existence, conquered, yet to be
An uncrowned partner still of dread eternity.

'T is done, o'erpowering Vision !   And no more
My simple numbers chronicle thy fame ;
'T is gone : the spirit of my voice is o'er,
Adventuring praises to thy mighty name.
To thee an atom am I, and in shame
I shrink from these aspirings to my doom ;
For all the world contains to praise or blame
Is but a garden hastening out of bloom
To fill up Nature's wreck—mere rubbish for the tomb.

Imperial Moralist !   Thy every page,
Like grand prophetic visions, doth instal
Truth for all creeds.   The savage, saint, and sage
In unison may answer to thy call.
Thy voice as universal, speaks to all ;
It tells us what all were and are to be ;
That evil deeds will evil hearts enthral,
And God the just maintain the grand decree,
That whoso righteous lives shall win eternity,

To John Milton,

" From his honoured Friend, William Davenant."

[This poem appeared in the " Sheffield Iris" of May the 16th, 1826, with this introductory note :— " The following stanzas are supposed to have been addressed to Milton by his friend and contemporary, Sir William Davenant. We cannot vouch for their authenticity, but for their excellency we can. They have been communicated to us by the late editor of the ' Iris,' who received them from Mr. John Clare, the ingenious poet of Northamptonshire."]

Poet of mighty power, I fain
Would court the muse that honoured thee,
And, like Elisha's spirit, gain
    A part of thy intensity ;
And share the mantle which she flung
Around thee, when thy lyre was strung.

Though faction's scorn at first did shun,
With coldness, thy inspired song,
Though clouds of malice pass'd thy sun,
    They could not hide it long ;
Its brightness soon exhaled away
Dark night, and gained eternal day.

The critics' wrath did darkly frown
Upon thy muse's mighty lay;
But blasts that break the blossom down
    Do only stir the bay;
And thine shall flourish, green and long,
In the eternity of song.

Thy genius saw, in quiet mood,
Gilt fashion's follies pass thee by,
And, like the monarch of the wood,
    Tower'd o'er it to the sky;
Where thou could'st sing of other spheres,
And feel the fame of future years.

Though bitter sneers and stinging scorns
Did throng the muse's dangerous way,
Thy powers were past such little thorns,
    They gave thee no dismay;
The scoffer's insult pass'd thee by,
Thou smild'st and mad'st him no reply.

Envy will gnaw its heart away
To see thy genius gather root;
And as its flowers their sweets display
    Scorn's malice shall be mute;
Hornets that summer warmed to fly,
Shall at the death of summer die.

Though friendly praise hath but its hour,
And little praise with thee hath been ;
The bay may lose its summer flower,
　　But still its leaves are green ;
And thine, whose buds are on the shoot,
Shall only fade to change to fruit.

Fame lives not in the breath of words,
In public praises' hue and cry ;
The music of these summer birds
　　Is silent in a winter sky,
When thine shall live and flourish on,
O'er wrecks where crowds of fames are gone.

The ivy shuns the city wall,
When busy-clamorous crowds intrude,
And climbs the desolated hall
　　In silent solitude ;
The time-worn arch, the fallen dome,
Are roots for its eternal home.

The bard his glory ne'er receives
Where summer's common flowers are seen,
But winter finds it when she leaves
　　The laurel only green ;
And time, from that eternal tree,
Shall weave a wreath to honour thee.

Nought but thy ashes shall expire;
Thy genius, at thy obsequies,
Shall kindle up its living fire
    And light the muse's skies;
Ay, it shall rise, and shine, and be
A sun in song's posterity.

The Birds and St. Valentine.

Sorrow came with downcast eyes,
And stole the lyre of love away.
VAN DYK.

[From ACKERMANN'S "*Juvenile Forget-me-not.*"]

Some two or three weeks before Valentine's day,
Sir Winter grew kind, and, minded to play,
Shook hands with Miss Flora, and woo'd her to spare
A few pretty snowdrops to stick in his hair,
Intending for truth, as he said, to resign
His throne to Miss Spring and her priest Valentine;
Which trifle he asked for before he set forth,
To remind him of all when he got in the North;
And this is the reason that snowdrops appear
'Mid the cold of the Winter, so soon in the year.
Flora complied, and, the instant she heard,
Flew away with the news to each bachelor bird,
Who in raptures half moved on Love's errand to start,
Their songs muttered over to get them by heart:
Nay, the Mavis at once sung aloud in his glee,
And looked for a spot where love's dwelling should be;
And ever since then, both in garden and grove,
The Mavis tunes first a short ditty to love,
While all the young gentlemen birds that were near
Fell to trimming their jackets anew for the year:

One and all they determined to seek for a mate,
And thought it a folly for seasons to wait,
So even agreed, before Valentine's day,
To join hearts in love; but the ladies said, Nay!
Yet each one consented at once to resign
Her heart unto Hymen on St. Valentine;
While Winter, who only pretended to go,
Lapt himself out of sight in some hillocks of snow,
That behind all the rest 'neath the wood hedges lay
So close that the sun could not drive them away:
Yet the gentlemen birds on their love errands flew,
Thinking all Flora told them was nothing but true,
Till out Winter came, and his frowns in a trice
Turned the lady birds' hearts all as hardened as ice.
In vain might the gentles in love sue and plead—
They heard, but not once did they notice or heed:
From Winter they crept, who, in tyranny proud,
Yoked his horses of storms to his coach of a cloud;
For on Valentine's morn he was raving so high,
Lady Spring for the life of her durst not come nigh;
While Flora's gay feet were so numbed with the snow
That she could not put on her best slippers to go.
Then the Spring she fell ill, and, her health to regain,
On a sunbeam rode back to her South once again;
And, as both were the bridesmaids, their teasing delay
Made the lady birds put off their weddings till May.
Some sighed their excuses, and feared to catch cold;
And the Redcap, in mantle all bordered with gold,
Sore feared that the weather would spoil her fine clothes,
And nought but complaints through the forest arose.

So St. Valentine came on his journey alone
In the coach of the Morn, for he 'd none of his own,
And put on his cassock and band, and went in
To the temple of Hymen, the rites to begin,
Where the Mavis Thrush waited along with his bride,
Nor in the whole place was a lady beside.
The gentlemen they came alone to the saint,
And instead of being married, each made a complaint
Of Sir Winter, whose folly had caused the delay,
And forced Love to put off the wedding till May;
So the priest shook his head, and unrobed to be gone,
As he had no day for his leisure but one.

And when the May came with Miss Flora and Spring,
They had nought but old cares and new sorrows to sing ;
For some of the lady birds ceased to be kind
To their old loves, and changed for new-comers their mind ;
And some had resolved to keep single that year,
Until St. Valentine with the next should appear.

The birds sung their sorrows the whole Summer long,
And the Robin first mixed up his ills with his song :
He sung of his griefs—how in love he 'd been crossed,
And gave up his heart as eternally lost ;
'T was burnt to a coal, as sly Cupid let fall
A spark that scorched through both the feathers and all.
To cure it Time tried, but ne'er found out the way,
So the mark on his bosom he wears to this day :
And when birds are all silent, and not a leaf seen
On the trees, but the ivy and holly so green,
In frost and in snow little Robin will sing,

To put off the sorrow that ruffles his wing.
And that is the cause in our gardens we hear
The Robin's sweet note at the close of the year.

The Wagtail, too, mourned in his doublet of grey,
As if powdered with rime on a dull winter's day;
He twittered of love—how he courted a fair,
Who altered her mind, and so made him despair.
In a stone-pit he chose her a place for a nest,
But she, like a wanton, but made it a jest.
Though he dabbled in brooks to convince her how kind
He would feed her with worms which he laboured to find,
Till he e'en got the ague, still nought could prevail,
So ever since then he's been wagging his tail.

In the whitethorn the Linnet bides lonely to sing
How his lady-love shunned his embraces in Spring,
Though he found out a bush that the sun had half drest
With leaves quite sufficient to shelter their nest;
And yet she forsook him, no more to be seen,
So that is the reason he dresses in green.

Then aloud in his grief sings the gay speckled Thrush,
That changes his music on every bush—
" My love she has left me to sorrow and mourn,
Yet I hope in my heart she'll repent and return;"
So he tries at all notes her approval to meet,
And that is the reason he singeth so sweet.

And as sweet sang the Bullfinch, although he confest
That the anguish he felt was more deep than the rest,

And they all marvelled much how he 'd spirits to sing,
When to show them his anguish he held up his wing;
From his throat to his tail not a feather was found
But what had been stained red with blood from the wound.

And sad chirped the Sparrow of joys fled and gone,
Of his love being lost he so doted upon;
So he vowed constant silence for that very thing,
And this is the reason why Sparrows don't sing.

Then next came the Rook and the sorrowful Crow,
To tell birds the cause why in mourning they go,
Ever since their old loves their embraces forsook;
And all seemed to pity the Crow and the Rook.

The Jay he affected to hide his despair,
And rather than mourn he had spirits to wear
A coat of all colours, but in it some blue
Denoted his passion; though crossed, 't was true;
So now in lone woods he will hide him all day,
And aloud he scolds all that intrude in his way.

The Magpie declared it should never be said
That he mourned for a lover, though fifty had fled;
Yet his heart all the while was so burnt and distrest,
That it turned all the feathers coal-black on his breast.
The birds they all marvelled, but still he denied,
And wore a black cap his deep blushes to hide;
So that is the reason himself and his kin
Wear hoods with the lappets quite under the chin.

Then last came the Owl, grieving loud as he flew,
Saying how his false lover had bade him adieu;

And though he knew not where to find her or follow,
Yet round their old haunts he would still whoop and halloo,
For no sleep could he get in his sorrowful plight,
So that is the reason Owls halloo at night.

And here ends the song of each woe-stricken bird.
Now was a more pitiful story e'er heard ?
The rest were all coupled, and happy, and they
Sung the old merry songs which they sing at this day :
And good little boys, when this tale they read o'er,
Will ne'er have the heart to hurt birds any more,
And add to the griefs they already have sung
By robbing their nests of their eggs and their young;
But feel for their sufferings, and pity their pain,
Nor give them new cause of their lot to complain.

Farewell and Defiance to Love.

[*After Sir John Harrington.*]

[From the "*European Magazine,*" March, 1826.]

Love and thy vain employs, away
From this too oft deluded breast!
No longer will I court thy stay,
To be my bosom's teasing guest.
Thou treacherous medicine—reckon'd pure;
Thou quackery of the harass'd heart,
That kills what it pretends to cure,
    Life's mountebank thou art,

With nostrums vain of boasted powers,
That, ta'en, a worse disorder leave;
An asp hid in a group of flowers,
That bites and stings when few perceive;
Thou mock-peace to the troubled mind,
Leading it more in sorrow's way,
Freedom that leaves us more confined,
    I bid thee hence away.

Dost taunt, and deem thy power beyond
The resolution reason gave?
Tut! Falsity hath snapt each bond,
That kept me once thy quiet slave,

And made thy snare a spider's thread,
Which e'en my breath can break in twain ;
Nor will I be, like Sampson, led
    To trust thy wiles again.

Tempt me no more with rosy cheeks,
Nor daze my reason with bright eyes ;
I'm wearied with thy wayward freaks,
And sicken at such vanities :
Be roses fine as e'er they will,
They, with the meanest, fade and die,
And eyes, tho' thick with darts to kill,
    Share all mortalities.

Feed the young bard, who madly sips
His nectar-draughts from folly's flowers,
Bright eyes, fair cheeks, and ruby lips,
Till music melts to honey showers;
Lure him to thrum thy empty lays,
While flattery listens to the chimes,
Till words themselves grow sick with praise
    And stop for want of rhymes.

Let such be still thy paramours,
And chaunt love's old and idle tune,
Robbing the spring of all its flowers,
And heaven of all her stars and moon,
To gild with dazzling similes
Blind folly's vain and empty lay :
I 'm sober'd from such phantasies,
    So get thee hence away,

Nor bid me sigh for mine own cost,
Nor count its loss, for mine annoy,
Nor say my stubbornness hath lost
A paradise of dainty joy :
I 'll not believe thee, till I know
That reason turns thy pampered ape,
And acts thy harlequin, to show
 That care 's in every shape.

Heart-achings, sighs, and grief-wrung tears,
Shame-blushes at betrayed distress,
Dissembled smiles, and jealous fears,
. Are aught but real happiness :
Then will I mourn what now I brave,
And suffer Celia's quirks to be
(Like a poor fate-bewilder'd slave,)
 The rulers of my destiny.

I 'll weep and sigh when e'er she wills
To frown—and when she deigns to smile
It will be cure for all my ills,
And, foolish still, I 'll laugh the while ;
But till that comes, I 'll bless the rules
Experience taught, and deem it wise
To hold thee as the game of fools,
 And all thy tricks despise.

The Gipsy's Song.

The gipsy's life is a merry life,
    And ranting boys we be;
We pay to none or rent or tax,
    And live untith'd and free.
None care for us, for none care we,
    And where we list we roam,
And merry boys we gipsies be,
    Though the wild woods are our home.

And come what will brings no dismay;
    Our minds are ne'er perplext;
For if to-day 's a swaly day,
    We meet with luck the next.
And thus we sing and kiss our mates,
    While our chorus still shall be,—
Bad luck to tyrant magistrates,
    And the gipsies' camp still free.

To mend old pans and bottom chairs
    Around the towns we tramp,
Then a day or two our purse repairs,
    And plenty fills our camp;
And our song we sing, and our fiddles sound
    Their catgut harmony,
While echo fills the woods around
    With gipsy liberty.

The green grass is our softest bed,
    The sun our clock we call,
The nightly sky hangs over head,
    Our curtains, house, and all.
Tho' houseless while the wild winds blow,
    Our joys are uncontroll'd ;
We barefoot dance through Winter's snow,
    When others die with cold.

Our maidens they are fond and free,
    And lasting are their charms ;
Brown as the berry on the tree,
    No sun their beauty harms :
Their beauties are no garden blooms,
    That fade before they flower ;
Unshelter'd where the tempest comes,
    They smile in sun and shower.

And they are wild as the woodland hare,
    That feeds on the evening lea ;
And what care we for ladies fair,
    Since ours are fond and free ?
False hearts hide in a lily skin,
    But ours are coarse and fond ;
No parson's fetters link us in,—
    Our love 's a stronger bond.

Tho' wild woods are our house and home,
    'T is a home of liberty ;
Free as the Summer clouds we roam,
    And merry boys we be.

We dance and sing the year along,
    And loud our fiddles play ;
And no day goes without its song,
    While every month is May.

The hare that haunts the fallow ground,
    And round the common feeds ;
The fox that tracks the woodland bounds,
    And in the thicket breeds ;
These are the neighbours where we dwell,
    And all the guests we see,
That share and love the quiet well
    Of gipsy liberty.

The elements are grown our friends,
    And leave our huts alone ;
The thunder-bolt, that shakes and rends
    The cotter's house of stone,
Flies harmless by the blanket roof,
    Where the winds may burst and blow,
For our camps, tho' thin, are tempest proof,
    We reck not rain and snow.

May the lot we 've met our lives befall,
    And nothing worse attend ;
So here 's success to gipsies all,
    And every gipsy's friend.
And while the ass that bears our camp
    Can find a common free,
Around old England's heaths we 'll tramp
    In gipsy liberty.

Peggy Band.

O it was a lorn and a dismal night,
    And the storm beat loud and high ;
Not a friendly light to guide me right
    Was there shining in the sky,
When a lonely hut my wanderings met,
    Lost in a foreign land,
And I found the dearest friend as yet
    In my lovely Peggy Band.

" O, father, here 's a soldier lad,
    And weary he seems to be."
" Then welcome in," the old man said,
    And she gave her seat to me.
The fire she trimmed, and my clothes she dried
    With her own sweet lily hand,
And o'er the soldier's lot she sighed,
    While I blest my Peggy Band.

When I told the tale of my wandering years,
    And the nights unknown to sleep,
She made excuse to hide her tears,
    And she stole away to weep.
A pilgrim's blessing I seemed to share,
    As saints of the Holy Land,
And I thought her a guardian angel there,
    Though *he* called her *his* Peggy Band.

The night it passed, and the hour to part
    With the morning winged away,
And I felt an anguish at my heart
    That vainly bid to stay.
I thanked the old man for all he did,
    And I took his daughter's hand,
But my heart was full, and I could not bid
    Farewell to my Peggy Band.

A blessing on that friendly cot,
    Where the soldier found repose,
And a blessing be her constant lot
    Who soothed the stranger's woes.
I turned a last look at the door,
    As she held it in her hand,
And my heart ached sore, as I crossed the moor,
    For to leave my Peggy Band.

To a Brook.

Sweet brook!   I've met thee many a summer's day,
And ventured fearless in thy shallow flood,
And rambled oft thy sweet unwearied way,
'Neath willows cool that on thy margin stood,
With crowds of partners in my artless play—
Grasshopper, beetle, bee, and butterfly—
That frisked about as though in merry mood
To see their old companion sporting by.
Sweet brook! life's glories then were mine and thine;
Shade clothed thy spring that now doth naked lie;
On thy white glistening sand the sweet woodbine
Darkened and dipt its flowers.   I mark, and sigh,
And muse o'er troubles since we met the last,
Like two fond friends whose happiness is past.

Prose Fragments.

PROSE FRAGMENTS.

A Confession of Faith.

My creed may be different from other creeds, but the
difference is nothing when the end is the same. If I did
not expect and hope for eternal happiness I should be ever
miserable; and as every religion is a rule leading to good
by its professor, the religions of all nations and creeds,
where that end is the aim, ought rather to be respected
than scoffed at. A final judgment of men by their deeds
and actions in life is inevitable, and the only difference
between an earthly assize and the eternal one is, that the
final one needs no counsellors to paint the bad or good
better or worse than they are. The Judge knows the
hearts of all men, and the sentence may be expected to be
just as well as final, whether it be for the worst or the
best. This ought to teach us to pause and think, and try
to lead our lives as well as we can.

Essay on Popularity.

——" Rumour and the popular voice
Some look to more than truth, and so confirm
Opinions."   CARY'S *Dante.*

Popularity is a busy talker : she catches hold of topics
and offers them to fame without giving herself time to
reflect whether they are true or false, and fashion is her
favourite disciple who sanctions and believes them as
eagerly, and with the same faith, as a young lady in the
last century read a new novel and a tavern-haunter in this
reads the news. It is natural, with such foundations, to
ask whether popularity is fame, for it often happens that
very slender names come to be popular from many causes
with which merit or genius has no sort of connection or
kindred. It may be some oddity in the manner, or
incident in the life, of the author that is whispered over
before his book comes out. This often macadamizes the
way to popularity, for gossip is a mighty spell in the
literary world, and a concealment of the author's name
often creates an anxiety in the public mind, for it leaves
room for guesses and conjectures, and as some are very
fond of appearing wise in such matters by saying they
know from good authority that such a one is the author,
it becomes the talk of the card party and tea-table, and he

gains a superficial notoriety. Such was the case with the
" Pursuits of Literature," a leaden-footed satire that had
as much claim to merit as the statue of Pasquin in the
Market-place of Rome, on which vulgar squibs were
pasted. Everybody knew the author, and nobody knew
him. The first names of the day were foisted into the
concern, and when the secret was found out that it
belonged to one of the lowest, the book sank to rise no
more. Sometimes a pompous, pretending title hits the
mark at once and wins a name. Who among the lower
orders of youth is ignorant of the " Young Man's Best
Companion" by Mr. Fisher, Accomptant, or the " Book
of Wisdom" by Mr. Fenning, Philomath? They are
almost as common as bibles and prayer-books in a cottage
library.

A guess is not hazarded in believing that popularity is not the omen of true fame. Sometimes the
trifling and ridiculous grow into the most extensive
popularity, such as the share of it which a man gained by
wearing a high brimmed hat, and another that cut off the
tails of his coat and thereby branded his name on the
remnant; and though the spencers are out of fashion they
have outlived many a poetical popularity. These are
instances of the ridiculous. The trifling are full as
extensive. Where is the poet who shares half the
popularity of Warren, Turner, or Day and Martin, whose
ebony fames are spread through every dirty little village in
England? These instances of the trifling and ridiculous
made as much noise and stir in their day as the best, and
noise and bustle are the essence and soul of popularity.

The nearest akin to popularity is common fame.
I mean names that are familiar among the common people.
It is not a very envious species, for they seldom know
how to value or appreciate what they are acquainted with.
The name of Chatterton is familiar to their ears as an
unfortunate poet, because they saw his history printed
on pocket handkerchiefs; and the name of Shakespeare
as a great play writer, because they have often seen him
nominated as such on the bills of strolling players, who
make shift with barns for theatres. But this sort of
revelry makes a corresponding idea in their minds, for the
paltry balladmongers, whose productions supply hawkers
with their wares, are poets with them, and they imagine
one as great as the other, common minds making no
distinction in these common fames. On the other hand
there is something in it to wish for, because there are
things as old as England that have outlived centuries of
popularity, nay, left half its history in darkness, and they
still live on, as common in every memory as the seasons,
and as familiar to children even as the rain and Spring
flowers. I allude to the old superstitious fragments of
legends and stories in rhyme that are said to be Norman,
or Saxon, or Danish. There are many desire this
common fame, and it is mostly met in a manner least
expected. While some affectations are striving for a lifetime to hit all tastes and always miss the mark by a wide
throw, an unconscious poet of little name writes a trifle
as he feels, without thinking of others, and he becomes a
common name.

Unaffected simplicity is the everyday picture of Nature. Thus, little children's favourites of "Cock Robin," "Little Red Riding Hood," and "Babes in the Wood," have impressions at the core that grow up with manhood and are always dear. Poets anxious after common fame, as some of the "naturals" seem to be, imitate these things by affecting simplicity, and become unnatural. These things found fame where the greatest names are still oblivions. A literary man might enquire after the names of Spenser and Milton in vain in half the villages in England, even among what are called its gentry, but I believe it would be difficult to find a corner in any county where the others are not known, nor an old woman in any hamlet with whom they are not familiar. In my days, some of the pieces of the modern poets have gained this common popularity, which must be distinguished from fame as it may only live for a season. Wordsworth's beautiful, simple ballad of "We are seven" I have seen hawked about for a penny, and Tannahill's song of "Jessy" has met with more popularity among the common people than all other songs, English and Scottish, put together. Lord Byron's hasty fame may be deemed a contradiction to the above opinion that popularity is not true fame, though at its greatest extent it is but an exception, and scarcely that, for his great and hurried popularity, that almost trampled on its own heels in its haste, must drop into a less bustling degree, and become cool and quiet, like the preaching of Irving. Shakespeare was hardly noticed in his lifetime by popularity, but he is known now, and Byron is hardly the tenth part of a Shakespeare. Every storm must have its calm, and Byron took fame by storm. By a desperate daring he over-swept petty control like a rebellious flood, or a tempest worked up into madness by the quarrel of the elements, and he seemed to value that daring as the attainment of true fame. He looked upon Horace's "Art of Poetry" no doubt with esteem as a reader, but he cared no more for it in the profession of a poet than the weather does for an almanack. He looked upon critics as the countryman does on a magistrate. He beheld them as a race of petty tyrants that stood in the way of genius. They were in his eyes more of stumbling-blocks than guides, and he treated them accordingly. He let them know there was another road to Parnassus without taking theirs, and being obliged to do them homage. Not stooping to the impediments of their authorities, like the paths of a besieged city encumbered with sentinels, he made a road for himself, and, like Napoleon crossing the Alps, he let the world see that even in the eye of a mortal their greatest obstacles were looked on "as the dust in a balance." He gained the envied eminence of living popularity by making a breach where it was thought impregnable. Where others had laid siege for a lifetime, and lost their hopes and their labour at last, he gained the heights of popularity by a single stride, and looked down as a freebooter on the world below, scorning the applause his labours had gained him, and scarcely returning a compliment for the laurels which fashion so eagerly bound round his brows, while he saw the alarm of his leaden-footed enemies, and withered them to nothings with his sneer. He was an Oliver Cromwell with the critics. He broke up their long-standing Parliament and placed his own will in the Speaker's chair, and his will they humbly accepted. They submitted to one that scorned to be shackled, and champed the bit in his stead. They praised and respected him, nay, they worshipped him. He was all in all in their mouths and in their writings, but I suspect their hearts had as much love for him as the peasantry had for witches in the last century, who spoke well of them to their faces because they dared not do otherwise for fear of meeting an injury.

Whether Byron hath won true fame or not I cannot say; my mind is too little to grasp that judgment. To say that he was the first of his age in his way is saying nothing, but we have sufficient illustration for the argument in saying that popularity is not the forerunner of fame's eternity. Among all the bustle of popularity there must be only a portion of it accepted as fame. Time will sift it of its drossy puffs and praises. He has been with others extolled as equal to Shakespeare, and I dare say the popular voice of "readers" thought him superior. But three centuries will wither every extravagance, and sober the picture of its glaring colours. He is no doubt one of the eternals, but he is one of those of the 19th century, and if all its elements be classed together in the next they would make but a poor substitute for a Shakespeare. Eternity will not rake the bottom of the sea of oblivion for puffs and praises, and all their attendant rubbish, the feelings that the fashion of the day created, and the flatteries uttered. Eternity will estimate things at their proper value, and no other. She will not even seek for the newspaper praise of Walter Scott. She will not look for Byron's immortality in the company of Warren's blacking, Prince's kalydor, and Atkinson's bear's grease. She looks for it in his own merit, and her impartial judgment will be his best reward. Wordsworth has had little share of popularity, though he bids fair to be as great in one species of poetry as Byron was in another, but to acknowledge such an opinion in the world's ear would only pucker the lips of fashion into a sneer against it. Yet his lack of living praise is no proof of his lack of genius. The trumpeting clamour of public praise is not to be relied on as the creditor of the future. The quiet progress of a name gaining ground by gentle degrees in the world's esteem is the best living shadow of fame to follow. The simplest trifle and the meanest thing in nature is the same now as it shall continue to be till the world's end.

> "Men trample grass and prize the flowers in May,
> But grass is green when flowers do fade away."

"Scraps for an Essay on Criticism and Fashion."

None need be surprised to see these two false prophets in partnership or conjunction for an essay, as they may be called brothers, for the one attests what it pleases and the other takes it for granted. Criticism is grown a sort of book milliner, who cuts a book to any pattern of abuse or praise, and Fashion readily wears the opinion. How many productions whose milk-and-water merits, or unintelligible stupidity, have been considered as novelties, have by that means gained the admiration of Criticism and the praise of Fashion, until a more absurd novelty pushed them from their preferments and caused them to be as suddenly forgotten! The vulgar, tasteless jargon of "Dr. Syntax," with all the above-mentioned excellencies to excite public notice from the butterflies of fashion, soon found what it sought, though some of the plates or illustrations possess the disadvantageous merit of being good. Yet the letter-press doubly made up for all, for it was prose trebly prosified into wire-drawn doggrel, and consequently met with a publicity and sale unprecedented. Edition multiplied on edition, till it was found needless to

number the title-page, and it was only necessary to say "A New Edition;" while the poems of Wordsworth scarcely found admirers enough to ensure a second edition. What will the admirers of poetry in the next age think of the taste of this, which has been called "the Golden Age of criticism, poetry, taste, and genius"?   *   *   *
Fashion is like a new book "elegantly bound and lettered." It cannot endure dust and cobwebs; but true criticism is like a newly-planted laurel: it thrives with age and gathers strength from antiquity, till it becomes a spreading tree and shelters the objects of its praise under its shadow.   *   *   *   Just Criticism is a stern but laudable prophet, and Time and Truth are the only disciples who can discern and appreciate his predictions.

✻

"Scraps for an Essay on Criticism."

Flowers must be sown and tended with care, like children, to grow up to maturity, but weeds grow of themselves and multiply without any attention, choking up those flowers that require it; and lies are propagated as easily as weeds, and choke up the blossoms of truth in the same manner. But the evils and misrepresentations of false criticism, though great and many, are not lasting. *   *   * Upon its principles fashion and flattery have made many Shakespeares, and these false prophets have flourished and will flourish for a season, for truth, when she cannot be heard by the opposition of falsehood, remains silent and leaves time to decide the difference, who cometh quietly and impartially to her assistance, hurling without ceremony, century after century, usurper after usurper from the throne of the mighty, and erasing their names from his altar as suddenly and as perfectly as the sunbeam passes over and washes away the stains of a shadow on the wall. Fame hath weighed the false criticisms and pretensions of centuries already, and found nothing as yet but dust in the balance. Shadows of Shakespeare are cast away as profane idols, and reality

hath fallen short of even a trinity. She acknowledges as sacred but one, and I fear that when she shall calculate the claims of ten centuries she will find the number of the mighty a unit. But why should fear be expressed for a repetition which we neither hope for nor need? We have but one sun in our firmament, and upwards of six thousand years have neither added to nor diminished its splendour, neither have vain desires been expressed for the existence of another. Needless wishes create painful expectations. When a man is warm and comfortable on a cold day he cannot wish for an excess that would burn him. Therefore we need neither hope for more Shakespeares nor regret that there is but one. When the Muses created him a poet they created him the sun of the firmament of genius, and time has proved, and will prove, that they glory in their creation, deeming it sufficient, without striving to find or create another, for nature knows the impossibility. There have been, both before and after, constellations of great and wonderful beauty, and many in this age will be found in the number who shine in their own light with becoming splendour, but whenever flattery or vanity places them near the great luminary their little lights lose their splendour and they vanish in his brightness as the stars are lost at noon.
*   *   *   The falling stars leave a stream of splendour behind them for a moment; then utter darkness follows, and not a spark is left to show where they fell.
*   *   *   It is said that Byron is not to have a monument in Westminster Abbey. To him it is no injury. Time is his monument, on whose scroll the name of

Byron shall be legible when the walls and tombs of Westminster Abbey shall have mingled with the refuse of ruins, and the sun, as in scorn, be left free again to smile upon the earth so long darkened with the pompous shadows of bigotry and intolerance.

Old Songs and Ballads.

OLD SONGS and BALLADS.

Respecting these compositions Clare says—" I commenced sometime ago with an intention of making a collection of Old Ballads, but when I had sought after them in places where I expected to find them, namely, the hayfield and the shepherd's hut on the pasture, I found that nearly all those old and beautiful recollections had vanished as so many old fashions, and those who knew fragments seemed ashamed to acknowledge it, as old people who sung old songs only sung to be laughed at; and those who were proud of their knowledge in such things knew nothing but the senseless balderdash that is bawled over and sung at country feasts, statutes, and fairs, where the most senseless jargon passes for the greatest excellence, and rudest indecency for the finest wit. So the matter was thrown by, and forgotten until last winter, when I used to spend the long evenings with my father and mother, and heard them by accident hum over scraps of the following old melodies, which I have collected and put into their present form." Two of the collection are omitted from this volume—the well-known ballad of " Lord Randall," and a second the subject of which appeared to render its inclusion inexpedient.

Adieu to my False Love for ever.

The week before Easter, the days long and clear,
So bright shone the sun and so cool blew the air,
I went in the meadow some flowers to find there,
    But the meadow would yield me no posies.

The weather, like love, did deceitful appear,
And I wandered alone when my sorrow was near,
For the thorn that wounds deeply doth bide the whole year,
    When the bush it is naked of roses.

I courted a girl that was handsome and gay,
I thought her as constant and true as the day,
Till she married for riches and said my love " Nay,"
    And so my poor heart got requited.

I was bid to the bridal; I could not say " No:"
The bridemen and maidens they made a fine show;
I smiled like the rest but my heart it was low,
    To think how its hopes they were blighted.

The bride started gaily, the weather was fine,
Her parents looked after, and thought her divine;
She smiled in their faces, but looked not in mine,
    Indeed I 'd no heart to regard her.

Old Songs and Ballads.

Though love like the poplar doth lift its head high,
The top it may fade and the root it may die,
And they may have heart-aches that now live in joy,
    But Heaven I 'll leave to reward her.

When I saw my false love in the merry church stand,
With her ring on her finger and her love in her hand,
Smiling out in the joy of her houses and land,
    My sighs I strove vainly to smother.

When my false love for dinner did dainties partake,
I sat me down also, but nothing could eat;
I thought her sweet company better than meat,
    Although she was tied to another.

When my false love had gone to her bride bed at night
My eyes filled with water which made double my sight;
I thought she was there when she 'd bade us "Good night"
    And her chair was put by till the morrow.

I drank to her joy with a tear on my face,
And the wine glass as usual I pushed on the space,
Nor knew she was gone till I looked at the place,
    Such a fool was I made of by sorrow.

Now make me a bed in yon river so deep,
Let its waves be my mourners; nought living will weep
And there let me lie and take a long sleep,
    So adieu to my false love for ever.

O Silly Love!   O Cunning Love!

O silly love !   O cunning love !
   An old maid to trepan :
I cannot go about my work
   For loving of a man.
I cannot bake, I cannot brew,
   And, do the best I can,
I burn the bread and chill the mash,
   Through loving of a man.

Shrove Tuesday last I tried, and tried,
   To turn the cakes in pan,
And dropt the batter on the floor,
   Through thinking of a man.
My mistress screamed, my master swore,
   Boys cursed me in a troop ;
The cat was all the friends I had,
   Who helped to clean it up.

Last Christmas eve, from off the spit
   I took the goose to table,
Or should have done, but teasing Love
   Did make me quite unable ;
And down slipt dish, and goose, and all,
   With din and clitter-clatter ;
All but the dog fell foul on me ;
   He licked the broken platter.

Although I 'm ten years past a score,
    Too old to play the fool,
My mistress says I must give o'er
    My service for a school.
Good faith !   What must I do, and do,
    To keep my service still;
I 'll give the winds my thoughts to love,
    Indeed and so I will.

And if the wind my love should lose,
    Right foolish were the play,
For I should mourn what I had lost,
    And love another day.
With crosses and with losses
    Right double were the ill,
So I 'll e'en bear with love and all,
    Alack, and so I will.

Nobody cometh to woo.

On Martinmas eve the dogs did bark,
　　And I opened the window to see,
When every maiden went by with her spark,
　　But ne'er a one came to me.
And O dear what will become of me?
　　And O dear what shall I do,
When nobody whispers to marry me—
　　Nobody cometh to woo?

None 's born for such troubles as I be:
　　If the sun wakens first in the morn
" Lazy hussy" my parents both call me,
　　And I must abide by their scorn,
For nobody cometh to marry me,
　　Nobody cometh to woo,
So here in distress must I tarry me—
　　What can a poor maiden do?

If I sigh through the window when Jerry
　　The ploughman goes by, I grow bold;
And if I'm disposed to be merry,
　　My parents do nothing but scold;
And Jerry the clown, and no other,
　　E'er cometh to marry or woo;
They think me the moral of mother,
　　And judge me a terrible shrew.

For mother she hateth all fellows,
    And spinning 's my father's desire,
While the old cat growls bass with the bellows
    If e'er I hitch up to the fire.
I make the whole house out of humour,
    I wish nothing else but to please,
Would fortune but bring a good comer
    To marry, and make me at ease!

When I 've nothing my leisure to hinder
    I scarce get as far as the eaves;
Her head 's instant out of the window,
    Calling out like a press after thieves.
The young men all fall to remarking,
    And laugh till they 're weary to see 't,
While the dogs at the noise begin barking,
    And I slink in with shame from the street.

My mother 's aye jealous of loving,
    My father 's aye jealous of play,
So what with them both there 's no moving,
    I 'm in durance for life and a day.
O who shall I get for me to marry me?
    Who will have pity to woo?
'T is death any longer to tarry me,
    And what shall a poor maiden do?

Fare=thee=well.

[With respect to this song, Clare has this note :—" Scraps
from my father and mother, completed."]

Here 's a sad good bye for thee, my love, .
    To friends and foes a smile :
I leave but one regret behind,
    That 's left with thee the while,
But hopes that fortune is our friend
    Already pays the toil.

Force bids me go, your friends to please.
    Would they were not so high !
But be my lot on land or seas,
    It matters not where by,
For I shall keep a thought for thee,
    In my heart's core to lie.

Winter shall lose its frost and snow,
    The spring its blossomed thorn,
The summer all its bloom forego,
    The autumn hound and horn
Ere I will lose that thought of thee,
    Or ever prove forsworn.

The dove shall change a hawk in kind,
    The cuckoo change its tune,

The nightingale at Christmas sing,
    The fieldfare come in June—
Ere I do change my love for thee
    These things shall change as soon.

So keep your heart at ease, my love,
    Nor waste a joy for me :
I 'll ne'er prove false to thee, my love,
    Till fish drown in the sea,
And birds forget to fly, my love,
    And then I 'll think of thee.

The red cock's wing may turn to grey,
    The crow's to silver white,
The night itself may be for day,
    And sunshine wake at night :
Till then—and then I 'll prove more true
    Than Nature, life, and light.

Though you may break your fondest vow,
    And take your heart from me,
And though my heart should break to hear
    What I may never see,
Yet never can'st thou break the link
    That binds my love to thee.

So fare-thee-well, my own true love ;
    No vow from thee I crave,
But thee I never will forego,
    Till no spark of life I have,
Nor will I ever thee forget
    Till we both lie in the grave.

Mary Neele.

[Notwithstanding the company in which it is found, this poem
may safely be attributed to Clare.]

My love is tall and handsome ;
    All hearts she might command ;
She 's matchless for her beauty,
    The queen of all the land.
She has my heart in keeping,
    For which there 's no repeal,
For the fairest of all woman kind
    Is my love, Mary Neele.

I felt my soul enchanted
    To view this turtle dove,
That lately seems descended
    From heavenly bowers of love ;
And might I have the fortune
    My wishes could reveal,
I 'd turn my back on splendour
    And fly to Mary Neele.

She is the flower of nations,
    The diamond of my eye ;
All others are but gloworms
    That in her splendour die.

As shining stars all vanish
    When suns their light reveal,
So beauties shrink to shadows
    At the feet of Mary Neele.

I ask no better fortune
    Than to embrace her charms;
Like Plato I would laugh at wealth
    While she was in my arms;
And if I cannot gain her
    From grief there's no appeal;
My joy, my pain, my life, my all
    Are fixed with Mary Neele.

The stone of vain philosophers,
    That wonder-working toy,
The golden fleece of Jason,
    That Helen stole from Troy,
The beauty and the riches
    That all these fames unseal,
Are nothing all, and less than that,
    Compared to Mary Neele.

O if I cannot gain her
    Right wretched must I be,
And caves and lonely mountains
    Must be the life for me,
To pine in gloom and sorrow,
    And hide the deaths I feel,
For light nor life I may not share
    When lost to Mary Neele.

Love scorned by Pride.

O far is fled the winter wind,
And far is fled the frost and snow,
But the cold scorn on my love's brow
Hath never yet prepared to go.

More lasting than ten winters' wind,
More cutting than ten weeks of frost,
Is the chill frowning of thy mind,
Where my poor heart was pledged and lost.

I see thee taunting down the street,
And by the frowning that I see
I might have known it long ere now,
Thy love was never meant for me,

And had I known ere I began
That love had been so hard to win,
I would have filled my heart with pride,
Nor left one hope to let love in

I would have wrapped it in my breast,
And pinned it with a silver pin,
Safe as a bird within its nest,
And 'scaped the trouble I am in.

I wish I was a happy bird,
And thou a true and timid dove :
O I would fly the land of grief,
And rest me in the land of love.

O I would rest where I love best ;
Where I love best I may not be :
A hawk doth on that rose-tree sit,
And drives young love to fear and flee.

O would I were the goldfinch gay !
My richer suit had tempted strong.
O would I were the nightingale !
Thou then had'st listened to my song.

Though deep my scorn I cannot hate,
Thy beauty 's sweet though sour thy pride ;
To praise thee is to love thee still,
And it doth cheer my heart beside.

For I could swim the deepest lake,
And I could climb the highest tree,
The greatest danger face and brave,
And all for one kind kiss of thee.

O love is here, and love is there :
O love is like no other thing :
Its frowns can make a king a slave,
Its smiles can make a slave a king.

Betrayed.

Dream not of love, to think it like
What waking love may prove to be,
For I dreamed so and broke my heart,
When my false lover slighted me.

Love, like to flowers, is sweet when green;
The rose in bud aye best appears;
And she that loves a handsome man
Should have more wit than she has years.

I put my finger in a bush,
Thinking the sweeter rose to find;
I pricked my finger to the bone,
And left the sweetest rose behind.

I threw a stone into the sea,
And deep it sunk into the sand,
And so did my poor heart in me
When my false lover left the land.

Old Songs and Ballads.

I watched the sun an hour too soon
Set into clouds behind the town ;
So my false lover left, and said
" Good night" before the day was down.

I cropt a lily from the stalk,
And in my hand it died away :
So did my joy, so will my heart,
In false love's cruel grasp decay.

The Maiden's Welcome.

Of all the swains that meet at eve
  Upon the green to play,
The shepherd is the lad for me,
  And I 'll ne'er say him nay.
Though father glowers beneath his hat,
  And mother talks of bed,
I 'll take my cloak up, late or soon,
  To meet my shepherd lad.

Aunt Kitty loved a soldier lad,
  Who left her love for war ;
A sailor loved my sister Sue,
  Whose jacket smelt of tar ;
But my love 's sweet as land new ploughed,
  He is my heart's delight,
And he ne'er leaves his love so far
  But he can come at night.

So father he may glower and frown,
  And mother scold about it ;
The shepherd has my heart to keep,
  And can I live without it ?
I 'm sure he will not part with it,
  In spite of what they say,
And if he would as sure I am
  It would not come away.

So friends may frown, while I can smile
    To know I 'm loved by one
Who has my heart, and him to seek
    What better can be done ?
And be it Spring or Summer both,
    Or be it Winter cold,
If pots should freeze upon the fire
    I 'd meet him at the fold.

I 'm fain to make my wedding gown,
    Which he has bought for me,
But it will wake my mother's thoughts,
    And evil they will be,
Although he has but stole my heart,
    Which gives me nought of pain,
For bye and bye he 'll buy the ring,
    And bring my heart again.

The False Knight's Tragedy.

[Students of ballad literature will be reminded by the following poem of the "May Collean" and "The Outlandish Knight" of other collections. The resemblance between the three ballads is general up to a certain point, but a striking contrast occurs in the *dénouement*, for whereas in other versions the maiden contrives by a simple stratagem to fling her false lover into the sea, where she leaves him to his fate, in the following she falls a victim to his treachery. His fitting end is, however, indicated in the remarkable stanza with which the ballad closes.]

A false knight wooed a maiden poor,
 And his high halls left he
To stoop in at her cottage door,
 When night left none to see.

And, well-a-day, it is a tale
 For pity too severe—
A tale would melt the sternest eye,
 And wake the deafest ear.

He stole her heart, he stole her love,
 'T was all the wealth she had;
Her truth and fame likewise stole he,

  * * * * *

And he gave gold, and promised more—
    That she his name should bear,
That she should share his love for aye,
    And live his lady fair.

But he ne'er meant a maid so low
    Should wear his haughty name,
And much he feared his guilty love
    Would work him muckle shame.

So underneath the mask of love
    He went to work her woe ;
And he did name the bridal day,
    And she prepared to go.

He brought her silks, unseen, to wear,
    And a milk-white steed to ride,
And not a word was to be known
    Till she was made a bride.

He brought for her a milk-white steed,
    And for himself a grey,
And they are off none knoweth where,
    Three hours before the day.

And as they rode she wished him speak,
    And not a word spoke he.
" You were not wont, loved knight," she said,
    " To be thus cold to me."

And they rode on, and they rode on;
    Far on this pair did ride,
Till the maiden's heart with fear and love
    Beat quick against her side.

And on they rode till rocks grew high.
    " Sir Knight, what have we here ? "
" Unsaddle, maid, for here we stop : "
    And death's tongue smote her ear.

Some ruffian rude she took him now,
    And wished she 'd barred the door,
Nor was it one that she could read
    Of having heard before.

" Thou art not my true love," she said,
    " But some rude robber loon ;
He 'd take me from the saddle bow,
    Nor leave me to get down."

" I ne'er was your true love," said he,
    " For I 'm more bold than true ;
Though I 'm the knight that came at dark
    To kiss and toy with you."

" I know you 're not my love," said she,
    " That came at night and wooed ;
Although ye try and mock his speech
    His way was ne'er so rude.

" He ne'er said word but called me dear,
    And dear he is to me :
Ye spake as ye ne'er knew the word,
    Rude ruffian as ye be.

" Ye never was my knight, I trow,
    Ye pay me no regard,
But he would take my arm in his
    If we but went a yard."

" No matter whose true love I am ;
    I 'm more than true to you,
For I 'll ne'er wed a shepherd wench,
    Although I came to woo."

And on to the rock's top they walked,
    Till they stood o'er the salt sea's brim.
" And there," said he, " 's your bridal bed,
    Where you may sink or swim."

A moonbeam shone upon his face,
    The maid sunk at his feet,
For 't was her own false love she saw,
    That once so fond did greet.

" And did ye promise love for this ?
    Is the grave my priest to be ?
And did ye bring this silken dress
    To wed me with the sea."

" O never mind your dress, quoth he,
     'T is well to dress for sea :
Mermaids will love to see you fine ;
     Your bridesmaids they will be."

" O let me cast this gown away,
     It 's brought no good to me,
And if my mother greets my clay
     Too wretched will she be.

" For she, for my sad sake, would keep
     This guilty bridal dress,
To break and tell her bursting heart
     She had a daughter less."

So off she threw her bridal gown,
     Likewise her gold clasped shoon :
His looks frowned hard as any stone,
     Hers pale turned as the moon.

" O false, false knight you 've wrapped me warm
     Ere I was cold before,
And now you strip me unto death,
     Although I 'm out of door.

" O dash away those thistles rude,
     That crowd about the shore ;
They 'll wound my tender feet, that ne'er
     Went barefoot thus before.

"O dash those stinging nettles down,
　　　And cut away the brier,
For deep they wound those lily arms
　　　Which you did once admire."

And he nor briers nor thistles cut,
　　　Although she grieved full sore,
And he nor shed one single tear,
　　　Nor kiss took evermore.

She shrieked—and sank, and is at rest,
　　　All in the deep, deep sea;
And home in base and scornful pride,
　　　With haunted heart, rode he.

Now o'er that rock there hangs a tree,
　　　And chains do creak thereon;
And in those chains his memory hangs,
　　　Though all beside is gone.

Love's Riddle.

" Unriddle this riddle, my own Jenny love,
  Unriddle this riddle for me,
 And if ye unriddle the riddle aright,
  A kiss your prize shall be,
 And if ye riddle the riddle all wrong,
  Ye 're treble the debt to me :—

 I 'll give thee an apple without any core ;
 I 'll give thee a cherry where stones never be ;
 I 'll give thee a palace, without any door,
 And thou shalt unlock it without any key ;
 I 'll give thee a fortune that kings cannot give,
  Nor any one take from thee."

" How can there be apples without any core ?
 How can there be cherries where stones never be ?
 How can there be houses without any door ?
 Or doors I may open without any key ?
 How can'st thou give fortunes that kings cannot give,
  When thou art no richer than me ?"

" My head is the apple without any core ;
In cherries in blossom no stones ever be ;
My mind is love's palace without any door,
Which thou can'st unlock, love, without any key.
My heart is the wealth, love, that kings cannot give,
   Nor any one take it from thee.

So there are love's riddles, my own Jenny love,
   Ye cannot unriddle to me,
And for the one kiss you 've so easily lost
   I 'll make ye give seven to me.
To kiss thee is sweet, but 't is sweeter by far
   To be kissed, my dear Jenny, by thee.

Come pay me the forfeit, my own Jenny love ;
   Thy kisses and cheeks are akin,
And for thy three sweet ones I 'll give thee a score
   On thy cheeks, and thy lips, and thy chin."
She laughed while he gave her, as much as to say,
   " 'T were better to lose than to win."

The Banks of Ivory.

'T was on the banks of Ivory, 'neath the hawthorn-scented
    shade,
Early one summer's morning, I met a lovely maid;
Her hair hung o'er her shoulders broad, her eyes like suns
    did shine,
And on the banks of Ivory O I wished the maid was
    mine.

Her face it wore the beauty of heaven's own broken
    mould;
The world's first charm seemed living still; her curls like
    hanks of gold,
Hung waving, and her eyes glittered timid as the dew,
When by the banks of Ivory I swore I loved her true.

"Kind sir," she said, "forsake me, while it is no pain to go,
For often after kissing and such wooing there comes woe;
And woman's heart is feeble; O I wish it were a stone;
So by the banks of Ivory I 'd rather walk alone.

For learned seems your gallant speech, and noble is your
    trim,
And thus to court an humble maid is just to please your
    whim;
So go and seek some lady fair, as high in pedigree,
Nor stoop so low by Ivory to flatter one like me."

"In sooth, fair maid, you mock at me, for truth ne'er
    harboured ill ;
I will not wrong your purity ; to love is all my will :
My hall looks over yonder groves ; its lady you shall be,
For on the banks of Ivory I 'm glad I met with thee."

He put his hands unto his lips, and whistled loud and
    shrill,
And thirty-six well-arméd men came at their master's
    will,
Said he "I 've flattered maids full long, but now the time
    is past,
And the bonny hills of Ivory a lady own at last.

My steed's back ne'er was graced for a lady's seat before ;
Fear not his speed ; I 'll guard thee, love, till we ride o'er
    the moor,
To seek the priest, and wed, and love until the day we
    die :"
So she that was but poor before is Lady Ivory.

Facsimile of Clare's sketch for his own gravestone, mentioned on page 89.

Opinions of the Press.

"A remarkable volume of poems, by a working shoemaker of Wellingborough, is among the books of verse that have appeared during the present year. . . . Mr. Askham sings of spring and snowdrops, of the morning, and the river, and the common grass; he has the poet's love for all the country sights and sounds, and memories of childhood in the country."—*The Examiner.*

"Mr. Askham's genius was already matured when he first challenged public opinion; and though his subsequent effusions would affirm and ratify the verdict of his earliest critics, he had no glaring faults to correct, few crudenesses of expression to ameliorate. The same sweet and pure tone pervades this second volume which was manifest in the first: there is the same deep sense of all natural beauty; the same power, too, of describing it, truthfully and vividly."—*Northampton Mercury.*

"Mr. Askham has both poetic feeling and skill in the handling of his native language. . . . . They may well be left to speak for themselves. If they do not aim to startle by the boldness of their imagery or to awe by the weird power of their words, they cannot fail to charm by a thousand simple beauties and delicate graces of expression."—*Chester Chronicle.*

"He has woven his thoughts and sentiments into verse very deftly, and has wreathed warm sympathies and generous impulses together in appropriate and unpretentious language."—*Leicester Chronicle.*

"This volume confirms Mr. Askham's claim to be regarded as a true poet. Not merely do his verses abound in poetical sentiment, but they have the ring and rhythm of genuine poetry, as distinguished from mere rhyme."—
Wellingborough Weekly News.

"The book should occupy an honourable position, if not amongst our standard minstrelsy, at least like the poems of John Clare, another Northamptonshire poet, among the curiosities of English literature."—*The Reader.*

"They are beautifully printed on toned paper, and are for the most part fully worthy of their elegant setting. They are marked by much natural force, and have a rhythmical ring which denotes the true metal. Some of the sonnets are especially sweet."—*Morning Star.*

"We should never have guessed that these poems were written by a working man. They have rather the characteristics of a higher culture, and their fault if, indeed, that are not 'faulty faultless,' is an over refinement doing away with inequalties by a levelling process. Yet the author has employed his eyes to some purpose, even though he has trusted too implicitly to his ears, and there are images in his verse, of which the thoughts and observations are his own, even if the language seems to have come from without."—*The Spectator.*

"We are glad to see another volume from the pen of Mr. Askham, of Wellingborough. Like its predecessor, it at once bespeaks for its author true nobility and refinement of mind, poetical genius, and steady perseverance."—
Midland Free Press.

"Our Shoemaker is none of the namby-pamby order of rhymesters who believe they are poets because they can make 'sigh' clink with 'die.' On the contrary, he uses a bold pen as the exponent of a healthy brain."—*The Train.*

"He has a true sense of rural beauty and considerable quiet descriptive power, and handles the sonnet neither unskilfully nor ungracefully."—*The Guardia.*

"His verse is always well constructed, his thought is healthy, and the book is pervaded throughout by a genuineness of feeling which arouses corresponding sympathy."—*Newcastle Courant.*

"The author of this attractive volume of poetry takes high rank among those humble 'sons of toil'—of whom we have several excellent samples amongst our own community—whose sense of the beautiful and innate love of 'harmonious numbers' are repressible by no condition of outward circumstances, however apparently unfavourable."—*Bristol Mercury.*

"John Askham, has, as a poet, a better claim to fame than some whose names are more familiar—than some even whose productions have brought them very agreeable recognition in the form of pensions from the government."
—*Norfolk News.*

"Mr. Askham can write the sonnet as it should be written—he can round it and make his meaning clear and complete. . . . . . There is real pleasure in meeting with a volume of poems, fresh and full of perfumes of the hill and valley from a working man, who has only the time that he can snatch from daily toil to gratify his taste. . . . . . The volume is the most remarkable one from a son of toil that we have seen for many years, and we hope so much talent will meet with deserved reward."— *Public Opinion.*

"A more thoughtful but less melodious poet is John Askham, a working shoemaker of Northampton, and the author of a collection of "descriptive poems, miscellaneous pieces, scriptural, descriptive, biographical, and miscellaneous sonnets.' His best pieces are his sonnets."—*New York Tribune.*

"The gentle craft can boast of many successful votaries of the Muse, among whom, perhaps, the most celebrated was Robert Bloomfield, the author of 'The Farmer's Boy.' Thomas Cooper, whose 'Purgatory of Suicides' is a most remarkable work, was also a shoemaker; and now we have John Askham of Wellingborough, with his earnest-toned and graceful lyrics, to tell us that the spirit of poetry has not yet passed away from the shoemaker's workshop."—
Working Man.

"The descriptive pieces are neat and truthful; but the sonnets and the biographical sonnets, in particular, will attract attention as being much superior to the every-day poetry, with which the literary world is inundated."—
Liverpool Albion.

"Many of the poems possess considerable merit. Some are simple and tender; others, and especially certain of the sonnets, manly and vigorous."—
Glasgow Daily Herald

TAYLOR & SON'S PUBLICATIONS.

Poems, Early and Late, by CHRISTOPHER HUGHES, sm. 8vo, cloth extra gilt, 3/6   1872

Tracts Relating to Northamptonshire, (chiefly Rare and Curious Reprints), *with illustrations*, 8vo, cloth extra, (pub. 21/) 10/6

Account of the Entertainment given to the Queen of James the First and Prince Henry, at Althorpe, the 25th of June, 1603, by T. F. DIBDIN, 8vo, 8pp., wrapper, 4d.

A Testimony against Periwig and Periwig-Making, and Playing on Instruments of Musick among Christians, or any other in the days of the Gospel. By JOHN MULLINER, 8vo, sewed, crayon wrapper, 24pp., 1/6

A Calendar of Papers of the Tresham Family, of the Reigns of Elizabeth and James I., 1580-1605, preserved at Rushton Hall, Northamptonshire, 8vo, sewed, crayon wrapper, 16pp., 1/6

Northampton Lenten Mission. Three Sermons, preached by the LORD BISHOP OF PETERBOROUGH, March 26th, 1871, 8vo, 36pp. 1/

Four Sermons on Special Occasions, by The Right Rev. Dr. MAGEE, Lord Bishop of Peterborough, 8vo, wrapper, 54pp, 1/

Sermons on Special Occasions, by the Rev. J. T. BROWN, 8vo, wrapper, 6d.

Some Pre-requisites of the Sunday School for the work of Religious Education, by Rev. T. Arnold, 8vo., sewed, 16pp., 1½d.

Memorials of the Independent Churches of Northamptonshire, with Biographical Notices of their Pastors, and Account of the Puritan Ministers who Laboured in the County, by the Rev. T. COLEMAN, 12mo, (pub. 4/) 1/3   1853

Early History of the Independent Church at Rothwell, from the 3rd year of the Protectorate to the Death of Queen Anne, by NORMAN GLASS, sm. 8vo, cloth extra, (pub. 3/6) 2/6   1871

Sketch of the Religious History of Northamptonshire, with an Account of some of the Baptist Churches in the County, sm. 8vo, 40pp., wrapper, 3d.   1871

Early History of College Lane Chapel, with Extracts from Original Documents, fcap. 8vo, 90pp., wrapper, 6d.

Historical Sketch of the Baptist Church AT WESTON-BY-WEEDON with particulars of its connection with the Churches at Towcester, Middleton Cheney, Stony Stratford, and others, by Rev. J. LEA, sm. 8vo, 30pp., wrapper, 6d.   1868

History of the Town of Northampton, with an Account of its Public Buildings and Institutions, Eminent Men, Members of Parliament, Mayors and Bailiffs, and the most Remarkable Events, *Plan of the Town*, 8vo, 112pp., cloth, 2/   1847

History and Antiquities of Higham Ferrers, with Historical Notices of Rushden and Irthlingborough, by JOHN COLE, *frontispiece*, 12mo, cloth, 3/6

History of Rothwell, with an Account of the Bone Caverns, by PAUL CYPHER, and Remarks on the Collection of Skulls by Prof. BUSK, *illustrations*, fcap, 8vo, 98pp., wrapper, 6d.

Henson's History of the County of Northampton, *illustrations*, 12mo, wrapper, 252pp, 6d.

Concise History of Northampton, from the Earliest Times to the Great Fire of 1675, 12mo, 22pp, wrapper, 2d.

Lightning Source UK Ltd.
Milton Keynes UK
UKHW010655090223
416681UK00007B/1901